THE CON

THE CON

An Organized Crime Cozy Mystery

Jackie Layton

First published by Level Best Books 2024

Copyright © 2024 by Jackie Layton

Author Photo Credit: Kellianne Layton

First edition

ISBN: 978-1-68512-726-8

Cover art by Level Best Designs

This book was professionally typeset on Reedsy.
Find out more at reedsy.com

This is dedicated to my wonderful readers. Thanks!

Praise for the Organized Crime Cozy Mysteries

CUTTER FREE

"This is a good beginning to what I hope is a long running series. The mystery was nicely done with fast-pacing and well-written narrative. The characters were developed enough to keep me interesting in the role they played and I enjoyed following the crumbs the author planted for us to solve the puzzle."—Dru's very short musing on *Clutter Free*

"*Clutter Free* is a cozy mystery with a dash of second chance romance set on Fox Island, where festivals may well hold secrets and the community is closer than you think. I enjoyed the setting as well as amateur sleuth and narrator Kate's organizational skills, with her dogged determination to clear her brother's name, along with the close friendships and protective natures of the men in her life."—Bookworlder

"I really enjoyed this cozy mystery. I loved the characters and the mystery. I loved how the story kept me engaged from the beginning of the story and I didn't know who had done it until the end. I liked how there were many twist and turns the author took us on as we tried to solve the mystery along with the characters. I also loved that the main character owned an organizing business. I thought that was a creative idea. I would definitely read more books by this author. Overall, I thought this book was enjoyable and one that I would recommend to anyone looking for a well written cozy mystery."—Holly's Book Corner

"I started reading this book and could not stop reading until I came to THE END! Kate is a very determined woman and she really wants to help her brother. I LOVE that her career, Professional Organizer, helps her with sleuthing and helping to "fix the problem". Her Brother, Paul, is well-liked in the Community and she knows this accusation could ruin his career. Reid is a GREAT Character in the book and I saw a bit of "sparks" as Reid was also Kate's High School Crush. I am glad I read this on a day where I could read from start to finish as it truly is a WONDERFUL BOOK! I highly recommend this book to anyone who loves Mystery!"—Blooming With Books

"*Clutter Free* is a fun mystery-type novel and also makes me wish I was more like the main character and could organize flawlessly! We live in a small house with lots of kids and I'm always looking for new organizational systems and ways to save my sanity a bit more.

"Kate is our main character/heroine. She's an organizer. Professionally. It's her job. She helps people organize and manage their homes. (Does anyone know a real-life Kate who wants to come to my house?!) But that new business takes a bit of a back burner when her brother is accused of having an affair. To make that accusation worse is the fact that he's a police chief!

"When she meets with the accuser to get her to recant the woman won't. And then to make it all worse that woman is found dead the next day by Kate and her assistant! Talk about an awkward and not good situation.

" This book read quickly and I loved the characters. They spoke to me and I wanted to be friends! I loved the book. Reid is another character that you're going to want to keep an eye on as he's quite the guy."—Erin from For Him and My Family

Chapter One

I slammed on the brakes of my old SUV. An osprey flew in front of me with an eagle hot on his trail. The first bird carried a large fish in its talons. The eagle drew alongside the osprey and swiped at the fish with its wings. The osprey dropped the fish. The eagle caught it midair with its talons; then the bigger bird flew away toward the pine trees between the road and the ocean.

A car honked.

"Sorry." I waved and turned my attention to pulling into Seaside Hideaway's parking lot. I wasn't here for a vacation. No, this was about work. As a professional organizer, I met a variety of people and saw interesting places. Today, I was tackling Ben Hauser's office. It was trendy, boring, disorganized, and cluttered. Ben's office was messy, but in this case, it didn't mean the man was a genius. Was there any truth behind that saying? Who cared if he was a genius or not?

Ben was the new owner of Fox Island, Georgia's historic resort, and he'd hired Let's Get Organized to transform his office. Bess Walker, my business partner, and I had impressed Ben at our first meeting the week before. Today, I was following up with specific plans and samples. Mondays always filled me with excitement for the week, and this was no different.

My creative juices stirred at the prospect of organizing Ben's office. When clients trusted me to meet their organizational needs, they ended up loving the results. I got to know the clients and asked specific questions to feel comfortable arranging their space for optimum efficiency. I credited the personal touch for the success I'd found in organizing spaces.

I parked near a pine tree in the resort's dusty parking lot. I hopped out and pulled my blue utility bag with white polka dots from the backseat of my old Wagoneer. After a recent car crash, I'd bought the biggest vehicle I could afford. Lucky for me, a client was downsizing and sold me his 1991 Jeep Wagoneer. The previous owner had shared a lot of the vehicle's details that meant nothing to me, but he'd loved the thing. I mostly wanted something safe to drive around the island, and I'd promised to take good care of his baby.

I strode to the entrance of the resort. Once inside, a visitor could go to the restaurant, the spa, the front desk, the pro shop, or the restrooms. Floor-to-ceiling windows revealed the pool area, an outdoor restaurant, and the beach. Beachy neutrals and fountains helped emphasize the beach, but I wasn't here to enjoy the view.

I waved to the staff and made my way down a short hall toward Ben's office.

"Calm down. You'll get your money." Ben's voice carried to the corridor. I was deaf in my right ear, and if I could hear the dispute, it must be bad. Ben's appeal to the other person stopped me from knocking on the office door. I stood frozen.

"This is no way to run a business, Ben." The angry tone matched the volume of Ben's voice. "Pay up, or I'm going to be forced to move my business."

"Don't do anything drastic." Ben's voice softened, and I couldn't distinguish more of his words.

I leaned closer to the office in hopes of hearing more.

The door swooshed open, and a weathered, gray-haired man appeared.

I jumped back, bumping my shoulder on the wall.

My gaze connected with his. The anger in his eyes diminished. "Pardon me. I hope I didn't hurt you."

"No, I'm fine. Thanks." I omitted sir, because the man didn't seem too much older than me despite the wrinkles lining his face.

"Well, I'm right sorry for startling you." He nodded, then stomped away.

I took a deep breath and once again turned toward Ben's office.

"Yeah, I'm still interested. Let's play a round of eighteen and discuss the situation." Ben's voice was clear. Did he always talk so loudly? Was it to make himself appear in charge, or did he have someone with hearing loss close to him?

I stood still, debating my next move. Was there another person in the room? There was no obvious reply.

"Yeah, man. See you then." Still Ben's loud voice.

When nobody appeared in the hall, I moved to the entrance of Ben's office.

The door remained open from the gray-haired man. "Knock, knock."

Ben looked up from his phone then slid it into his gray shorts. "Kate, please come in."

"Hi, Ben. Is this a good time?" We had an appointment, but he appeared to be dealing with a lot.

"Absolutely. What do you have for me?" He motioned for me to join him in the sitting area. He took the chair facing the wall of windows overlooking the golf course. I was left to sit on the couch, facing him.

The coffee table was an uncomfortable distance from the couch, but I would manage. "You've got a good space here, but it's not being utilized to its full potential. For instance, the shelves look cluttered. What are all the stacks of paper?" They hadn't been there the week before.

He turned his attention from whatever was happening outside to me. "Each stack is a different business deal."

"Do you have the same information stored on your computer?"

His face reddened. "Well, some of it is, but I like the feel of papers in my hand."

I was fifty-three, and Ben was thirty-two. It flabbergasted me that he liked paperwork. My son was in his late twenties, and he preferred to keep important information on his computer. "Okay, that's good to know. If you prefer physical paperwork, we need a system to file it and keep your office tidy. You're revamping the resort, and you want your office to give a good impression. What do you have in the cabinets under the shelves?"

"Mostly junk." Ben laughed. "I'm starting to feel like a teenager getting scolded for having a messy room."

Uh-oh. My face warmed. "I am so sorry. You hired me to organize your space. I work for you, but I need to figure out what's important versus what we can change or get rid of."

"Just kidding." He moved to the nearest cabinet and opened the door. "Oh, this is really embarrassing. I've got a box of old video games and other junk." He pulled a cardboard box out, and it thunked on the ground. "Here's a box of trophies."

I hadn't counted on organizing to that level of detail. "How about focusing on the most important stuff first? Do you like file cabinets?" I pulled out a folder featuring modern file cabinets and passed it to the man. "There are many great options for your paperwork. We've got traditional, mid-century modern, and some that look like furniture. See for yourself."

Ben returned to his seat and looked at the options and tapped one. "This would work. Can you lock the drawers?"

"Yes, and this company has a good reputation for locks that actually work." His papers were all over the place, yet he wanted to lock them in a file cabinet. Interesting.

We discussed more ways to declutter his workspace. He had been distracted at the original meeting, and the job was going to be more intense than we'd expected. At last, I quoted him an estimate plus a figure for the down payment for our services.

"Kate, I usually pay as I go. You do the work, then I'll pay."

He'd already accused me of treating him like a kid, and I couldn't lecture him. Still, I wasn't planning to get burned financially. I smiled. "I'm sorry, Ben. We don't operate that way. A lot of items we order cannot be returned. There's also the time we spend drawing up plans and ordering the supplies you need. You're a businessman and must understand we can't work for free. If we're going to continue to organize your office, I need a down payment."

He looked out at the golf course and squinted. "Okay. I see your point."

I packed my belongings but remained seated on the couch. Was he going to pay me or let me go? The silence lengthened.

At last, Ben moved to his desk. "Who do I make the check out to?"

"Let's Get Organized, and thanks for understanding."

Ben's phone rang before he finished writing the check. He pulled it out and frowned at whoever's name popped up. He placed it on a stack of papers and finished with the check. He tore it out with a flourish, and I handed him a receipt.

"One of the local office supply stores carries these file cabinets. If they have yours on-site, I'll bring it by in the next couple of days. Otherwise, I'll order it."

"Great. I'm going to walk around the property. Besides my office, we're updating the spa and the suites on the top floor. They are two of my biggest money-makers, and they deserve my attention. Feel free to stick around."

Yay. I needed to get a grip on what else would be required to accomplish this job. "Is it okay if I look through your cabinets and your shelves? It'll give me a better idea what we're working with."

"Knock yourself out." He moved to a side door. "This is a quick way to get to the golf course. It's kinda like my secret passageway. Whenever I walk through the lobby, somebody always stops me with questions. The little corridor allows me to avoid those time suckers."

"That's pretty clever." I smiled at the man. "If I'm not here when you return, I'll be in touch."

"Sounds good." He mock-saluted me and disappeared.

Now for some alone time in Ben's office. I wanted to discover what was hidden behind those cabinet doors. Why hadn't he mentioned they were full the first time we'd met? He hadn't owned Seaside Hideaway for long, and I'd been under the mistaken impression they were empty.

It was a good thing I'd worn khaki shorts and a capri blue polo shirt advertising Let's Get Organized. My outfit was comfy and perfect for crawling around. I began with the cabinet nearest the large floor-to-ceiling windows.

A quick survey revealed it only needed some organization. The next cabinet was full of files stuffed with papers. I began calculating how much space would be needed for file cabinets. By the time I crawled to the sixth cabinet, I'd begun loading some items into utility bags. Boxes were needed to clear out all the junk, so we could start fresh.

Voices reached me from the hall leading to the lobby, and they didn't sound happy. If this resort was going to succeed, Ben had better get a handle on the conflict saturating the resort. Otherwise, it didn't matter how many renovations and updates he did, nobody would want to stay here.

I gathered my bags and notes and left. After pulling the door shut behind me, I walked right into the same man I'd seen earlier. There was a young woman with strawberry blonde hair standing near him. Her face was redder than her hair.

I turned my attention to the man and smiled. "We've got to stop meeting this way. I'm Kate Sloan."

He chuckled. "Rory Ledger. I run the golf shop here. This here is Sue Porter. She's the receptionist at the spa."

Sue wore a pink spa tunic over black slacks. "Nice to meet you, Kate. Rory, I'll see you later."

Rory said, "Don't worry. Together, we'll figure out a solution."

"That's usually easier said than done when dealing with—well, you know who." She waved and walked toward the main entrance.

"Rory, is the spa connected to the pro shop?" We strolled down the hall.

"No, but we're both across the lobby from check-in. You can enter the spa from the pool area, the parking lot, or the lobby. They take appointments, and there are usually not enough guests at the resort, so they accept outsiders. Sue and I've become friends. Are you a new employee?" The man's wide smile was full of warmth.

I pulled a business card out of a bag and passed it to him. "Ben hired my store to organize his office, but I don't think of myself as an employee. Although, in a way, I guess I am."

"Professional organizer? Hunh. If my granddaughter gets wind of this, she might hire you to organize my trailer." He chuckled.

"I'd be happy to take the job if one of you gives me a call. Have a good day, Rory." We parted ways at the main doors.

After stashing my bags in the SUV's backseat, I sat in the driver's seat and jotted down ideas on a fresh notepad about what I needed to do for Ben's office.

After Ben's reaction to paying me today, I decided to head straight to the bank just in case the check bounced.

Chapter Two

Driving back to the store, I spotted an SUV parallel parked along Ocean Boulevard with Texas tags. The sight lightened my heart, making me feel like my only son didn't live so far away. I parked in my designated spot for Let's Get Organized and lugged the utility bags through the back door of our business.

The sound of Bess having a conversation with a man made me happy. The voices didn't sound angry, like at the resort. I didn't believe Seaside Hideaway could succeed if there was strife around every corner.

Our business had only been open a few weeks, and money was tight. Bess and I were a two-woman operation. At some point, we'd be financially solid, but it would take time. As a real estate agent in Kentucky, I'd grown used to not having a steady paycheck. Back then, some months had been better than others, and the experience taught me to plan accordingly.

I placed the heavy bags on a work table in the back room. The man's voice sounded familiar, but it wasn't Pastor Tom Cross, the man Bess had a crush on. I headed to the front room of our store to join Bess out front in case she needed my assistance.

The room grew silent when I entered.

The man talking to Bess met my gaze.

It couldn't be.

I blinked.

Ethan. My Ethan stood beside Bess.

Tears sprang to my eyes.

"Hey, Mom. Surprise." He moved to me.

Joyful tears trickled down my face. I hugged my twenty-seven-year-old son. "Oh, honey. It's so good to see you, but what are you doing here?"

He patted my back. "Don't panic. I still have a job, but the position has changed. The company wants me to work remotely now, and I decided to move to Fox Island."

I stepped back and studied my dark-haired son. His brown eyes shone. "But why? I thought you liked Texas."

"Hey, I do like Texas."

"But?" Something fishy was going on. When he took his job and moved, I'd become an empty nester. It had seemed like the perfect opportunity to move back to Georgia, where I'd grown up. Ethan's formative years had been in Kentucky, and it didn't make sense for him to move here. My brothers and friends lived here, but this had never been Ethan's home.

"After you put yourself in danger trying to catch a killer—"

"Hey, I was instrumental in catching the killer." There was no trying to it.

"You're right, but it occurred to me that you might be more than your brothers can handle. When we lived in Kentucky, you were never in mortal danger, and I decided it was best to move here."

I gasped. "You're not serious. Are you?"

"Let's go to lunch and discuss it." He turned toward Bess. "Can you join us?"

Bess was like family, even though we hadn't lived near each other for years until I returned to Fox Island a few months earlier. Ethan had always been comfortable around my best friend. She shook her head. "Next time, but thanks for the invite."

"Shall we?" Ethan raised his eyebrows.

"Absolutely. We can walk to a new restaurant that I've been wanting to try. It's getting rave reviews." I took a moment to grab my purse; then we walked to Shrimp and Grits. A hostess took us to a table for two.

In no time, we had glasses of iced tea, and we placed our orders.

Ethan leaned back in his chair. "I wonder how many times this restaurant has reinvented itself?"

"At least four in my lifetime, but let's discuss your reason for being here."

As much as I loved my son, I didn't want him to change his life for me.

"Mom, you had me worried, and I felt helpless, living so far away."

"I'm a grown woman who's been taking care of myself for years, plus I raised you. Ethan, you can't give up your freedom, your life, to babysit me."

"Hey now, I have no intentions of giving up my freedom. I'm going to crash with you until I can find a home. It might be on the island, or it could be in Savannah, or somewhere else nearby." The stubborn look on my son's face spoke volumes. I'd seen that look plenty of times when he'd been growing up.

Ben Hauser entered the restaurant and slid into a nearby booth.

"See that man over there? He's close to your age. Dark wavy hair and in good shape." I gave a discrete motion with my head to indicate where I wanted Ethan to look.

My son glanced in Ben's direction. "Yeah, what about him?"

"He's the new owner of Seaside Hideaway, and he's updating it to attract tourists. I understand the golf course is nice."

"If the course is nice, he could hold golf tournaments. When managed the right way, they're big moneymakers."

A young woman with wavy shoulder-length hair entered the restaurant and looked around. She made a straight shot to Ben.

Would this be a nice interaction, or would there be a dispute like Ben's interaction with Rory? "This place is hopping."

"The month of May on the coast is tourist season." Ethan took a drink of his tea.

The young woman raised a book sealed in a clear plastic bag and frowned at Ben. I couldn't hear her words.

"Ethan, what's that girl saying?"

My son did a double take. Soon he said, "The woman told your friend that he owes her twelve-hundred dollars for the book in her hand. It sounds like she ordered it just for him, and now he doesn't want to pay her."

My stomach clenched. Good thing I'd already gone to the bank and deposited Ben's check. "He's a client, but I'm not sure if he's a friend."

"How about the woman? Who is she?"

"I haven't met her, but I've heard a bookstore was moving into the old art gallery. She's got a book, so it's possible she's the new owner."

Ben motioned that the young lady should sit across from him, and she did. The stiff set of her shoulders indicated she'd rather go anywhere else. She'd probably agreed, hoping he'd pay her for the book.

Our waitress appeared and placed a Caesar salad in front of me and the grouper special at Ethan's place. My attention drifted back to Ben.

"Mom, quit staring."

I smiled at him. "Sorry. Ben has been in arguments with at least three people today, and it's just lunchtime. I hope Bess and I don't regret working for him."

"I'm sure it'll be fine. Try not to worry." He glanced toward the table again.

"You're right." I stabbed my salad and took the first bite of cold crispiness. "When you see my place, you might decide to crash with one of your uncles. My apartment is tiny."

"I'm surprised you settled for something that doesn't live up to your high standards."

"It's clean and close to the beach, plus it's temporary." It made sense my son would be surprised at my choice. When he was growing up, we always had nice homes. "Again, feel free to stay with your uncles."

He shrugged. "I don't mind crashing on your couch. Uncle Paul already warned me about your apartment, but I don't need much space. He agreed that the best part is your location to the beach."

"It's pretty sweet, and there's a coffee shop across the street. But my new place will be awesome once Reid renovates it. Do you remember Reid?"

"I think I met him once. He and Uncle Paul are friends, right?"

"We all grew up together, and he was my friend too." I needed to start preparing Ethan to know about my relationship with Reid. Baby steps seemed appropriate.

Ethan paused, dragging a French fry through ketchup. He leaned over the table. "Am I missing something?"

My chest, neck, and face grew warm, and I didn't think it was a hot flash. So much for taking it slow.

"Mom?"

"Reid and I are dating." May as well go for broke. "Exclusively."

"Okay." He ate his French fry.

His calm acceptance surprised me. "You don't mind?"

"No, ma'am. Dad passed away years ago. You deserve to be happy."

"Thanks, honey."

"I figure he'd be an idiot to hurt you with your brothers living here, and now I'm in town."

I bit back a smile. "True, and he's no idiot. Let's talk about your decision to live in the area." We discussed real estate agents and possible areas where Ethan might enjoy living. "If you consider a fixer-upper, Reid can help with your renovations."

"Good to know."

Movement at Ben's table caught my eye. The young woman left with the book in her hand, and she wasn't walking to the exit.

"I'm finished, and I need to use the restroom. I'll be right back." I made my way to the ladies' room and got lucky. The young woman was washing her hands, and the book was secured between her arm and ribs.

"Do you need help?"

Her eyes widened, and she nodded. "Thanks."

I took the book. "It looks old."

"It is. I'm Madison Ledger, and I own the FUN Book Shop. Fun stands for Fine, Unique, and New Book Shop. I moved my business into the old Fox Island Art Gallery." She reached for a paper towel and dried her hands.

"I'll have to come by. I love to read. I'm Kate Sloan, and I work at Let's Get Organized. Actually, my friend Bess Walker and I are the owners. If you need support from other women business owners, please reach out to us."

"Thanks. It's kind of you to offer."

"I saw you having lunch with Ben Hauser."

She huffed. "Watch your back with that guy. The book you're holding cost me over twelve hundred dollars. Ben asked me to locate a copy, and he promised to pay the price once I found it. He even agreed to go as high as three thousand dollars. I should've known better, but the auction was

winding down, and I didn't want to miss out. Now Ben's refusing to pay."
She reached for the book.

"I'm curious. What's the title?"

"*Atlantic Coast Guide.*"

"What makes it so valuable?" I typed the title into my phone.

"I honestly don't know. It's not written by a famous author or politician. It's old, but that alone doesn't make it worth so much money. I blame myself for making a poor choice."

"I'm sorry this happened to you, and I hope you won't hold Ben's actions against the rest of us. Fox Island is a lovely place to live, and Ben just recently moved here."

Her shoulders slumped. "I should go. It was nice meeting you."

"You too, Madison. Bess and I recently remodeled the offices at the art gallery, now your store. Let me know if you'd like us to tweak them for your needs. Also, stop by if you'd like to grab a cup of coffee." I handed a business card to her. "Welcome to Fox Island."

"Thanks." She left, and I followed.

Ethan wasn't at the table, and Ben had also left. I found my son outside on the sidewalk, and we returned to Let's Get Organized.

"Thanks for lunch. What do you have planned for this afternoon?"

"I took off a few days to get settled. How can I help you today?"

There were so many options, and I didn't have an appointment scheduled. "The biggest way you can help might be to go to Seaside Hideaway with me. It'll require lifting and moving a few things."

He flexed his arms the way he'd done as a young boy. "I should be able to handle it."

"Great. My Wagoneer is in back. Come on."

"Wagoneer?" When we reached my vehicle, Ethan laughed. "Mom, where's your Bug?"

"You know I had an accident in it?"

"Yeah, but why not just fix it?"

"Yuck. It was full of pluff mud and water—"

"Um, it sounds like more than a fender bender."

I nodded. "Yeah. After crashing into the marsh, I decided it was time to get something bigger."

He whistled and walked around the SUV. "Did you consider a newer replacement?"

"Yeah, but this suits my purposes. It's safe, it's solid as a tank, and I can fit a lot into it." I unlocked my door, then his door. "Get this, there's even a cassette player."

"I'm pretty sure nobody makes cassettes anymore. Most people listen to music and podcasts by linking their phones to the car's audio system with Bluetooth."

"I know, now buckle up. Prepare to be amazed at how great this baby drives."

By two o'clock, Ethan and I were moving a new file cabinet into Ben's office. The woman at the front desk remembered me from earlier and told me to go on into the office even though she wasn't sure exactly where Ben was.

"Mom, how do you know he's going to pay you for this?"

"Before I fill it with his files, I'm going to get the money, or else it'll go back to the store." We placed the cabinet near Ben's desk, then returned the hand truck to my SUV. We carried empty boxes back to the building.

Madison Ledger exited the pro shop, and Rory Ledger followed her. The young woman looked like she might have been crying.

"Ethan, wait a second. I want to introduce you to these two." I changed directions and joined them. "Hi, there. Madison, when I met you, it didn't occur to me you were related to Rory."

She sniffed. "Yes, ma'am. He's my uncle."

"How nice for you to have family nearby. This is my son, Ethan. He's also moving to the area." We made a quick round of introductions. "I'm organizing Ben's office space, and I roped Ethan into helping me. We better get to it, but it was nice to see you again."

Madison's eyes widened. "Don't forget my warning."

"I won't, but thanks for the reminder. See you later."

Once Ethan and I returned to the office, I assembled a box. "The files will go in here until I can get Ben to sort through them. There's no need to haphazardly put files in the cabinet."

"Hey, let me build the boxes, and you organize."

"Thanks, honey."

Ethan played a sports podcast on his phone, and we got busy. My son had participated in different sports, growing up. He was working for a professional sports team in Texas, and it didn't make sense that he could work remotely.

I searched the shelves and removed anything that didn't fit. Once we had boxes filled, I looked at my son. "Will you take all these to the car? I'm going to leave Ben a note with his homework assignment."

"His what?"

"Once Ben pays me, I need him to put the important files in the cabinet. There's only so much an organizer can do without input from the client." I placed a sticky note on the top colorful folder. "I wonder where Ben is."

"It seems like owning a resort requires a lot of work, but there are plenty of distractions here. In fact, I believe that golf course is calling my name. After I put the boxes in your Wagoneer, I'm going to take a quick look."

"Take your time."

I sat at the desk, found paper and pen, and wrote a detailed note to Ben, explaining what I'd done. I also gave brief directions about filing his papers and suggested a theme for each file color. At the end of the day, he needed a system that would work for him. I ran my hand over the note and looked out the big windows.

It was a beautiful day, and fresh air would do me some good. I walked down Ben's private hallway and stepped into the sunshine.

A warm breeze blew back my hair. I gathered it into a ponytail and looked around. There was Ben in a golf cart. "Hey, Ben. I need to talk to you a minute."

Something wasn't right.

He was slumped over the steering wheel of the golf cart.

Had he passed out from the heat? It was probably only in the high eighties, but was that enough to affect a young person so badly? Had he drunk too much at lunch? I approached him. "Ben, are you okay?"

He didn't respond.

My mouth grew dry as a saltine cracker, but I forced myself to step closer.

"Ben?" I touched his shoulder, and his body fell toward me. I tried to catch him, but my knees buckled. He was too heavy. "Help! Help!"

Ben's dead weight pushed me down onto the cart path.

Dead weight. Yeah, because I suspected Ben Hauser was dead.

Chapter Three

"Katie, what are you doing?" Reid ran to me. He reached down and began lifting Ben's body off me.

"Mom!" Ethan joined us and helped Reid move the body.

"I think he's dead." My voice shook, and my body trembled.

Reid and Ethan lay the body flat on a shady patch of grass, and Ethan felt for a pulse.

I fell back on my arms, trying to catch my breath. Deep breath in, then exhale slowly.

Reid knelt beside me in the position men often use for proposing. "Katie, are you okay?"

"Yes. No. I don't know. Is Ben alive?"

Ethan said, "I don't feel a pulse, and there's blood on his shirt."

A woman screamed.

The scene played out in slow motion before my eyes.

The screamer was the spa girl. What was her name? Sue. Sue Porter. Yeah.

Ethan looked at her. "Call for help. Hurry."

She pulled a phone out of the pocket in her pink tunic.

"Katie, let's get you in the shade." Reid helped me to my feet, and we walked to a bench under a group of palm trees. My back was to Ethan and Ben.

"No pulse means he's—"

"Unless they can do CPR and revive him." He squeezed my shoulder.

"Isn't that mainly for drowning victims and heart attacks?"

Before Reid answered, Madison appeared with a bottle of water and a soft drink. "Uncle Rory thought you might need a cold drink. You could be in shock."

"Thanks." I took both drinks and sipped on the sugary one first, hoping it'd give me some energy. "Ethan's alone with Ben's body."

Reid said, "No, Rory Ledger and Sue Porter are with him. An ambulance is on the way."

Madison glanced at the cart path area where I'd found Ben. "That's why Uncle Rory disappeared while I was getting the drinks. It makes sense he'd want to help."

Reid sat on my left. He knew of my hearing loss and was always conscientious to make it easier for me to hear him. "Katie, did you hear me say that an ambulance is on the way?"

"Good, that's very good."

Madison rocked from one foot to the other, and I felt sorry for her.

"I feel so guilty. My last conversation with Ben was an argument." Madison met my gaze. "You were there."

"Ben wasn't easy to like. Given the circumstances, you treated him better than he deserved." I leaned against Reid's shoulder. Ben was probably dead, and I had been one of the last people to see him. "Reid, we need to tell Paul right away. The 9-1-1 operator might have reported an emergency and not a murder."

"Good thinking." He removed his phone, then stepped away.

Paul Wright was my brother and the police chief of Fox Island. He'd want to know about the murder, and he needed to know I was the one who'd found the body.

Madison pulled her dark hair into a messy bun and paced.

"Do you want to sit beside me?" I took a sip of my water.

"No, ma'am. I should check on Uncle Rory." She walked away, dragging her feet. Her flat sandals scuffed along the concrete sidewalk.

I avoided looking toward Ben, even though I hated the thought of Ethan dealing with the situation. The birds had grown silent. There was no more noise coming from the swimming pool. A somber mood fell over the area.

A few weeks earlier, I had found a dead body. This time, a dead body fell on me, pushing me to the ground. The memory made me feel nauseous, then cold. I shivered despite the warm, humid day.

Reid rejoined me. "Paul's on the way."

"Good. Why are you at the resort, Reid?"

"I was inspecting the suites to give Ben a bid. He was looking for local contractors to renovate them. I assume you're here for a job, too."

"Yes, Ben hired Bess and me to organize his office. From what I learned in a short time, he didn't seem to get along with many people. It's odd, because I bet he hasn't lived here over six months."

"I wasn't around him enough to know. We met in his office, and he told me he wanted to update the suites. He asked for a proposal and an estimate of the price. I was surprised at the freedom, but he didn't have time to answer questions. Our conversation was brief, then a staff person appeared and took me to one of the areas to be renovated."

Two firemen ran past us with what appeared to be life-saving equipment.

Reid gave me a one-arm hug. "Just breathe."

"I'm trying."

The sound of a siren grew louder as we sat there with me pulling myself together; at least I tried to get a grip on my emotions.

The first policeman on the scene was Officer Drake Collins. He'd helped me in the past, and he slowed when he spotted me. "Mrs. Sloan, are you okay?"

I nodded. "Yes. The body's over there."

The young man with a crew cut jogged in the direction I'd pointed.

Officer Emerson Diaz and my brother arrived together. Emerson headed toward the body, but Paul detoured to Reid and me. "Sis, what's happening? Reid said you found another dead body."

"I'm afraid so, but it was purely by accident. I only stepped outside for a breath of fresh air."

He raised his hand. "Stop. We'll officially question you in a bit."

"Okay. I'll stay here."

Paul hustled toward the crowd but slowed when he crossed paths with Ethan. The men hugged, then held a short conversation. Soon, my son joined us on the bench. He dropped his head into his hands and shuddered. "I don't see how they can revive him. He's got to be dead."

I rubbed Ethan's back but didn't speak.

Ben's death would affect all of us in different ways. Ethan had never met Ben, yet he'd been the one with the body when paramedics arrived. I barely knew Ben, and it seemed cruel to think negative thoughts about the man. Reid had only met him briefly.

Ben was in his early thirties and had appeared to be in good shape. The way his body had been draped over the steering wheel had given me the impression he'd passed out.

Ethan sat straight. "Where'd you get the drinks?"

"Oh, Madison brought them to me. She may have gone to the pro shop with her uncle."

"I'll be back." His head hung as he walked away.

"Oh, Reid. I don't know what to say to him right now."

"This is a tough situation. He knows you're here for him, and he'll talk when he's ready. Do you want me to reach out to Tom Cross? Maybe he's willing to speak to Ethan."

The pastor of the community church was not my biggest fan, but we were beginning to accept each other. "Let's give it a few days."

Reid laced his fingers with mine.

"Ethan and I had lunch at Shrimp and Grits and saw Ben. Madison Ledger confronted him about owing her over a thousand dollars for a book. "

Reid whistled. "That's pricey. Now, who is Madison?"

"She owns the new bookstore, and she moved her business into the abandoned Fox Island Art Gallery."

"That was fast, but I'm glad nobody is tearing it down." Reid gave me a lopsided smile. One of his passions was to renovate old buildings and homes.

"Her uncle runs the golf shop here." I shared what little I knew about the two of them. "Did you smell alcohol on Ben?"

"There was a slight odor, but it wasn't strong enough to make me think he was drunk."

"I felt the same way. Did you see blood?"

"From the gash on his head?"

"I was so distraught that I didn't know exactly where the wound was." I shivered again.

"It was a head wound. Why are you asking so many questions?"

"I did a pretty good job-solving Carissa Ruffalo's murder. The police might need my help again."

"They humored you last time, because your brother was a potential suspect." His gentle tone softened the words.

"You might be right." Motion caught my eye. "Here comes Officer Collins."

"It's going to be okay."

My heartbeat skittered. There was no reason to feel nervous, so why did I?

Chapter Four

Ben Hauser was no longer among the living. It was past suppertime before Reid, Ethan, and I were finally able to compare stories. We'd grabbed sandwiches and salads at Danny's Deli and had eaten them there, saying very little. Now we sat in my little living room. Reid and I were on the couch, and Ethan sat in the comfortable chair.

Reid rubbed his thighs. "Do y'all want to discuss what happened today?"

I sighed. "A man died today, and we should compare notes about what we know. Officer Diaz questioned me for hours, but what if you all saw something that would trigger a memory for me? Plus, Ethan, you were with the body the longest. How are you processing the situation?"

"I'm still processing." His head dropped back and rested on the chair. "When you hold a warm, dead body that was alive earlier, it makes you assess what you're doing with your life."

"What do you mean?" I hated that this experience was my fault. If he hadn't been worried about me, he'd still be in Texas.

"You know. Life." He grimaced. "I'm making good money, but am I making a difference in the world? I'm not helping orphans, the elderly, animals, or the environment. What is my purpose?"

Reid said, "I get it. Why'd you move to Fox Island?"

"The primary reason was to keep an eye on Mom. As you know, that's a bust. We were only together a few hours before she found a dead body." Again, Ethan grimaced.

"Hey, that's not your fault. We were just unlucky to find Ben." I shook my head. "That sounds incredibly selfish, but why did he have to get murdered today? Why'd we find him? Again, I hear myself, and I know it's selfish."

Reid took my hand in his. "This is a safe place to express how you feel. There's no judgment from me, and probably not Ethan."

"He's right, Mom. All afternoon, I kept thinking about the purpose of life. What am I doing with my life, as well as why did we find the body. Er, mostly you. Is there a reason I was with you, or at least nearby? Why didn't he get killed this morning? You were with him then. It might have been both of you. Also, why didn't he get murdered later today, say in the dark? There are so many questions, and they are rolling around in my brain like pool balls, but they are not going into the holes. They bounce off each other and go in different directions."

My heart ached for Ethan. "For my sake, I'm glad you were around to help. I don't know what I would've done if you and Reid hadn't appeared. Thank you both."

"Would anyone like some chamomile tea?" Ethan stood. "None of us will probably get much sleep tonight, but it might help."

"I'll take a cup." If the action gave my son a reason, no a purpose, for being here tonight, I'd drink a gallon of the tea.

Reid said, "That sounds good to me."

The kitchen was only a few steps away. While Ethan moved to the kitchen, I opened the sliding glass door to the little balcony. "The fresh sea air might help us relax too. Why don't I start with my conversation with the police?"

I walked to my desk and retrieved a journal. The first few pages had been used for making notes on my new house, but I flipped it over and began writing from the back. "I saw Ben this morning. There seemed to be a conflict between him and Rory Ledger. There was also something going on between Ben and Sue Porter; she works in the spa."

Ethan filled the tea kettle with water and placed it on the stove. "Romantically?"

"I doubt it." I sat beside Reid again and wrote Sue's name on the top of the page. "While I was finishing up in Ben's office, I heard voices in the hallway. I ran into Rory and Sue. He appeared to be comforting her, in a fatherly way. I felt like it had to do with a situation between Ben and Sue. It'd be good to know if the spa rents the space at the resort, or do the employees work for Ben?"

Reid tapped the page where I was writing. "Now that Ben has passed, it'd be interesting to know who inherits the resort."

"What is happening here? It sounds like you two plan to solve the murder." Ethan placed a mug on the counter so hard it broke. He growled and threw away the broken pieces. "Sorry."

"Don't worry about it. This isn't like trying to catch the killer in order to prove Paul was innocent. I'm just curious, and it's possible I forgot something in the stress of the day."

"Mom, I just don't like it." The teakettle whistled, and he began pouring hot water in mugs.

I indented and wrote down another name. "That cute Madison Ledger confronted Ben at lunch. Remember?"

"How could I forget? Now that you mention her, did you follow her to the restroom on purpose?"

Busted. "Well, yeah. Ben had tried to get me to work without a down payment. I had to insist. I told him flat out that if he didn't, we wouldn't do the work for him. So, I was curious. It turns out that Ben refused to pay Madison for a very expensive book."

Reid helped Ethan carry over the mugs of tea. "We're adding to our list of suspects. Today, Ben upset Rory Ledger, Sue Porter, and Madison Ledger. Those are only the people I know about."

I jotted down Sue's name. "Yes, and all three were at the resort around the time we found Ben's body."

Ethan returned to his seat. "You found the body. I heard you scream and came to help."

"Right."

"There's another person you don't know about." My son sipped his tea.

"Don't leave me hanging."

"While you were in the restroom with Madison, another man approached Ben, and they argued. Ben threw a wad of money on the table, and they walked out together."

Chapter Five

"Another man? What did he look like?" It was a good thing I wasn't investigating this murder. It never occurred to me I might have missed a clue at the restaurant. Some detective I was, but there was really no reason for me to investigate the murder. My notes were only to satisfy my own curiosity.

Ethan cocked his head. "I'd guess he's around your age. He's tall with salt and pepper hair. He appeared to be in decent shape. Bottom line is he was mad, and Ben laughed at him. That's when Ben threw money on the table and walked out with the angry dude."

Reid set his mug on a side table. "Did you tell the cops?"

"No. I mainly focused on what happened at the hotel. You know, Mom and I worked in the office. I took boxes to the car, then looked at the golf course. That's when I heard Mom scream. Officer Collins asked if I saw anything unusual before or after the scream." He turned his focus on me. "Besides the dead body knocking you to the ground, nothing else seemed unusual or suspicious." He sipped his tea. "By the way, he mentioned he helped you out of a deadly situation."

"That's true." Goosebumps broke out on my arms, and I shivered. "Don't worry. I won't try to solve this murder mystery."

Ethan swiped his phone. "I don't find your words very reassuring while you taking notes on the murder."

"Nobody likes a smarty pants."

Reid said, "I've never met Sue Porter. How did she act around you?"

Ethan glanced at Reid. "She called 9-1-1 for me. She relayed questions to me from the operator. I grabbed a golf towel and held it over the wound. It was probably stupid, because I don't know that he was still bleeding."

"It wasn't stupid." Reid's calm demeanor seemed to soothe Ethan.

"I asked Sue if she knew Ben. She said they were work associates, but she didn't know him very well."

I turned the page in my notebook. "Tell me about the wound."

"Of course, I'm no authority, but there was a gash in his head. The shape of the dent made me think a golf club had struck him." He closed his eyes. "It was near the hairline and would've been easy to miss, depending on the angle of his head."

"Did you see the club?"

"No, but I wasn't looking either."

"Did you see any other wounds or signs of a fight?"

Ethan shook his head. "Mom, the only dead body I've ever seen was Dad, and that was in the casket. Today, I was doing my best not to flip out. I was not looking for clues, and I didn't see any other wounds. I saw Ben with a bruise and blood around the wound. It appeared to have run down his face. I didn't see any other bruises or cuts."

I recognized Ethan's tone. It was the same tone he always used when he was fed up with a situation. "Okay. Maybe we should call it a day." I stood and put away my notebook.

A breeze ruffled the curtains, and I smelled the ocean. It was almost a full moon, and from my balcony, I could see a sliver of the beach.

Ethan finished the tea in his mug. "Is your WiFi always so spotty?"

"It depends on how many people are in the building, and the weather, and, well, yeah. It's not the best."

"I won't be able to deal with it. Are there any good apartment complexes on the island? Maybe I can get a six-month rental while deciding what to do."

"There's Pelican Shores Apartments. I know a young man who lives there. At least, I think he's still there. Ian Wilson. He's a financial adviser. If you'd like to talk to him about the reality of living there, I'll set it up. Or I can send you his contact information."

"I'm afraid to ask why you have the phone number of a guy my age in your phone."

Reid said, "You probably don't want to know. I'll shove off."

"I'm going to take a shower." Ethan disappeared into the bathroom.

I walked to the community front porch with Reid. Sand Piper Apartments consisted of eight apartments. The place was old, and the apartments were small. The beauty of the place was the location. It also didn't hurt that you could rent for a short period of time. I wasn't convinced Ethan would be able to do the same at Pelican Shores.

Reid wrapped me in his arms. "I'm sure you're trying to be strong for your son, but how are you really holding up?"

I met his gaze in the porch light's reflection. "I've certainly been better."

"That's understandable." He played with a loose strand of my hair. "On a happy note, we caught a break on your kitchen remodel. The cabinet people have the cabinets ready, and they look spectacular with the stripped and freshly polished wood floors in the kitchen. The drywall looks good, and it's all coming together. I had hoped to take you over tonight."

My heart leapt. "What if I pick up breakfast and meet you there tomorrow morning?"

"Is seven too early? I've got a full day."

"It's no problem at all. I'll see you then."

"It's going to be a great way to start our morning." Reid's lips touched mine.

My knees grew weak from the kiss. I'd had a crush on Reid in high school, but life had taken us in different directions. We were back together, and I'd never felt so loved and cherished.

My apartment door opened.

The kiss ended.

Ethan appeared with wet hair and wearing athletic shorts. "Uh, sorry, guys."

Reid said, "I best shove off. See you tomorrow, Katie. Night, Ethan."

"Night, Reid." My son made no move to leave.

"Goodnight." I entered the apartment. At last, Ethan followed, locking the door behind us.

"Sorry, Mom. I think Ben's death has me a little freaked out, and it surprised me when you weren't here. I thought I should look for you."

"Thanks, honey." I glanced out the window. Across the street was Island Perk Coffee Shop. They opened at six every morning, and I could swing by there and pick up breakfast.

Movement across the street caught my attention.

I stood back but continued to watch.

A man stood in the shadows, talking on a cell phone, and he stared straight at me.

"Mom, whatcha doing?"

I jumped but stifled a scream. "Look at the man across the street."

Ethan reached for the curtain.

"No, wait. Don't let him see you." My pulse thundered like waves on a stormy day. "Be subtle."

My son stood at the corner of the window and peeked out. "I don't see anyone."

I looked again.

The man had disappeared.

Coincidence? Or something sinister?

"It was probably my overactive imagination, but let's shut the sliding glass door." I was glad to have another person staying in the apartment with me. Otherwise, I probably wouldn't get any sleep.

Chapter Six

Tuesday morning, I left Ethan a note and slipped out of the apartment. I ordered breakfast sandwiches and coffee at Island Perk, then met Reid at my new house.

He was waiting and smiled when I hopped out of my old Wagoneer.

"Food first or see your house first?"

"It'd be a shame for our food to get cold, and I want to take my time walking through the house."

"My crew is ahead of schedule, which is unheard of these days. Remodeling is also quicker than building from scratch. If you weren't competing in the Memorial Day Triathlon, you'd probably be able to move in that weekend."

"Oh, man. I'd really hoped you'd forgotten." I laughed. When we first reconnected, I shot off my big mouth and claimed I could beat him in a triathlon.

"Not a chance. You can't challenge a man and expect him to forget." He pointed to the front steps. "Let's eat there. I don't let the workers eat inside, and I want to set a good example."

"Perfect." We got settled and ate our sandwiches. Fried egg, turkey bacon, and avocado slices on multigrain toast. Birds chirped, and I could hear the ocean waves. One huge perk to this house was its proximity to the beach, and it was off the beaten path.

A young man drove by in his golf cart with a baby strapped to his chest. He waved, but his strained smile made me wonder if the purpose of the ride was for the baby to sleep.

"Do you think you'll buy a golf cart when you move here?"

"Maybe, or I might ride my bike around." My thoughts drifted to Ben's body draped over the steering wheel. "It's been a while since I drove a golf cart. Do you think Ben was attacked on the golf course and drove back for help? Maybe he died before he could walk inside."

"I don't know, and I'm sorry you had to be the one to find him." Reid rubbed my shoulder.

"Me, too, and I need to quit thinking about his murder." I sighed. "I can't believe I stayed away from Fox Island for so long."

"Yeah, roughly thirty years. It was way too long, but you're home now. If only people wouldn't get murdered, life would be near perfect." He tossed his food wrapper into the paper bag, then he leaned back and drank his coffee.

I finished eating. "I can't wait any longer. Let's tour the house, and I'll drink my coffee later."

We walked up the stairs to the front door and entered. The interior was nearly two thousand square feet, and it'd be plenty of room for me. The best part of this home was the outside living spaces. Front porch, side porch, rear deck, and a roof deck. The house was raised over a carport and storage area.

I walked through the family room, dining area, and the kitchen. The space was open and inviting. There were two bedrooms and two full bathrooms. Upstairs was a third bedroom and a loft leading to the roof deck. I planned to use the loft to take up painting in my free time. The third bedroom could be an office or guest room.

I practically danced through the house, oohing and aahing over the progress. Back in the family room, I spun to Reid and hugged him. "I can't thank you enough. You suggested this house, and you're remodeling it to be the house of my dreams."

He wrapped his arms around me. "I can't take all of the credit. I mean, you are paying me for the remodel."

I laughed. "Of course I am. Are you sure I can't move in before Memorial Day?"

One side of Reid's mouth quirked up. "I don't want to get your hopes up, but it's possible."

I kissed him. "This is better than I ever dreamed."

"If you keep kissing me like that, I'll make sure it's move-in ready before Memorial Day."

Clomping footsteps, climbing the front steps, ended our embrace.

"Probably some workmen." Reid chuckled. "We can't seem to catch a break."

"Let's get out of here so they can finish sooner." Once I moved in, there'd be plenty of time to cuddle and kiss.

Reid laughed. "I like the way you think."

Two HVAC employees entered and stopped to speak to Reid.

I left them alone and walked out to the carport, slowing to snag my coffee cup. I took a sip of the honey vanilla coffee and wandered around the open area. The coffee smelled and tasted delicious, and I took my time to savor it. There were tools, water hoses, and crumpled boxes pushed into a corner of the space. I tried the storage room door, but it was locked. If I kept anything here, it'd need to have some kind of insulation to protect it from the salt air.

An official police truck eased into the driveway, and Paul hopped out. "Hey, sis. You're up early."

"How'd you know where to find me?"

"I tried your apartment first and woke up Ethan. He found your note, so I drove here. Will this place be ready soon?"

"Hopefully before Memorial Day."

"That's impressive. Most builders are hitting delays for various reasons."

"Reid said the same thing, but he's not ordering many new items. You know how much he likes to protect the environment and improve what's available?"

"Boy, do I. He's called me to help him pull out cabinets and countertops from one project to be used at another site. I don't know why he works out at the gym when he does so much grunt work on his own."

"He goes to get a cardio workout. None of us are getting any younger."

"True. Listen, I read the interview notes of Ben Hauser's death. I'm curious if you remembered anything else since you gave your official statement."

I sipped my coffee again. Paul would be upset if I told him I'd begun an investigation. Although, I really hadn't. Nobody had been questioned by me. "Last night, Ethan, Reid, and I discussed the murder. You know, to kinda decompress."

"Right." Doubt laced his tone.

"Ethan mentioned that a man spoke to Ben at the restaurant while I wasn't at the table. He said they weren't exactly friendly, but they left together. Maybe that's a clue."

"I'll check with Ethan and the staff. Where'd you eat?"

"Shrimp and Grits."

"Nice. Anything else?"

I sighed. "This is probably nothing, and I wouldn't report it, but since you asked. I thought someone was watching my apartment last night, but when I tried to show Ethan, the man was gone."

Paul's eyes widened. "You found Ben's body, and it's possible the killer knows that. Try not to worry, but stay alert just in case. Let me know if you spot him again. Also, I may have the night patrol keep a closer watch on your place. Be careful." My brother hugged me and left.

Reid returned, and we finished our coffees together before going our separate ways.

As I drove to work, I kept my eyes open for the stranger. It was probably the reason I spotted Madison Ledger at the front door of the bookstore. I whipped into the parking lot, intending to ask about the book she'd ordered for Ben.

Paul probably wouldn't be happy, but I was the one who'd found Ben's dead body. He'd fallen on me. I'd seen him hours before his death. While we hadn't exactly been friends, a sense of urgency filled me, pushing me to help catch the killer.

Chapter Seven

"Hi, Madison. Can I give you a hand?" I walked across the sandy parking lot of FUN Bookstore.

The young lady's arms were full, and she was fumbling with a ring full of keys. "Oh, hi. Mrs. Sloan, right? My mind is jumbled from yesterday."

"Call me Kate. Here, let me help." I held out my hands, and she dumped the books and folders in them. "You know, a utility bag might be helpful for days like this."

Madison returned to inserting different keys into the lock. "That's right. You're the organizer. Sorry. I'm meeting so many people, and it's hard to keep everyone straight."

"I understand. Have you been in town long?"

"Six weeks. It started out as a visit with Uncle Rory, and before you know it, I own my own bookstore. My head's spinning with all I need to accomplish before the opening. I'm wearing down."

"Ben Hauser's death has hit our community hard, and it probably isn't helping your stress level."

"I thought he was a newcomer. Why do so many people care?"

"Fox Island is a small town. Plus, murder is always disturbing." Her words reminded me that the previous murder victim hadn't lived here all that long, either.

"At last." Madison turned the key in the lock and hurried inside to turn off the alarm.

I followed her at a polite distance. "Would you like me to take this to your office?"

"Sure, it's just—oh yeah, you organized it for the previous owner. Can you believe when I bought his place, it came furnished? Too bad all the artwork was confiscated."

"It's amazing you were able to buy it so quickly." I elbowed on light switches as I walked to Madison's office. Once there, I placed the items on an empty chair. This place needed some attention.

"Uncle Rory knows the owner of the building and helped speed up the process. Sorry about the mess. I hope to open the store this weekend, but I'm nowhere near ready. At least I built the shelves for displaying the books."

"Will you sell books in the section that used to be the art gallery?"

"Yes." She spun in a slow circle as if looking for something. "I have plans for expansion, but in the beginning, it'll be simple. One advantage to this building is the ability to grow."

"What about the coffee shop?"

"Down the road, I'll find someone to run it for me." Her eyes widened, and she strode to an open box. "These books are by a local author who agreed to sign them and meet customers this Saturday. I need to get busy, but how can I help you?"

"I'm curious about the book you ordered for Ben. I don't mind to help you for a few minutes, if you would answer some questions."

"You sound like a cop or a reporter."

"No, I'm just an organizer."

She eyed me up and down, then waved for me to follow. "Come on. The book Ben wanted had to do with the coast of Georgia. It's the most I have ever spent on a book, and now I'm stuck with it."

"Do you have proof that he requested it? Maybe the estate will pay you."

Madison placed the box of books on a small rectangular table. "Good idea. I'll try to find out if the executor of the estate will pay for it. Uncle Rory may know who it is."

Discussion about the pricey book seemed to trigger Madison's anger. It was time to change the subject. I pointed at the square table. "Is this where the autographing will take place?"

"It sure is."

"I can arrange the display and let you work on something else."

"Oh, thanks."

"Is there any possibility you'd let me look at the book you ordered for Ben?" I pulled books out of the box and stacked them neatly.

"For twelve hundred dollars, you can buy it. Shoot, I might give it to you at cost just to get rid of it."

"Sorry, that's not in my budget. Don't forget, I'm a new business owner, just like you."

"I figured as much. If I decide to let you look at it, you'll need to wear gloves, and I'm not letting it out of my sight."

"I understand." The first book I removed from the box was a romance written by a Georgia author. *Love and the Lighthouse Keeper* by Darby Meadows was the newest release by the author. "You say this is a local author?"

"Yes. She lives on the island full time."

"That is so cool." I arranged the books, pens, bookmarks, and a bowl of candy on the table. "I like the color you painted the walls, and the place seems brighter."

"The previous owner had black curtains over the windows, probably to highlight the artwork. So, I painted, added more lights, and removed the window treatments."

"I like all your improvements." I removed the cardboard boxes from the table. "If you add fresh cut flowers near the table, it'll be even more inviting. What do you think?"

Madison studied the display, then nodded. "It looks terrific. You placed the items on the table so it looks inviting and not crowded."

"Thanks. Is the book here?" Oh, that probably sounded abrupt. "I mean, the one Ben asked you to order."

"Yes, ma'am. It's secure in the office safe."

"May I see it?"

"I'm not sure." Madison jutted out her chin. "Did you tell the police about my discussion with Ben?"

"I told the police officer everything that happened to me yesterday, especially if Ben was involved. I found the body, and they questioned me. I really didn't have a choice. What about you? Were you questioned by the authorities?"

"Yes, thanks to you. I've never done anything wrong. The worst thing on my record is a parking ticket, and I paid it the next day. I don't appreciate being questioned about a murder."

"Look, I don't know where you're from, but Fox Island is a small town. People talk. If I hadn't told the police, somebody else in the restaurant would have. Your bookstore will probably do well, because we have tourists and events to bring visitors to the island. At the heart, though, we're a little town. On the plus side, we'll be there for you." I removed a business card from my black and white polka dot purse. "For instance, you don't have a lot of time before your opening. If you get in a bind, give me a call. I have appointments scheduled for today, but I can come back later."

She took a deep breath. "Thanks. I see your point, and I'm sorry about my attitude. I'm under a lot of financial stress, and that's probably why I overreacted. Let me think about showing the book to you."

It was a start. "Thank you, Madison. Would you at least tell me the title again?"

"Sure, it's *Atlantic Coast Guide*." She walked me out and locked the door behind me.

The conversation hadn't been a complete bust, but I hadn't seen the book either.

"Katelyn dear, what are you doing here?"

I looked into the familiar blue eyes of Joy Barrett. Reid's mother.

Chapter Eight

"Joy, what a nice surprise. What are you doing here?"

Reid's mom wore hot pink capris with a pink, green, and white paisley knit top. "There's a new bookstore going in here, and it's called Fun. Fine, Unique and New Books. You know I'm always up for a good time, hon." Pink feather earrings dangled from her ears and almost touched her shoulders.

"I know that's true." I laughed with her. "I met the owner yesterday. The store isn't opening until this weekend."

"Yes, dear. That's right, but I work for Madison now."

Whoa. That was news. "Really? Does Reid know?"

She took my hand in her soft one. "You know, ever since Sam returned to town, things have been a little tense between Reid and me. I wasn't sure how he'd feel about his seventy-four-year-old mother working."

Sam Barrett was Reid's father. When returning from war and suffering from PTSD, he abandoned his family. Sam was back in town and dating Joy, and Reid was worried his mom would get hurt again.

"If working at the bookstore makes you happy, I'm sure Reid will be happy for you. But you need to tell him." Joy had lots of energy, and her personality fit her name. It didn't surprise me that she'd gotten a job.

"I'm not as confident as you that Reid will approve, but this opportunity was too good to ignore. I better scoot inside."

"Real quick. I'm trying to get on Madison's good side. I'd like to get a look at a history book she bought for Ben Hauser. Would you put in a good word for me?"

"It'd be my pleasure. See you later, Kate." She gave me a quick hug and knocked on the door.

I returned to my vehicle and tried to remember the name of the book. Oh, yeah. I put the name in my phone earlier. I opened the app for taking notes and found the answer.

Atlantic Coast Guide.

I Googled the title and found some information. The book was an old guide to the East Coast of the United States. It provided information on moons, tides, rocky shores, channels, and safe places to stop. A map was included with the book.

Interesting, but it didn't explain why it was valuable. The book was old, so it couldn't be useful to Ben. He was a businessman and golfer. Nothing I'd seen in his office indicated an interest in boating or fishing. Plus, how relevant could the book be today?

I checked an online auction site, and the price seemed right. The copy in Madison's possession was a bargain compared to online sellers. Maybe Madison could sell it and make a small profit.

Sitting here wouldn't pay my bills or solve a murder. I drove to work.

It was still early, and I opened the store. Two appointments were noted on my calendar.

One customer had hired us to organize her rental condo. The owner was recovering from hip replacement surgery and had asked us to get her unit ready. Her list had been specific, and we had signed the contract.

In the afternoon, Bess had us booked to organize the children's area of the Fox Island Community Church. Bess used to work there with Tom Cross. He was a widower with an adult son, and the son struggled with addiction problems. We had bought supplies for both projects, and the jobs should go smoothly. If I was lucky, I'd pay a visit to Seaside Hideaway and see if I could learn anything else about Ben.

The morning flew by, and soon it was time for lunch. Bess and I decided to grab sandwiches at the pier and eat on the benches. At a cute kiosk with a red and white awning, I ordered chicken salad on whole wheat and iced coffee.

Seagulls circled us until children on the sand threw bread crumbs in the air. Then, it became hard to distinguish the cries of the seagulls from the delighted laughter of the children.

Bess elbowed me. "Hey, there's Ethan."

I looked toward the pier parking lot and waved. He turned around and jogged to us. Once he reached us, he pulled on the T-shirt he had wadded in his hands. "I finished my online call and went for a run. What a beautiful day."

"It sure is. Do you have plans for the afternoon?"

"Yeah, I'm going to look at the apartments you suggested, then I might play a round of golf."

"Oh, can I play with you?"

He narrowed his eyes. "Are you going back to the resort?"

I couldn't lie to my son. "Yes, and if you're going to golf, maybe I can join you. I mean, that is if you're going to play at Seaside Hideaway."

"I knew what you meant. I'll meet you there; just don't go without me."

"Did your uncle tell you to watch me?"

"No. I don't want anything bad to happen to you. One person was murdered there yesterday, and I don't want you to get hurt, or worse. So, please, don't go over there without me."

"Okay. Let me know when you're ready to golf, and hopefully, I'll be through with our afternoon project."

Bess wadded up her sandwich wrapper. "I'll make sure she's finished in time. Don't you worry."

If I didn't know better, I'd think my friends and family were ganging up on me.

Chapter Nine

Ethan was standing in front of Seaside Hideaway when I pulled into the parking lot. He wore gray golf shorts, a blue polo, and a white hat. He appeared to be inspecting his clubs.

I parked near his gray SUV and hopped out. "Hi, honey."

"Hey, Mom. You ready for this?"

"Yes, and I have a plan." I had devised a strategy for everything right down to needing clubs. "My clubs are still in storage, and I thought maybe I could rent some from the pro shop."

"You mean, Mr. Ledger."

"Yes, Rory. If he doesn't have a set to rent, I'll use yours."

Ethan shook his head. "They're not the right size, but you might get lucky. Let's go."

We entered the front doors of the resort and veered left to Rory Ledger's golf shop. I glanced at the spa, hoping to spot Sue Porter. No luck there.

Ethan held the golf shop door open, and I entered the space. It was bigger than I had imagined. There were racks of clothes, and a section of one wall displayed golf shoes, balls, tees, and, of course, clubs and bags.

Rory hung up the phone and looked our way. "Good afternoon. It's Kate, isn't it?"

"Yes. Hi, Rory. You probably remember my son, Ethan."

His expression was grim, but he reached out and shook Ethan's hand. "Yes. Yesterday was like a nightmare. No, make it a horror movie, and it keeps playing in my mind. Death. The Grim Reaper."

I nodded. "The violence adds to the shock. Were you and Ben close?"

"Not sure close is the right word."

"But you worked here with Ben."

"True, but I pay to run the pro shop. I bought the golf carts and fixed them. So, I guess you could say we were business partners who got along."

"Okay. I understand, but I heard you two arguing yesterday morning. What was that about?"

He stuck his hand in his pockets and pulled out a couple of used golf balls. "Ben threatened to raise my rent. We had a contract, but he always pushed the limits."

"Was that all?"

He removed his straw golf hat and revealed flattened-down gray hair. "In the beginning, Ben approached me. He asked me to take over the shop. One of the terms of our agreement was for me to find golf carts, and he'd pay to have them overhauled. So, I found some good, used carts and bought them with the understanding Ben was paying for the purchase. Then, I got an estimate on getting them repaired. Ben agreed to the expense. I decided to fix some myself and pocket the extra money. Nothing wrong with that. The worst carts were sent to professionals."

"Did Ben know you were going to do that?"

"Didn't matter. He agreed to a price to get the carts ready for the golfers. It shouldn't have mattered who did the fixing." He tugged his hat back on.

Ethan said, "Sounds like good business to me."

I appreciated my son's comment. "Rory, do you have any thoughts on who might have murdered Ben?"

"Well, I can't rightly say that I do." He frowned. "Is there anything I can do for you today?"

Ethan stepped closer to the golf pro. "We were hoping to play a round of golf. Can anyone play on your course, or just resort guests?"

"Nah, anyone can play. Even if the resort was full and each guest golfed, it wouldn't be sustainable. We need others to come play. How long are you in town, Ethan? Maybe I can cut you a deal."

"I'm planning to move here, but thanks for the offer."

"Hmm, I bet we can work something out. Play this round on me, and see how you like it. Then we'll discuss options." He scratched his neck. "Did you come here for a job?"

"Well, that's a long story, and I'd rather not go into it."

"I hear ya." Rory's gaze shifted to me. "You're playing too?"

"Yes, I thought I would. I just need to rent a set of clubs for today."

"Fine, we can do that. Will you two want to rent a cart?"

Ethan said, "Because we're starting late, I think a cart will help us move along quicker. Is the course crowded this afternoon?"

"This morning, I couldn't keep people away. Morbid curiosity, if you ask me. But it's reasonable now." He wound his way through a group of golf bags with clubs. "This is my best option for you, Kate."

The clubs looked in good shape. "Okay. Thanks."

"I'll load it on a cart, and you two can be on your way." He carried a bag and exited through the glass door leading to the back of the property.

Ethan grinned at me. "I'm curious to see how the clubs work for you. He didn't even let you hold one."

"Oh well, I'm more excited to spend time with you than I am about playing golf." I touched his arm. "I want to hear what you meant about your job."

He shrugged. "Ben's death hit me hard even though we were strangers. I keep questioning what I'm doing with my life."

"I'm a good listener, if you need me." I knew better than to push Ethan into a conversation before he was ready to talk.

"Thanks, Mom."

I spotted Sue Porter in the lobby area. "Let me run to the restroom, and I'll meet you outside."

He narrowed his eyes at me. "Last time you said that, you questioned Madison, and I just saw the lady from the spa walk by. I'm beginning to think that's code for questioning a person of interest."

I waved him off and left to find Sue.

She was talking to an older lady at the front desk.

"Excuse me. Sue, can I speak to you a minute?"

She jerked away from the desk, and both women gave me wide-eyed looks. Sue said, "Sure. I remember you from yesterday. Would you like a massage or something?"

I motioned for her to follow me, and we stood by a large plant near the pool exit. "How are you today? It can't have been easy—" No good words came to me for what she'd experienced. "Do you have somebody you can talk to? A counselor, best friend, or maybe a pastor?"

Her strawberry blond hair fell forward and partially hid her face. Her posture was stiff. "I'm friends with some of the other staff. We're talking to each other."

"Okay, well, if you need somebody fresh to listen to you, feel free to give me a call." I decided to be direct. "Who do you think murdered Ben?"

"Why would you ask me that?" She glanced at her watch. "I need to get back to work." She took off before I could say another word.

That young lady's superpower was quick getaways. It made me question if she had something to hide. If so, what was it?

Chapter Ten

Tuesday evening, Reid was working on my new house when I arrived with sandwiches, cut-up fruit, and veggie strips. He met me in the driveway and changed into a clean T-shirt. "Hey."

"Hey, there." Butterflies stirred in my belly.

He wrapped one arm around me and locked his lips on mine.

Mercy. The butterflies multiplied.

Woof! A dog raced by and interrupted our kiss.

I laughed. "Wonder where he's heading in such a hurry?"

"And where is his owner?" Reid placed his hands on his hips.

The golden dog disappeared.

"It really ticks me off when people don't take care of their pets."

That was another new thing I didn't know about Reid, or I'd forgotten. "Are you hungry? I brought supper, er, it's more like a simple picnic."

"I'm starved. There are a couple of beach chairs under the house. Why don't we eat on the front porch? You can catch me up on your day."

"Sounds good." I pulled the small cooler from my vehicle and met Reid on the porch.

Waves sounded in the distance, and the ocean breeze caressed my face. "I can't believe how lucky I am to live here again."

"Some people take island life for granted. They get involved in work and other stuff and ignore the beauty all around us."

"That's a real shame." I chomped on a carrot stick. "Why don't you have a dog?"

He stretched out his long legs. "I used to have a beagle. Named him

Snoopy."

"Aw, that's cute. What happened?"

"He died. Then, I got suckered into adopting a boxer. Called him Shorty."

I smiled. "As in boxer shorts?"

"Pretty much." He grinned. "Shorty wanted to go everywhere with me, and a lot of the time, I took him. Work sites aren't always the safest places to take a dog, so I'd put him in doggy daycare at least once a week to keep up his socialization skills. When he crossed the rainbow bridge, it about did me in. I just haven't had to heart to look for another best friend since then."

Reid might have the softest heart of anybody I knew. He looked out for veterans, dogs, the environment, his mom, me, and people in general. "Something tells me when the time is right, you'll get another dog."

"Hmm. You're probably right. Tell me about your day."

"Bess and I worked on a couple of projects, then I played golf with Ethan."

"How'd that go?"

"Mercy, the clubs I rented from Rory Ledger were for a woman much shorter than me. Plus, I haven't played in years, so that was unfortunate. But it was nice to spend time with Ethan."

"You played at the resort?"

"Well, yeah. I was hoping to pick up a clue."

A car approached and pulled into the drive.

Reid leaned forward to get a better look. "It's your brother. Were you expecting him?"

"No. Maybe he caught the killer." I wiped my hands on the paper napkin and threw my trash into a plastic bag.

We walked down the stairs, and Reid tossed the bag into the site dumpster, and we walked to Paul who was on his phone.

My brother wore his uniform, and he looked tired. He ended the call and turned his attention on us. "Hey, guys." His voice was flat.

"What's wrong?"

"You mean besides the murder? I keep hitting brick walls in this investigation." He rubbed the back of his neck. "It appears that not everyone in town trusts me after being cleared of Carissa Ruffalo's murder."

"But the killer was caught." How had I not heard any of the rumors?

"True, but you know how people are with conspiracy theories and all. There have been accusations of police corruption and arresting an innocent person."

My heart beat faster. "That's ridiculous. Why I—"

"Steady now, Katie." Reid touched my back. "Paul, what do you need us to do?"

"The best way to put an end to the gossip is to solve the murder. The sooner, the better."

"Which you can't do if people won't talk to you. Do you want us to snoop around?" I wouldn't mind pulling out my vision board to get a better visual of the crime. It'd be helpful in organizing clues and suspects.

Reid cleared his throat. "Paul, your sister's already begun taking notes, and she's legit asking people what they think about Ben's murder."

His eyes bulged, then his body lost fight like a popped balloon loses air. "I guess there's no sense in lecturing you, because I'm asking for help. I need to hear what you've got."

"My notebook is in my purse, and that's in the car."

Reid said, "Why don't we go to my house? We can discuss the murder without interruptions."

"I'll follow you over, and Paul, why don't you ride with me? That way, nobody will be suspicious about your Charger being at Reid's place."

"Better yet, let's drop my car at the station."

Reid flicked sawdust off his shirt. "I'm going to lock up here, then hit the shower when I get home, but the front door will be unlocked. Go ahead and let yourselves in."

We agreed to the plan, and I called Ethan on my way to the police station.

"Mom, I was just about to call you. I met your friend Ian, and we're going to grab burgers tonight."

"Good. I'm with Paul and Reid, so there's no need to worry about me. But I appreciate that you were going to call."

"Yeah. Between the murder and living in the same town, it seemed like the considerate thing to do."

"Aw, I'm so proud. Have fun, honey." I pulled into the parking lot and stopped where Paul stood.

"Sis, you can't be talking on the phone and driving. Georgia is a hands-free state."

My body heated up, and it was not a hot flash. "How do you know I was on my phone?"

"Your phone is in your lap. I'm literally looking at it." He picked it up and held it in front of my face to open it. "Yep. I see you were talking to Ethan a few seconds ago."

I tapped my deaf ear. "I'm sorry, but I can't hear you."

"Don't do it again, or buy a car with Bluetooth technology so you can talk on your phone safely." He buckled his seatbelt.

"You know I normally follow all the rules and laws. I just forgot. It won't happen again. Unless, you know, I'm running for my life or something."

"Let's hope that doesn't happen again." He pointed to my purse. "Do you mind if I read your notes?"

"Go for it." I kept both hands on the steering wheel, and my eyes stared straight ahead for the rest of the drive.

Paul pulled the journal out of my purse and flipped through the pages.

I turned onto Reid's street, keeping at or below the speed limit. If Paul was paying attention, he'd be aware that I was a Fox Island law abiding citizen. I passed a black Dodge Ram truck parked on the other side of the street near Reid's place. Most of the homes were spread out with cars parked in driveways or even in the grass.

The truck was solid black, including the hubcaps. Tinted windows added to the darkness.

I caught a glimpse of a man sitting with the window down. His arms were propped on the steering wheel.

A sense of déjà vu hit me.

Ben had been slumped over the steering wheel of the golf cart when I found his body.

I turned into Reid's driveway. My pulse pounded in my temple. "Paul, do you see that truck?"

He closed my journal. "Yeah. What about it?"

"There's a man. His arms are on the steering wheel." My voice squeaked. "Like Ben."

Paul leapt out of my Wagoneer, leaving the door open.

I turned off the engine.

I didn't want to follow my brother.

What if somebody else had been murdered?

I didn't really have a choice. Paul might need assistance. With slow steps, I walked toward the blacker than black pickup truck.

Chapter Eleven

"Are you hurt, sir?" Paul stood near the driver's side of the black truck with his hand hovering near his gun.

The man sat up and turned his face to Paul. Shoe-wee. He was alive.

I approached Paul and the driver of the black truck but didn't hear the response.

"I need to see your license and registration." Paul glanced at me. "Nothing to worry about." The underlying message was for me to let him do his job.

I walked to Reid's white raised house and climbed the wooden steps to his front door. The shutters were teal, and the front door was a bold yellow, making me wonder if his mother had painted it without his knowledge. Joy was all about bright colors.

I sat on the porch swing and kept my eye on Paul. Even though Reid had given us permission to enter his house, it felt like I should remain on the porch. Something was off with the man in the truck, and I'd be ready to call for help if the situation went sideways.

Reid came out to the porch, wearing faded jeans and an old Braves T-shirt. His hair was damp, and his eyes sparkled. "Where's Paul?"

"He's talking to a man parked on the street." I scooted over and patted the empty space. "Want to sit with me?"

"Always." He claimed the spot and slid his arm around me. His woodsy scent enveloped me. With a barefoot, he rocked the swing. "So, what's the deal? Was the driver speeding?"

"No. He's just parked on the street. For a minute, I was freaking out that he was dead too."

"I'm glad he's alive. One murder this week is more than enough." He played with a strand of my hair that had escaped the ponytail. "I pulled out a fresh sketchbook and an easel pad to keep bullet points on."

"Let's get started. I'm sure Paul won't take much longer."

Reid stood first and held his hand out for me. Once I was on my feet, he pulled me to him and gave me a quick kiss. "We better go inside before I lose focus on the reason you're here."

"Yeah, plus we have a chaperone."

Reid took two steps, then stopped. He leaned over the porch rail. "Did you see the driver?"

"Only enough to know it's a man. Paul asked for his license, so I figure it's a stranger."

"I've seen a truck just like that before." His grip tightened on the rail. "It's got to be my dad. What is he doing here?"

My happiness dissipated. Reid's distress was like an early morning fog rolling off the ocean and making life gray. I placed my hand on Reid's taut back. "What do you want to do?"

Seconds ticked by.

What was taking Paul so long?

Reid pushed back. "I'm not going to interfere. Let's get to work before it's so late we can't think straight."

It was almost eight o'clock and nearly sunset. One thing I was still adjusting to was the earlier sunsets in Georgia than in Kentucky. I followed Reid inside. The main floor was pretty much an open floor plan. You entered the open living room with a vaulted ceiling, dining room, and kitchen. The stairs led to a large loft with built-in shelving and a closet. Reid had told me he used it as his home office.

I followed him to the dining table and sat beside him. It killed me that Sam Barrett caused Reid so much pain. "Have you forgiven your dad?"

"I thought so, until he returned to Fox Island. I'm not worried for my sake, but he better not hurt my mother again." He slid the sketch pad and a fat marker to me. "Who is your first person of interest?"

Okay. End of discussion. "There are so many people to consider, but let's start chronologically. Ben and Rory Ledger argued yesterday morning." I wrote Rory's name at the top of the first page. "What do we know about him?"

"He works at the resort's pro shop. He knew the victim, and he was there the day Ben was murdered."

I made bullet points of these facts. "He's able to repair golf carts, and Ben's body was found in a cart."

"His niece is Madison Ledger, and Ben owed Madison money for the book."

"Ben also owed Rory money. As far as Rory goes, is his motive financial loss? Or he may have been mad that Ben didn't play fair with Madison." I added this to the list.

"Is either motive enough to commit murder? I wonder how much money Ben owed Rory? I bet the whole town knows he owed Madison twelve hundred dollars." Reid rubbed his chin. "If someone stole that much money from me, I'd be mad. I wouldn't be murderous. If they stole twelve million dollars, I might consider shooting the scoundrel."

I patted Reid's arm. "No, you wouldn't."

"Yeah, you're right."

"On the other hand, you're a loyal guy with good friends. If someone wrecked my life, you might be more tempted to shoot them."

"True, but still, I wouldn't plan a murder. It'd more likely be the heat of the moment."

It was inconceivable to me that Reid could hurt someone on purpose. But if he was defending a friend, that would be a different story. It wasn't so hard to picture Reid defending his mother, even if it cost his own life in the process. "That's one question we need to figure out about Ben's death. Was it planned out and intentional? Or did an argument get out of hand?"

Reid stood and paced. "You found the body slumped over in the golf cart. To our knowledge, there was no sign of the murder weapon. We need to ask Paul."

"Right." I made a note to ask.

There was a knock at the front door, and Paul walked inside. "Hey, guys. There's somebody here who'd like to talk to you."

I leapt to my feet and hurried to Reid's side. I took his hand in mine and squeezed encouragement, at least I hoped he felt encouraged.

Solving the murder could wait. I was glad to support Reid in this conversation.

Sam walked into the room. He was tall and thin. Not trim, but he gave off more of a malnourished impression. "Son, we need to talk."

Reid pointed to the khaki couch placed against the front windows. "Have a seat."

Without uttering a word, Sam sat on the couch.

Reid and I sat across from him.

Paul settled into the leather chair and rubbed his hands together.

Of all the awkward situations I'd been in, this was one of the worst.

Chapter Twelve

An uncomfortable silence filled Reid's living room. From the kitchen, the ice maker dumped ice. It was followed by the sound of water running.

Still, nobody spoke.

Reid stared at his dad, and Sam looked at the floor.

"Mr. Barrett, I'm Kate Sloan."

"Pleased to meet ya." He rose and shook my hand. "This is probably a mistake."

"Are you okay? I was worried about you when I saw you leaning on the steering wheel."

"I was praying, young lady."

It'd been decades since anyone called me a young lady.

Reid stood. His feet were shoulder-length apart, and he stuffed his hands into the front pockets of his jeans. "Why are you here, Dad?"

"I can't make up for the past, but I'd like us to begin to have a real relationship. It won't be because your momma and I are reconnecting, but I'd like to have you back in my life. You and me. Simple as that." Just like Reid had done, Sam stuffed his hands into the pockets of his threadbare but clean jeans. "What do you think?"

"It's not a good time to talk. We're working on something tonight."

"How about breakfast tomorrow? The Pancake House? They open at six. You set the time." Mr. Barrett's voice was deeper than Reid's.

I held my breath. Reid needed his dad, and Mr. Barrett needed his son.

Reid sighed. "Fine. I'll be there at six."

"See you then." Mr. Barrett hurried away as if scared Reid might change his mind.

Reid let out a slow exhale. "Katie, don't you have a question for Paul?"

I shifted mental gears. "Yes. Have you found the murder weapon yet?"

"No, but we're confident a golf club was used to strike Ben in the head."

I moved to the dining table and added this to my notes. "Where do you think the crime took place? Have you searched the golf course and the grounds of the resort?"

"We've looked, but when you consider the resort is on the beach, that club could be just about anywhere. On the beach, in the dunes, hidden in the beachgrass, or out to sea. It's possible we won't recover the club."

Reid paced. "It's probably nothing a K-9 police dog could search for."

"We have one K-9, and he's trained to find drugs. His name is Cody, and Officer Troy Merrick is his handler. Cody might be able to find a cadaver, but I doubt he can find a golf club. Unless the dog can sniff blood, and if there's blood on the golf club." Paul shrugged. "It's possible."

"What about a metal detector?"

"To my knowledge, we haven't tried that. I'll check with my people. What are you thinking, Reid?"

"I know tonight was weird with my dad and all. I have talked to him some, but it was either on neutral turf or at Mom's house. What I'm trying to say is that I know he has a metal detector. He told me using it is a good way for him to block out the world. If he finds something, it's just a bonus."

Paul said, "Instead of a therapy dog, he's got a therapy metal detector. It works for me."

Reid looked at Paul. "Your sister asked if I've forgiven my dad. I thought I had, but having him back on the island has stirred up old feelings. If I push myself to hang out with him, like breakfast tomorrow, then maybe I can begin to trust him. If breakfast goes smoothly, maybe I'll ask him to use his metal detector on the beach around the resort."

I wanted to hug Reid but didn't want to embarrass him. "I think that's a great idea. I can't think of a good reason to talk to Rory right now. Why don't we come up with our second person of interest?"

"Sis, you can just say suspect. I pretty much only say person of interest when speaking to the public."

"Why?"

"I'm less likely to get sued. Why don't I share what I know about Rory?"

"Go ahead." I motioned for him to continue.

He smirked at me. "Thanks, sis. Rory moved here without much money. In Florida, he tried to be a professional golfer, but he never made the cut. So, he was a golf pro and gave lessons. The man's a likable guy. But he's also a gambler and found himself in a financial pickle. He moved to Georgia for a fresh start."

Reid sat beside me. "What about his niece? How did they both end up in Fox Island at the same time?"

"Madison was living in Myrtle Beach and came to visit Rory. She was working for a grocery chain while waiting for a job opening at a bookstore. She went to college and majored in literature and business. Madison met Ben while visiting her uncle. Somehow, Ben inspired her to move here and open a bookstore. He said he'd be her first customer if she could find a copy of the Atlantic something. Rory encouraged her also, and she has a soft spot for her uncle."

"*Atlantic Coast Guide.* I've become very familiar with the title. I want to see it, but Madison was hesitant to let me. Joy may be able to help me, though."

"What's my mother got to do with this?"

Uh oh. Joy must not have told Reid she was working at FUN. "I've said too much. When's the last time you talked to her?"

"It's been a few days, but I'm about to fix that. Excuse me." He walked out the front door.

"Oh, Paul. I blew it. Joy's working for Madison at the bookstore, and obviously, she hasn't told Reid." I sighed. "What else do you have for me?"

Paul opened the easel pad and wrote Rory and Madison's names on a fresh page. "Sue Porter was also at the resort when you found Ben."

"Yeah. She was upset with Ben, too. He made her cry, and Rory tried to comfort her."

"Is that so?" Paul quirked an eyebrow.

"Yes, Ben drove her to tears."

"What about the relationship between Sue and Rory?"

"I think it was more like a father-daughter relationship. I doubt it was romantic. At least it appeared that way to me." I turned the page and began writing Sue's information on it. "She's a receptionist at the spa, and she's not the warmest person around."

"That doesn't make her a killer."

"True. Who arrived on the island first? Rory or Ben?"

"Rory hit town first. He did odd jobs and bought a trailer. Ben contacted him, and Rory mentioned that the resort was for sale. Rory's been here almost a year. Ben arrived before Christmas, best that I can tell. Madison has been in town six weeks. I believe Rory has a soft spot for Madison. He may have known she was frustrated waiting for a good job. Maybe he and Ben cooked up a plot for her to start a bookstore here."

"That's a nice theory. Have you talked to Ethan about the man who confronted Ben at the restaurant? They argued then left together."

"I'll give him a call." Paul pulled out his cell phone. "Oops, I missed a call from Susie."

"Call your wife. Ethan's out with a new friend tonight."

"Be right back." He headed out, and Reid returned.

"Are you mad at me?" I walked to him and wrapped my arms around his midsection.

"No. Mom said you encouraged her to tell me. I don't understand why she kept it a secret."

"Maybe it wasn't so much of a secret, but more like she hadn't found the time to tell you. Are you okay?"

"She's a grown woman, and I've never tried to stop her before. I couldn't even if I wanted to. She's an independent person and won't take orders from anyone." He held me close. "Let's don't keep secrets from each other."

"I'm sorry about Joy. I thought she should be the one to tell you. In the future, I won't keep anything from you." I sagged against him, relieved at his response.

"Same here. Secrets only fester and can ruin relationships."

My head snapped back. "If Ben was killed because of a secret, maybe I should take a hard look at his life. That could lead me to his killer."

"Sounds like we've got a plan. I'll talk to Pop, and you see what you can learn about Ben."

I gave him a quick kiss, then pulled away. "Paul's on the phone with Susie. I better get him home and let you get some sleep."

He walked me outside. "See you tomorrow."

"Definitely." I motioned to Paul to get in my vehicle, and I drove him to the police station.

He continued his conversation with his wife, and my thoughts drifted to Ben Hauser.

The guy had given off the impression of being likable. Had it been an act? Had he been a con artist? Could that be what kept him in conflict with others?

My goals for Wednesday, besides work, would be to find out more about Ben. I'd also beg Madison to let me see the book he'd asked her to order.

Chapter Thirteen

Ethan walked me to work Wednesday morning. "So, I liked the Pelican Shores Apartments, but they won't rent me a place for less than a year. That will make it harder to get settled if I know it's temporary. Do you mind if I crash with you a little longer?"

"That's no problem. I hope to move into my new house by the end of May. I can't wait for you to see it, and there's a guest room if you need time to find a temporary place. There may also be the option of taking over my current apartment. It comes furnished." I stopped at an intersection and waited for the light to walk across.

"If I'm going to stay with my job, I need good WiFi."

"That rules out my current apartment. Tell me what you're thinking." The crosswalk light showed it was our turn to go.

After we crossed, Ethan said, "Besides making money, what good am I doing at my current job?"

"Do you donate to charitable organizations?"

"Yeah, but I want to be more hands-on. Know what I mean?"

"I get it. Maybe Uncle Paul knows of some opportunities for volunteer work around here and in Savannah."

Ethan stopped when we came to a bike rental shop. "You know what? I'm going to rent a bike and get to know the island better. Then, I'll look for Uncle Paul."

"Reid is all about fixing up old houses. He thinks it's better for the environment, and he found my house. If you find a place on your ride that needs renovations, give him a chance."

"You make it sound like I don't like the guy. I barely know him, but if he makes you happy, he's all right in my book."

"Thanks, honey. Besides exploring the island, what are your plans today? Did you meet any new people last night?"

"Ha, are you trying to ditch me?"

"No, but if you get bored, I can find ways to put you to work."

"Oh, man. This brings back memories. There's no telling how many times you said that to me when I was growing up. But not to worry. I'm having lunch with a lady about my age. If I get bored later, I'll find you." My grown son gave me a boyish grin.

"Well, okay. Have a good day." I left Ethan at the bike shop and walked to Let's Get Organized.

"Good morning, Bess." My best friend had the coffee going, and I headed straight there. "What's on our agenda today?"

Bess stirred creamer into her coffee. "This morning, we'll divide and conquer. Would you rather organize a country music star's trophy room, or would you rather tackle an author's library? The author lives here, and the singer lives in Savannah."

"I'd love to do the library project. I don't remember booking either of these jobs, though."

"I did when you were out drumming up other business. I have plans drawn up for the library and supplies organized. The secret to any good library is comfy chairs and good lighting."

"Don't forget the books." I poured coffee into a mug with our business logo and added creamer.

"Never. The books have been moved to a guest room because the library was painted white. There's a desk, and she'd like the room to serve as her office as well as a library."

"Anything else?"

"I think that's all. She'd prefer if we can do it today."

"Are you sure it's a one-woman job?"

"I have faith in you. When I finish the trophy room, I'll check in." She looked at her phone. "I'm sending you her address now."

"I need to get my car—"

"You mean that beast."

"Hey, now. That's a little offensive. My old Wagoneer deserves the same respect you show the elderly." I took a large gulp of coffee and burned my tongue. "I'll be back."

"I'll help you load up. Soon, we need to discuss hiring an assistant."

"I couldn't agree more." I left her and hurried to get my Grand Wagoneer. I was glad I'd worn our uniform of shorts and a T-shirt with the store's logo. It made one less thing to do before arriving at the author's house, and it'd probably take every minute of the day to organize her library.

***

By three o'clock that afternoon, the furniture had been efficiently placed in Darby's library. She was an author of historical fiction with close to twenty published books. She was also the person who would sign books at FUN Bookstore on Saturday. I'd learned the stories were all set on the coast of Georgia. I'd be sure to buy one of her books at the signing.

I placed the books she wrote on a shelf with good visibility and at eye level. When she had guests, they needed to easily find what she'd written. I created an organization system for everything else. Nonfiction titles would probably fill three shelves. There were enough books by authors in the surrounding towns to fill one section. Fiction titles were organized by author name. Now, I just needed to get them all on the library bookshelves.

The doorbell rang, and I went to answer it because I was the only one at the author's house. I wasn't expecting another delivery, but maybe Bess had forgotten to tell me something. I opened the door and faced Ethan.

"Hey, Mom. I saw your SUV and decided to see if you need help." He was perspiring, but he wore a big smile.

"Yes. You can help move books into the library." I explained my plan.

"How about I carry the books in and lay them on the desk? You arrange them whatever way you like."

"Great. I'll treat you to supper."

"Thanks." Ethan made a few trips back and forth, and I shelved them as fast as I could. I made sure research books went on a side shelf near the desk. Fiction was placed on shelves near Darby's books.

"Mom, you won't believe this. There's a copy of *Atlantic Coast Guide*."

I gasped. "You're kidding me. Did she buy it from Madison?"

"I don't think so."

"Oh, I wonder if she'd possibly let me look at it? Madison said I'd need to wear gloves to see her copy. Maybe if I offer to do the same here, Darby will let me look at it. No, wait." I ran to the powder room off the hall and washed my hands. I dried them on the fluffy towel and even shook them in the air as I walked back to the library. "I can't resist taking a peek."

Ethan began snapping fingers on both hands. "Do I need to be your lookout? What if you get caught?"

I sat at Darby's desk and gently opened the book. "Relax. It's not like I'm stealing."

"You're stealing a look at her book without permission."

"I've touched every book in this room today. Look at the slips of paper she's used to mark pages." I focused on the pages she had marked. "Oh, here's a map. Hand me my phone, please."

"Here you go. I'm not going to watch, then if the police question me after she decides to press charges, I'll be free to hire a defense attorney—"

"Shh, honey, it's going to be okay. Stand in the hall, if it makes you feel better." Mercy. He would've flipped out if he'd been around during my first murder investigation. The book wasn't thick, but I chose only to take pictures of the maps and sketches. When I finished, I set the book on the desk. "It's safe to come back."

He returned with his hands stuffed in the pockets of his wrinkled cargo shorts.

"I did the same kind of things to prove Paul was innocent, and your uncle asked for help on this case. If you're ever in a bind, I'll do anything humanly possible to prove you're innocent."

"Yeah. I remember you got your passport when I spent the summer in France, working at tennis clinics."

"You also left the country for youth mission trips. If you'd been kidnapped, I was planning to come look for you, or negotiate, or do whatever I could to find you."

He laughed and scratched his head. "I didn't realize how spunky you were then. I guess it just seemed annoying."

"Spunky? I'll take it." I shelved more books.

He cleared his throat. "By the way, I had lunch with Madison."

"So, you saw her last night, too? Where?"

"At a smoothie shop near Ian's apartment."

"Sammy's Smoothies. I like that place." I glanced at my watch. Time marched on too fast. "And Madison was there?"

"Yes, ma'am. We talked about how intimidating you are." He snorted.

"Ethan, that's not true."

"I don't know what to say. Growing up, you were the strictest parent around."

"It didn't seem to stop your friends from coming over." I reached for more books and was thankful he'd brought them to me in the order I'd arranged them.

"You were also the coolest. If they wanted to drink or do something stupid, they went to Jake's house."

I was aware that Jake's parents partied with the kids. "Teens need boundaries."

"You're right. You gave us boundaries, but you also showed us you respected us and cared. Our house was a fun and safe place to be."

"Aw, thanks. Would you like to look for nonfiction books that Darby might use for research? They need to go on that shelf." I pointed out the spot. "But you didn't defend me to Madison?"

"I told her you're all right. She knows you solved a murder here."

"Did she mention Ben?"

"Only because of the book."

Did that mean Madison and Ben only had a business relationship? If so, her motive would have been related to money and not a bad romance. "Darby will be back soon. See those plants? I've left room on shelves for either a plant or a small painting. It'll add pops of color and interest."

"What's your system?" He raised a spider plant.

"This is one time I don't have an exact system. If it looks good, leave it."

We finished placing everything on the shelves. I looked around the room. Comfy chairs, a two-drawer file cabinet next to the antique desk, plenty of lamps, throw blankets, and shelves of books. "It looks like a library to me. Thanks for your help."

"Hello." Darby appeared and clapped her hands. Her thick red hair bounced with the movement, and she beamed. "It looks so inviting. My guests will enjoy it, and I'm sure I'll write lots of books in here."

"That's good to hear. Darby, I'd like you to meet my son, Ethan. He's going to move to the island."

"Do you work for your mother?"

"No, ma'am. I was on a bike ride when I spotted Mom's vehicle. I decided to see if she needed any help."

"How nice. Kate, I love your old Grand Wagoneer. If you haven't given it a fun name, I can help. Maybe Vinny because it's a vintage Jeep."

"Cute. I'll think about it."

"Oh." She walked to the shelf with her books. "I love, love, love how you spotlighted my books."

"You might hire an electrician to install a little spotlight to shine on them. I put your files in the file cabinet, and your reference books are right here. Do you have any questions for me?"

"No. I'll be sure to recommend you to others, because I'm sure everyone will ask who created this amazing space." She handed a check to me.

"Thanks." I placed it in my pocket, then pointed at the only book not on a shelf. "Is there any chance you'd be willing to let me look at your copy of *Atlantic Coast Guide*?"

"Sure. It's a great resource, but I'm promoting my new book the next couple of weeks." She laughed. "It's the only reason I could step away from my computer long enough to have this space organized."

"I appreciate it so much."

Darby handed the book to me. "I'll need it back when I return to writing."

I'd never imagined she'd let me borrow the book for a few days. "Not a problem. You've got my number, and I'll take good care of it."

We said our goodbyes and left.

Ethan stopped at the Wagoneer and patted the hood. "Do you think we can squeeze my bike into Vinny?"

"At this point, I'm not calling him Vinny, but yes. If we pop off the bike's front tire, it should easily fit." My stomach growled.

"Gosh, Mom. Did you eat lunch?"

"I was on a tight timeline, and Bess got stuck in Savannah. There wasn't time to eat."

"How about an early supper? What's quick and casual?"

"At the beach, everything is casual. We've got Danny's Deli, Poppa's Pizzeria, and Dairy Barn."

"Pizza sounds good." He loaded the bike in back. "Would you like me to drive so you can take a look at the book?"

"Yes." I tossed the keys to Ethan and jumped into the passenger seat. I didn't get past the author's notes, but it was a start.

Chapter Fourteen

I'd conquered the job for Darby Meadows, but I hadn't gotten far on the murder investigation. After we ate pizza, I drove Ethan to my new house.

My heart leapt at the sight of Reid's white truck in the driveway. I parked behind it and freshened my lipstick.

By the time I popped a breath mint and reached for the book, Ethan was on the porch talking to Reid. It did my heart good to see the two most important men in my life getting along.

Ethan headed inside, but Reid waited for me. "Busy day, huh?"

"Yes, and I got a copy of *Atlantic Coast Guide*."

He kissed me. "It's good to have you home again. Have I told you that?"

We were the classic star-crossed lovers, and life was sweet now that we were together again. "Once or twice, and I feel the same way."

"Do you want to look at the book inside? It might be less humid in there, and I have a card table set up."

"Let's go." I entered the neat workspace. "It smells like a new house. How was breakfast with your dad?"

"Fine. He agreed to search for the golf club."

"Thanks for asking him. You know, one of the first things your momma told me when I returned to Fox Island was that you always keep a neat work site. She's right. This isn't the only place you're working on, is it?"

"The house for vets is almost finished, and I have a couple of small projects going. There's also a bid on a small house I'd like to flip, but I'm waiting to hear back from the owner."

"Okay. Let's look at this." I sat at the card table, and Reid looked over my shoulder.

Ethan ran down the stairs and landed with a light thud. "Mom, this place is sick. You've got great views and lots of space. I better not crash with you here, or it'll be hard to leave."

I laughed. "I'm confident you'll find a great place, too, but you can stay here as long as you need."

"Or until we get on each other's nerves." He grinned. "I'm going to shove off and explore this area of the island. I'll get my bike out of Vinny and see you at the apartment later."

"Vinny?"

Ethan nodded. "It's the name of Mom's Jeep. A famous author suggested the name."

"No, I'm not calling it Vinny. Next thing you know, I'll have a conversation with my car." I smiled at the guys. "Be careful, honey."

"If I beat you home, is there anything you'd like me to do?"

"Would you see what you can find out about Ben on those work sites? Link me to a job or whatever they're called."

"No problem. It won't hurt for me to look for a job, too. I've got an idea brewing."

"Brew? As in a coffee shop?" Would that add purpose to his life?

"Nah. Let me keep thinking about it. See y'all later." He took off with a smile.

"So, Vinny?"

"Yeah. I worked for Darby Meadows today, and she suggested I name my Wagoneer Vinny because it's vintage. Unfortunately, Ethan was there, and he likes the name. Unless I come up with a better name soon, Vinny is going to stick."

"And you don't like it?"

"Ugh. No, but a famous author suggested the name."

Reid leaned against the kitchen counter and crossed his arms. "It's big. How about Tank? Rusty? Max? Oh, T-Rex would be fun."

"No. Doesn't it seem silly to name my 1991 hunter-green Jeep Wagoneer?"

"Life doesn't always have to be serious. What about Hunter? Frog? Greenie? Roadrunner?"

"I don't know." I focused on the book. "Darby loaned this to me for a couple of weeks. What was so important in here that Ben would pay twelve hundred dollars for it?"

"Let's go for a walk before the rain moves in. Maybe it'll clear your head, then we can study the book."

"You're right. I've been cooped up most of the day working. Fresh air will do me good."

We took the path to the beach and found it near empty. Music drifted to us from the pier, but I couldn't distinguish much about it.

"Summer's coming, and the sooner we get you into the house, the better. The crowds and music are fun, but night after night, it'll wear on you."

We walked in the direction of the lighthouse and away from the pier. There was no breeze, and perspiration beaded my hairline. "Is that why you're working so hard on my place?"

He took my hand in his. "You come first."

I'd never come first to my husband when he was alive. There was always a new story to chase on his climb up the ladder to news anchor. He hadn't been supportive of me, but I'd always supported him. At least until I discovered the other woman.

"Katie, where'd you go?" Reid stopped walking and drew me to him.

"Sorry. My mind drifted back to my disaster of a marriage. I can't believe how blessed I am to be with you now."

"Get used to it. I'm not going anywhere. Part of me is concerned that after your bad experience with David, you're scared to fully commit."

"To be honest, I am a little scared. After I discovered David had broken our marriage vows, I began to put up shields to protect my heart. Then I got the acoustic neuroma diagnosis and had to take care of myself. Before I could decide how to handle the situation, David died in the carjacking."

"I waited too many years to be with you, and I have no intention of screwing up our relationship. I'd propose and marry you tomorrow, if I thought you wouldn't freak out."

I laughed. No, it was more of a combination between a gasp and a bark.

"And there you go, flipping out on me. We'll proceed at your pace, Katie." He kissed my forehead.

My stomach knotted. Why couldn't I allow myself to completely let go?

Paul appeared. "Hi, guys. I got a report about a sea turtle nest. The head of the turtle rescue organization asked me to mark it off. Trouble is, I can't find it."

Reid said, "Don't they know you've got a murder to solve?"

Paul grimaced. "It's all about priorities."

Paul's appearance gave me time to pull my thoughts together regarding Reid's statement. "How can we help? Do we look for turtle tracks?"

"Yeah. Thank goodness we're not on a popular section of the beach."

"How did the turtle lady know about it?"

"Somebody reported it to her, but they didn't have supplies to protect it. I'll go this direction, and y'all go that way."

It was still daylight but shadowy. I reached for Reid's hand, and we took our time searching for loggerhead turtle tracks.

A few minutes later, Reid stopped. "Katie, Paul found the nest."

I looked over my shoulder, and Paul was putting wood stakes in the sand. "Good. Can we walk a little longer?"

"Yeah. Do you see what I see?" He pointed to a woman walking toward us. "That looks like Sue Porter."

"You're right, and I've been wanting to talk to Sue. Let's try to intercept her."

"Lead the way."

We angled toward the woman walking by herself, and it was obvious the minute she spotted us, because she broke into a run.

Chapter Fifteen

I glanced at Reid. "Are we too old to run after Sue?"

"We can run, but I don't know if we'll catch her. I'm willing to try, though."

"She's a spa receptionist, not a physical trainer. Let's try." I broke into a jog.

Reid matched my pace. "She's heading toward the resort. I'll try to cut her off, and you come up behind."

"Are we overreacting?"

"We won't physically restrain her, but you have questions. May as well try."

"Okay. Don't forget that her superpower is quick getaways."

"Understood." Reid took off, and I increased my pace. Low tide made it easier to run on the beach. The hard-packed sand wasn't hazardous like the thick, fluffy sand near the dunes.

My phone vibrated in my pocket, but I couldn't waste time answering it. I kept my focus on Sue.

Reid ran past her like a normal runner might pass a beachcomber. Only thing was he wore jeans.

Sue slowed her pace and held her side.

Surprisingly, I caught up with my target. "Sue, wait."

Reid U-turned and came back to us.

"Leave me alone." The young woman huffed.

"We're not going to hurt you." Reid raised his hands, palms out. He even took a step back.

"Please, Sue. I just have some questions about Ben."

She came to a dead stop. "I don't know what you want me to say. I worked at Ben's resort. We didn't get along. I called for help after you and your son found Ben's body. End of story."

"Why didn't you get along? Did he treat you unfairly?" I stood close enough to hear her answer.

"It depends on your definition of fair. Ben was always ready for a good time. He tricked people. It's like the old joke. How do you know Ben is lying? His mouth is moving." Her chest heaved. "Was he fair to you?"

"I didn't give him an opportunity to cheat me, but I think he might have tried if I hadn't been so insistent. What did he do to you?"

"I need to sit down."

Reid said, "Let's talk by the pool."

She glanced at the resort and hung her head. "I have a passkey, but if I answer your questions, will you leave me alone?"

I studied the young lady. She looked more sad than mad. Dark circles under bloodshot eyes made me wonder if she had trouble sleeping. "If you're honest with me, then yes. I'm not trying to upset you, but the sooner Ben's killer is caught, the sooner we'll be safe."

Sue turned and trudged through the sand toward the resort.

Reid and I followed.

Soon, the three of us sat at a round table along the back fence of the pool area. A man swam laps, and a group of women sat at a table on the other side of the pool. The bar was packed with people drinking and cheering for their favorite NBA basketball teams.

A young man came over and asked if we'd like anything to drink or eat. We ordered drinks, and he walked away.

"You seem to be taking Ben's death harder than I would expect for coworkers."

"Porter is my married name, but I'm divorced." She crossed and uncrossed her legs. "Some family issues wrecked my marriage. I don't blame my husband for wanting out. He deserved better."

"I'm sorry." How was this information relevant?

"Phoenix Sue Stewart Porter is my full, and legal, name. Most people call me Phoenix, but I came here as Sue. I came here a few weeks ago to confront Ben."

"Why?"

"Because Ben killed my brother."

Chapter Sixteen

Our drinks appeared, and Sue told the man to put them on her tab. I sipped my fruity concoction and tried to process what Sue had just shared. Ben was responsible for her brother's death.

Reid said, "Will you tell us what happened?"

"My brother was in college when he met Ben. They became friends. Eli wasn't one of the popular kids when we were growing up, but for some reason, Ben took him under his wing. I think it was because Ben could manipulate him."

I scooted my chair closer to hear better. "How did he manipulate him?"

"Eli was so excited to have fun friends, and he'd do just about anything Ben asked. Ben was in school on a golf scholarship. He gave Eli golf lessons, for a price. I guess that's fair. But then he'd give Eli a sob story, and my brother ended up writing some of his papers so Ben wouldn't lose his scholarship. Eli shouldn't have done that, but he was under some kind of spell when it came to Ben." She took a sip of her green smoothie.

Clouds appeared and floated by. The air smelled like the ocean and rain.

Sue said, "One day, Ben and Eli were playing golf. Some of Eli's friends claimed that Ben started drinking before they teed off on the first hole, and he bought more drinks along the way from the cart girls."

"Was he old enough to legally drink?"

"He was of legal age. The more Ben drank, the more belligerent he became. Anyway, the others left after playing nine holes, but Ben insisted on finishing all eighteen." She pulled a tissue from her purse.

"Did your brother stay?"

"Yes, and Ben lost control of the golf cart. They ended up on the road. A distracted young mother was driving and T-boned the golf cart. Eli flew out of the cart, hit an oak tree, broke his neck, and died. Ben only had a few scratches."

"Oh, Sue. I'm so sorry." My heart sank. "Did Ben serve time for driving under the influence?"

"No, ma'am. There were lots of excuses, but nobody was arrested. Then Ben disappeared. I thought all was lost. Recently, a friend of Eli's heard that Ben had bought the resort, and I came here with the intention of making him pay for killing my brother."

I gasped. "So, you murdered Ben?"

"It turns out that despite the anger building inside me for years, I don't have the killer instinct. I couldn't do it." With the tissue, she blotted tears running down her face.

Would she have told me all that if she had murdered Ben?

No.

I believed she grieved her brother's death, but I also believed she was innocent. Where did that leave us?

Reid said, "I'm sorry for your loss, and thanks for sharing your story with us. You've been around Ben for a few weeks. Who do you think might have killed him?"

"I'd look at his brother. Craig Hauser."

Her words surprised me. "Do you know where we can find Craig?"

"He's staying at the resort. He and Ben argued about something, and the next thing you know, Craig is a guest. He's in a modest suite. Not one of the luxurious ones on the top floor, but it's still nice."

"Do you know what they argued about?"

"You'll have to ask him yourself." She took a drink of her smoothie.

"Can you tell me what he looks like?"

She pointed to the bar. "See the guy on the end? With the dark hair?"

"And the muscles?"

"Yep." She frowned. "That's Craig."

"Oh, he doesn't look happy."

"I doubt it's because he's mourning his brother's passing. Craig is a serious guy with some serious issues. I've got to open the spa early tomorrow, so good night."

"Sue, is there anything I can do for you?"

"No, ma'am."

"If you need a friend, I'm here."

She walked away without replying.

Reid changed spots to sit next to me. "What do you think?"

"I believe her story."

"Me, too. Do you want to talk to Craig?"

"This might be our best opportunity."

"I'll go ask him to join us, and you think about what you want to say."

"Deal." I didn't have questions prepared to ask Craig, because I hadn't even known of his existence until now. I'd play the conversation by ear if he agreed to join us.

Chapter Seventeen

Paul had called and texted, wondering what happened to us. I texted and told him we were at the resort and we were fine.

Reid returned with Ben's brother. "Katie, I'd like you to meet Craig Hauser."

I shook his hand. Up close, he was even bigger than I imagined from a distance. His muscles probably had muscled. "I'm so sorry it's under these circumstances."

"Thanks." He sat across from me, and Reid sat on my right. "I understand you have some questions for me."

"Yes, and I'm willing to answer any questions you might have. First, you should know that I'm the one who found Ben. I'm an organizer and was working on Ben's office. When I stepped outside for some fresh air, he was on the golf cart. He didn't respond to me, and I touched his arm. That's when he fell on me. Reid and my son were on the property and heard me yell." I gave him minimum details of finding Ben's body. "Again, I'm sorry for your loss."

Craig waved off my comments. "Did he scam or steal from you?"

"No, but I was firm. He didn't want to pay upfront, and I explained to him that Let's Get Organized doesn't work that way."

Craig's eyes widened. "That worked?"

"It did for me. Maybe he didn't want to take advantage of me because I'm old enough to be his mother."

"Huh, that wasn't it. He scammed my entire family." He cracked his knuckles. "We didn't grow up rich. Ben was two years older than me, and he was the first one of us to work for money. He cut yards, walked dogs, pretty much anything. But in his defense, he was never a bully. He didn't threaten small kids for their lunch or anything."

Interesting. He'd also taken Eli under his wing. Was that Ben's redeeming quality? He watched out for those he believed were less fortunate.

Reid flagged down a waiter and asked for coffee. He looked back at us. "Sorry, it's been a long day. I probably won't sleep, but that's okay. Sorry to interrupt Craig. Go on. You said Ben wasn't a bully."

"Right. At least back then, he was a good guy. He discovered his talent for golf when he helped one of the older neighborhood ladies prepare for a yard sale. Her deceased husband's golf clubs were part of the sale, and she gave them to Ben. That's how he discovered his talent for golf."

"My son and I play golf, and clubs don't come cheap. That was a nice gift, but you mentioned he scammed your family."

"That's right, and if I know my brother, there was a scam connected to this resort. I just haven't figured it out yet."

The waiter returned with Reid's coffee. He reached for his wallet. "Man, I don't know what I was thinking. Katie. I don't have my wallet."

I sighed. "My purse is at the house. Maybe I can stay here and you run back and get your wallet. I don't mind waiting."

"Guys, this is silly." Craig motioned for the waiter to return. His arm muscles strained his shirt. "We'll charge it to my room."

"Yes, sir." The waiter stood politely waiting.

Craig signed the receipt with a flourish, and the waiter walked away.

Reid cleared his throat. "Craig, thanks. We started out on a romantic stroll. When we saw Sue Porter, our plans got blown off course. I'd be happy to drop by and pay you back."

"It's just a cup of coffee. No sweat."

Reid fidgeted with the neck of his shirt. "Thanks again."

I cleared my throat. "Will you tell us more about how Ben took advantage of your family?"

"I'm sure he was running a Ponzi scheme. He asked us all to invest, and he promised a big return on our money. There was no way we could lose if we invested with Ben. I still believed in my brother. It was only later that I learned you can't make an absolute promise on any investment." Craig's blue-green eyes flicked from me to Reid.

"I can't believe he involved your family."

His attention drifted back to me. "Yeah, and we're not wealthy. Both my parents work, and they've taken second jobs in the evenings to recover from their losses. Mom sits with an older adult, and Dad is the host at a fancy restaurant. They invested their retirement money with Ben. I mean all of it." He pressed his forehead.

"Did you invest?" Reid drank his coffee.

"Yes. Like I said, at that point, I still believed in my big brother. I'm sure Sue told you about the golf cart accident that killed her brother."

"She did." My leg bounced, and I forced myself to sit still.

"He fed us a story about how he was really the victim. He claimed that Eli was driving the cart even though every witness said it was Ben. I'll never figure out how he didn't pay for that."

"When I heard he didn't serve time, I figured your family must have paid off the police or something." If it'd been Ethan, I would've stood by his side, but I wouldn't have tried to bribe officials to let him go.

Craig groaned. "Like I said, we didn't have a lot of money. My parents have always worked hard. They just caught some bad breaks, but that's another story. When Ben approached us with his scam, I was all in. It did make me nervous for our parents to invest so much. But it was Ben. He wouldn't take advantage of family, right? Wrong. Not only did he take our money, when his business venture fell apart, he asked my parents for money to leave town. Luckily, I stopped by to check on my parents. Ben was sitting at the kitchen table with them, begging for money. I burst into the kitchen and told Ben to leave. It was a terrible scene, but my brother left, then I had a heart-to-heart conversation with my folks."

The wind picked up, and the night had grown black. Clouds filled the sky, and not a star could be seen.

Reid rubbed his chin like he often did when deep in thought. "How did he get away with a Ponzi scheme? Didn't anyone suspect?"

"No. First, he kept it local, which also means he only stole money from people who knew our family. Everyone felt sorry for my parents. They started a secret support group. People scammed by Ben Hauser, or something like that. They decided not to file charges, and Ben got away."

Reid's eyes widened. "That's amazing and speaks volumes about what good people your parents are. How'd you feel about your brother then?"

"I've got a love-hate relationship with Ben. Er, I did."

I tapped a finger on the table. "Why'd you come to Fox Island?"

"It was time to confront Ben. I refused to let him hurt more innocent people." He took in a deep breath and slowly exhaled. "Hatred hurts you more than the person you hate, and I believed there was still some good in my brother."

"Did you have a plan for the confrontation?" Reid finished his coffee and set the cup down.

At last, Craig answered. "Not really, and the resort surprised me."

"How did your brother afford this place?" Reid's low voice forced me to lean forward.

"That is a very good question. For the life of me, I can't figure it out." Craig looked at his watch. "I've got an early meeting tomorrow. I'll be in town at least until after the funeral."

I said, "Do you have a business card?"

Craig opened his wallet and gave each of us his contact information. According to the card, he worked for a small chain of fitness centers. That explained a lot.

"Thank you. Craig, who do you believe murdered your brother?"

"My best guess is a client who got burned. Although, he's left a lot of broken hearts along the way. Kate, in case you're wondering, I was mad at Ben. Still am. Personally, I'm young enough to recover from the money I lost. But my parents are close to retirement age. They scrimped and saved. Ben couldn't see beyond his own selfish desires. I guess you could say my motive was revenge." Craig stood. "It's starting to rain. Be careful getting home."

"I'll text my son for a ride." I pretended to fumble with my phone and snapped a picture of Craig in the process.

Reid stood and shook Craig's hand. "Thanks for the coffee."

"Anytime."

I texted Ethan. *Can you pick us up at the resort?*

Raindrops splattered on my work polo.

Random drops of water. Soon, it'd be steady rain. Maybe a downpour. This is how I'd work the case. A clue here and there until I collected enough clues to solve the case.

Chapter Eighteen

Ethan picked up Reid and me at the resort and drove us to my new house. "Mom, I'm glad you only needed a ride because of the rain and not because you had too much to drink. I would hate to lecture you on that. Although, you can call me anytime you find yourself in a bad situation."

"Very funny." How many times had I given him practically the same speech?

"I never imagined saying that to you." He chuckled.

"It's doubtful you'll need to repeat yourself." When he stopped the SUV, I passed my phone to him from the backseat. "This isn't a great picture, but is it the person you saw talking to Ben at Shrimp and Grits?"

"No."

"You didn't look at it very long."

"That's because he looks nothing like the guy. This one is dark-haired, young, and muscular. The man I saw was older and taller. He was fit. Not skinny, but he doesn't have bulky muscles either."

"That's disappointing."

"Who is this?"

The wipers swooshed.

"Craig Hauser. He's Ben's brother, and he was at the resort the day of the murder."

Reid opened the passenger door. "Why don't we take this conversation inside? I'm a little cramped. No offense to your Land Rover, Ethan."

"None taken."

"Good." Reid dashed to the house.

Ethan looked at me. "What's with him?"

"He's had a long day and drank coffee while we questioned Craig. I imagine he's wired and restless. He probably found sitting in your nice SUV confining. Do you have time to discuss the murder?"

"I don't have anything better to do." He passed the phone back to me. We hurried up the stairs and met Reid inside.

Light filled the sky, and thunder rumbled over the ocean.

Ethan said, "Cool echo. Do y'all believe Craig is a suspect?"

"It's possible, but we ruled out Sue Porter." Reid paced and explained why we'd made that decision.

Ethan ran his hands through his hair. "Sue, aka Phoenix, is innocent. I don't guess the golf club has been found?"

"No. Did Paul ever explain why he thinks a golf club was used to kill Ben?" I glanced at my watch. Eleven o'clock. Wow. I rarely stayed up this late, at least when I lived in Lexington I hadn't. "It's too late to ask him, but let's find out tomorrow."

"Guys, the marking on Ben's face was the shape of a golf club head. I won't be surprised if Uncle Paul confirms it's the murder weapon."

Reid nodded. "Good to know. Katie, we were also going to delve into Ben's life."

Ethan said, "I might help there. He was a business major. He seems to appear and disappear. For instance, he ran a Ponzi scheme in his hometown. Once it fell apart, Ben left."

Reid yawned. "Sorry. I'm shocked the coffee isn't working better. Craig told us about that so-called business opportunity. You're right. It wasn't legit, and he stole from his family. Your mom can tell you more, but I think we need to call it a night."

I felt terrible for keeping Reid so busy. "I'm sorry. We can talk more tomorrow."

"I'm meeting a potential client early in the morning, then I'll check on progress at the creek house. Do you have time to meet for breakfast? Say around seven-thirty?"

Ethan laughed. "We'll meet you."

It didn't take long to lock up my new house, and we all left in our individual vehicles. The rain was lighter, but it hadn't quit.

My phone rang. A glance indicated it was Ethan, and I pulled to the curb. "Hey."

"Why'd you pull over?" He parked behind me.

"Your Uncle Paul already lectured me once today about Georgia being a hands-free state. I'm not going to get a ticket, at least not tonight. What'd you need?"

"We ate early, and I'm hungry. Thoughts?"

It was way too late for me to eat. I didn't have the metabolism for it. Plus, I'd just had a smoothie at the resort. "I'm good, but I'll go somewhere with you. The pancake place is open until midnight."

"Nah. I'll swing by the grocery store. See you at the apartment."

I pulled away from the curb and drove home. Once I backed into a parking place and gathered my purse and notebook, I reached for the door handle, then pushed it open.

It slammed back on me, jamming my wrist.

A person wearing a dark hoodie and a mask stood at my car door.

I locked my door. Were the other doors locked?

"Leave Ben's murder alone." He pounded the roof of my vehicle, then ran off.

My heart was in my throat. I restarted my vehicle and pushed the button to lock all the doors.

My hands shook hard, and I struggled to swipe my phone. At last, I dialed nine-one-one. I reported my emergency and sat in my old Grand Jeep Wagoneer, waiting for help to arrive.

Grand? Definitely. I felt somewhat safe in the big vehicle. Vinny. Yeah, I might name it Vinny. No, the Grand Dame seemed fitting.

I was losing my mind, sitting here thinking what to call my vehicle. I'd just been threatened. If the culprit had carried a gun, I might not still be alive.

The rain beat harder on my windshield.

Good. When the police and Ethan showed up, maybe they wouldn't realize I was crying.

83

Chapter Nineteen

Sweet Officer Drake Collins came to my rescue. Again. He'd helped me more than once when I worked to clear Paul's name in the last murder investigation. Poor guy was probably sorry I'd moved to Fox Island.

"Mrs. Sloan, are you all right, ma'am?" He wore a rain slicker and plastic cover on his hat.

I nodded. "Yes."

Lightning flashed, and thunder rumbled.

"Can you please open the car door?"

My belongings were still in my lap. I opened the door and stepped out, holding the stuff tight against my chest. "Thanks for coming."

"Of course. Why don't we go to your front porch and talk?" He touched my elbow, and we walked up the wide wood stairs and stood by one of the lights. "What happened?"

My legs shook, and I took a deep breath. "Some guy pushed my door closed when I tried to get out of the Wagoneer. He told me to quit asking questions about Ben Hauser's murder."

Officer Collins took notes on his phone. "Are you sure it was a man?"

I thought about it. "Not really. The person was dressed in black, and their face was obscured. It didn't see hair. The hoodie was black. No markings. It didn't advertise a college or any kind of team. I didn't notice if it was Nike, Adidas, Under Armour—"

"I get your point. We'll go with plain black. Did the person say anything else?"

"No. At least, nothing I heard. I'm completely deaf in my right ear. I've learned to compensate by reading lips sometimes, but it was too dark. And again, he, or she, wore a mask."

Footsteps splashed on the sidewalk.

"Stand back." Officer Collins reached for his gun.

I spotted Ethan. "No, wait. That's my son."

"Mom, what happened?" He splashed up the steps.

"I'm fine now. Honey, this is Officer Drake Collins. Or did you two meet the other day?"

"We met." Ethan spoke to the police officer, and I watched the rain fall.

Thunder eerily echoed off the water. I shivered. Storms always seemed worse at the beach.

What was I doing? I was fifty-three years old. I had reunited with the love of my life. My son disrupted his life so he could watch after me. That wasn't fair to him. He should be in Texas, working at a job he'd been thrilled to have.

"Mom, let's go inside."

Officer Collins said, "I'll follow you and make sure there's nobody else lurking around."

Ethan used his key to unlock the door. He pushed it open, and a piece of paper fluttered to the porch.

"Don't touch it." The officer pulled out gloves and reached for the paper. "Wait, I'm going to get it wet." Water sluiced down his rain jacket.

"Officer Collins—"

"At the rate we're getting to know each other, you should call me Drake."

"Okay. Drake. We're all wet, but I have plastic zipper bags in the kitchen."

He nodded. "I'll go first."

I stood back and allowed him to enter my apartment.

Drake removed his gun and held it up like I'd seen on TV shows. He looked in each direction, then walked to the kitchen counter and placed the paper on it. He disappeared down the short hall that would lead him to my bedroom and bathroom. Soon, he returned. "It's clear."

Ethan waited for me to go first, then he followed and closed the door.

"Drake, take off your coat. Would you like a hot drink?"

"No thanks." He walked down the little hall again and returned without his hat or coat. "I put them in your shower for now. Let's see what the note says."

I turned on every light in the apartment.

Drake picked the paper up with his gloved hands. "Leave the evidence in the lighthouse parking lot tomorrow before midnight."

I gasped. "Evidence? Somebody thinks I have evidence?"

"Mom, do you have something that could incriminate the killer?"

I looked at my son, then the cop. "No. This person must think I found a file or a contract in Ben's office, but we left all the files there. Remember? That was Ben's homework. Organize and put away the files. I even left him colorful folders with tabs to make it easy to find the documents when he needed them."

Drake said, "We need to start spreading the word that you never took any paperwork out of Ben's office. I also think first thing in the morning, we, as in other police officers and myself, need to take a closer look at Ben's files. We'll make our presence known at the resort."

"What about protecting my mom?"

"I'll have another officer patrol this area while I take this note to the station. There could be fingerprints on it. Then, I'll come back and see if we might find the sleazeball who was here tonight."

We thanked Drake, and he geared up and left.

"Mom, I should've come straight home with you. Sorry."

I shook my head. "Don't be silly. There's no way we could have anticipated the killer would think I had any evidence."

"Why don't you get ready for bed first? I'm probably going to sleep with one eye open tonight."

I hugged my grown son. "If you weren't here, I wouldn't be able to get a wink of sleep. Thanks, honey."

Chapter Twenty

Reid's meeting ran longer than expected, and he had to back out of our breakfast plans. My son was still disturbed from the night before. Ethan drove me to work and even went inside with me.

Bess stood at the coffee station, filling her mug. "How are y'all this beautiful morning? I always sleep better when it rains, don't you?"

Ethan laughed. "If you don't mind, I'll help myself to a cup of coffee. Neither one of us got much sleep."

"Make yourself at home." She moved aside.

I sat down at my desk, trying to motivate myself to work.

Ethan filled a mug. "Mom, I meant to tell you that I have a job interview this morning."

"Oh, who is it with?" I hadn't brought up the issue of him returning to Texas and his real life yet. Maybe this would be a better opportunity than his other job.

"The local parks and recreation department. They're looking for a new director. Yesterday, on my bike ride, I saw a rundown park. The disc golf course is overgrown, but it appears to be in decent shape. The ball fields aren't terrible, but the bleachers look dubious. I'm not sure they're sturdy. The tennis courts have some cracks, but I've seen worse. I want to get a look at the indoor facilities." His voice was peppy and excited. "Programs for the kids and youth can really draw a community closer. I also want to see what the budget is for improvements and growth."

"I doubt the city can pay anything near what you've been making in Texas."

Bess said, "That's the truth."

"It's not about the money. I feel like I can make a difference here. Maybe Ben Hauser only needed an adult, a coach, or a friend to believe in him. If he hadn't turned into such a manipulator, maybe he'd be alive today. Who knows?" He poured a second cup of coffee and added French vanilla creamer. He stirred it and put the cream carton in the mini-fridge before bringing me the doctored coffee. "This one is for you. It looks like you could fall asleep at your desk."

"Thanks. I'm proud of you honey, but don't make a drastic decision because of Ben's murder."

He sat on the edge of my desk. "Maybe this was the direction I should've gone after college. It's possible I got sidetracked because of the amazing salary with my job now. Yeah, I've enjoyed the money and what I've been able to do with it. But Ben's death was a wake-up call. There's more to life than making money."

I patted his knee. "The city will be lucky if you take the job."

"I appreciate the vote of confidence."

The conversation shifted to the events of the night before, then Ethan left for his job interview.

"Kate, what am I going to do with you? You can't keep digging into murder investigations as if you'd been trained at the police academy. What are you thinking?"

"Do I get credit for not dragging you into it?" I gave her a half-hearted smile.

"A little bit." She sat at her desk and studied me. "Seriously, are you okay? Or are you just putting on a brave face for your son?"

"If you'd seen me last night, you'd realize there was no bravery going on. That guy really scared me, and I have no idea what he thinks I have." I sipped my coffee. It was sweeter than I would've prepared, but I enjoyed it. "What do we have scheduled for today?"

"You make it seem like I'm the boss, but we're partners. No matter, I'll review the calendar with you. One of us is going to the senior center to discuss downsizing with a group of older adults. That's early this afternoon. I've given a talk on that subject before, if you'd like me to do it. I've also arranged for some door prizes, and there are business cards and pamphlets to hand out."

"If you have a speech ready, go ahead. I'll make one for the future, so you're not always stuck."

"That would be fine, or you can come up with your own topics. What about preparing your teen to live in a dorm? Bringing home a new baby?"

"I love your ideas, Bess. I'll work on the dorm rooms. With it being summer, it's probably a good time to have that and advertise our availability to speak. Is our goal to get ourselves hired, and the talk is free?" My creative juices began to flow.

"Yeah."

"Perfect. I'll think about what to say and who to speak to. In the meantime, what do I need to tackle today?"

"Would you rather call some people who've left messages for us? Or would you prefer to create plans for people who've already hired us?"

I took another sip of my coffee. While I loved to create organizational schemes, exhaustion weighed on me. My brain was stuck in the pluff mud. I clenched my teeth to suppress a yawn. "I'll make calls, and afterward, I can order items we'll need for your plans." My phone vibrated on my desk. "I should take this. Hi, Paul."

"Sis, where are you?" His voice sounded strained.

"I'm at work. Why?"

"Ben Hauser's office. It's been ransacked, and Officer Collins mentioned your incident last night. So, I had to make sure you're okay."

"I'm fine."

"Why didn't you call me?"

"Because it was close to midnight, and I didn't want to disturb you. Drake and Ethan took good care of me. Listen, after you dust for fingerprints and do your crime scene investigation stuff, I'd be happy to meet you there. My fingerprints will be everywhere because he hired me to organize his office, and I mean everywhere. If you think it'll help you, I'd be happy to have a look and see if I can tell what's missing."

"Great. You have a good ability to notice details. I'll be in touch." He ended the call.

Bess's eye twitched. "Now what?"

"Somebody ransacked Ben Hauser's office. I wonder if it's the same person who threatened me. If it is, what are they looking for?"

"Did you inventory his office while you were there?"

"There's a partial inventory." I turned on my computer. "After I found the body, I didn't update my notes."

"That makes sense. Who's going to take over the resort? Will they want us to finish the job?"

"Good question. I'll call Ben's brother." I rooted through my purse, found Craig's business card, and used our landline to place the call.

"Hello."

"Hi, Craig. This is Kate Sloan. We talked last night."

"Yes, of course. Did you make it home okay?"

What did he mean? Could he possibly know about the threat? "What?"

"With the rain? Did your son pick you up?"

"Yes." Was Craig innocent or messing with my mind? "Listen, who will take over the resort now that Ben's gone?"

"I guess it's either me or one of his business partners. Zeke McCarthy is a likely candidate, or it could be somebody I never met."

I jotted down the name. "Do you think Zeke will want me to finish working on the office? Or if you take over, do you want it organized? Ben has paid me for work done, but that's all."

"I'll let Zeke know about you. It'll probably be easier if we have you organize it before we move into Ben's chaos."

"Chaos?" Did he know the office had been ransacked?

"Don't forget I grew up with Ben. I know he's a slob."

"Say, are you staying in Ben's hotel room or suite? Or do you have your own?" I was curious to see if his answer matched what Sue had told me.

"He assigned me to a small suite, but he didn't make me pay. I'll stick around until after the attorney reads the will."

His answer matched what Sue had shared. "Is there going to be a funeral?"

"No, he wanted to be cremated. We'll spread his ashes later. I've got to go.

If I inherit this place, I'll call you about the office."

"Okay, thanks. Bye." I looked at Bess. "I'm not sure I trust Craig Hauser. He may turn out to be as conniving as his big brother."

"I recognize that look on your face. You're dying to find out about Craig."

"True."

The door burst open, and wind rushed in.

I leapt from my chair. Had the creep come back?

Chapter Twenty-One

"Katie, why didn't you call me?" Reid rushed to me in Let's Get Organized. He wrapped me in his arms. "I came as soon as I heard."

"Mercy, Reid. You liked to scare us to death." Bess shook her finger at him.

"How'd you find out?" I patted his back and eased out of his arms to study his face.

"Small town life. One of the employees at the convenience store was talking about it." He wrapped me in his arms again.

"I'm sorry, but you were tired and had to get up this morning. After I called the police, I just sat in my car doing nothing. Discombobulated." My voice shook, and memories of the previous night made me weak. I held tight to Reid.

"Honey, you should always call me."

I nodded.

Bess's eye twitched. "Kate isn't going to stop until the killer is caught. Can you believe that?"

Reid placed his hands on my shoulders, and looked me straight in the eyes. "Is that true?"

"I won't lie to you." I hated to think about him being disappointed in me.

"Okay. Then let me make some calls. Don't do anything until I come back." He left as fast as he'd appeared.

"Uh, oh. It looks like Hurricane Reid is heading your way. Or is Hurricane Kate about to sweep Reid off his feet? Does he know you love him?"

"Yes." I hated to talk about my relationship with Reid while a killer was loose. "I'm going to investigate Craig now."

"Go ahead, just don't leave the store. I don't want to face Reid if you take off." I'll make some business calls."

"Bess, are you okay?"

"I'm fine, but I don't like you tackling murder investigations."

Her closed expression didn't give me enough to decide if she was being completely open. "I'm sorry. Trust me, I'm as surprised as anybody that I have a knack for solving mysteries. Do you regret leaving your job at the church to go into business with me? Do you miss spending time with Tom?"

"Kate, you're my best friend, and I'm glad we've started a new business together. Let's leave Tom out of the equation."

"All right." I gave her a quick hug. "Who would've imagined we'd take on this business venture in our fifties? There's nobody I'd rather be doing this with."

"Same here, sister." She smiled. "I best get to making calls."

Thirty minutes later, Reid appeared. "I rescheduled my appointments, and I've got the day off. What can I do to help your investigation?"

The thought of spending the day with Reid lifted my spirits. "Let's go to the resort. I want to talk to Rory."

Bess said, "I thought you were going to investigate Craig Hauser."

"I learned a little online, and I'll get back to him." I turned to Reid. "You game?"

"You bet. My truck's out front."

It didn't take long to get to the resort, and we found Rory in the pro shop.

"Kate, good to see you. Planning to play golf today?"

"Not today. Who's running the resort now that Ben's gone?"

"Some kid. He was friends with Ben. They worked together on some business deals in the past. He showed up Monday."

Monday was the day of the murder. "Do you remember if he was here before we found Ben's body?"

"Yeah." He scratched his head. "At least, I think so."

"Who put him in charge?" I moved to the rack of golf shoes. "Do you have these in a size nine?"

"Let me check in back." Rory disappeared.

Reid leaned toward my left ear. "What are you doing?"

"If I can keep him distracted, will you check out all the clubs? Make sure none of them have blood."

"I'll do my best." He moved to the golf club area and began inspecting each club from top to bottom. At the sound of Rory's heavy-footed gait, Reid moved to look at gloves.

"I've got your size, and I brought another option in case you don't like these. You got socks?"

"Sure do." I moved to the bench near the shoe display.

Instead of standing, Rory sat beside me and handed a box to me. "I've invested everything I own into this business. Plus, Ben died owing me money, but you know that. Go ahead and try the shoes on. Act like we're just talking about shoes." His voice was low, and he glanced toward the door and windows.

"Is someone watching us?" I untied my tennis shoes and set them to the side. One by one, I put on the golf shoes, ever so slowly, to give Rory more time to talk.

"I don't know for sure, but something feels off. All the employees around here are worried because the killer hasn't been caught. What if one of us is arrested for a crime we didn't commit? Worse yet, what if we're the next on the hit list?"

I gasped. "Rory, why do you think there's a hit list? Is there something else going on here besides being a resort?"

He cleared his throat. "Go on and walk around in them."

I stood and moved around the shop.

Rory joined me. "What do you think?"

"I'd like to try on the other pair for comparison." And to extend our conversation.

Reid had gone back to inspecting the clubs. He even swung a wedge in a clear area.

I sat and swapped shoes.

Again, Rory claimed the empty spot. "We don't have a hidden casino or anything like that. But I was filling the ball washers the other day, and I overheard something disturbing. Ben and another man were talking about the suites on the top floors. Executive suites. Anyhow, the other guy was talking about some European plan where you buy a hotel room."

"Like a timeshare?"

"I don't think so. Madison helped me look it up. Seems like there are some hotels that let you buy a room. You can access it whenever you want. The other days, the hotel tries to book them. They get a cut, of course."

An elderly golfer entered the store, and Rory went to assist him. "Howdy. How can I help you?"

I walked over to Reid in the second pair of golf shoes and reached for a club. "Any luck?"

"No, but Rory's turning out to be quite talkative. Like a baseball commentator during a game tied at zero to zero."

Rory showed the elderly man a new golf ball that would fly straighter no matter if you teed off with it or were putting. Sounded dubious to me, but I wasn't an engineer. "Yeah, he's something else. I'll tell you all about it."

"I've looked at every club I could find but came up empty. No apparent blood stains. Are you getting those shoes?"

"Nah." I swung the club as if I was going to chip. "This one is pretty nice." I glanced at the price, then did a doubletake. No way it could be that cheap. I put it back and checked another club. It wasn't expensive either. What was going on? Usually, clubs were more expensive at resorts. People paid, if for no other reason than the convenience.

"I'll meet you on the back patio."

"Sounds good." I returned the second club, boxed up the golf shoes, and put on my tennis shoes. "Thanks for your help, Rory. Neither pair fit quite right, but I'll come back another day."

"Alrighty. We have new inventory coming in every day."

I entered the lobby on my way to join Reid. As I walked through the area, I passed by Craig. He was in a deep conversation with a lean man wearing a quirky golf shirt. Craig had mentioned Ben had a good number of business associates, but Zeke McCarthy was the only one he named. Could this possibly be Zeke? Was Zeke the same guy Rory overheard talking to Ben on the golf course about the resort suites?

It was impossible to snap a picture on my phone, but I tried to commit his image to memory. In the meantime, I wanted to know about the European model of hotel rooms.

Chapter Twenty-Two

"Hey, Ben asked you to give him a bid on the suites, but he died before you gave him a number." I joined Reid on the back patio area between the resort's lobby and the swimming pool.

"True."

I took his arm and led him to a shady spot where nobody lurked. I'd already discovered people eavesdropped around this place. "Did he mention if he'd be paying you?"

"I wouldn't do it for free."

"Because you're so smart, but did he mention a European model hotel?"

Reid rubbed his chin. "Seems like I've heard of it, but I can't remember the details for sure. As far as Ben goes, he only asked me for a bid to renovate the suites."

"We need to investigate the European model. According to Rory, it goes something like this. An individual buys one room in your hotel and gets a cut every time it's used. But how do you know it's fair?"

"Good question. I can imagine different ways to rig the system. First, just don't report when the room is booked."

"And how about when people contact your hotel for a vacation, you could always give guests your rooms. It would be tempting to only rent out the investors' rooms when all of yours are booked. I mean, if you were a bad person."

Reid said, "Do you believe Ben was trying to get investors for rooms and suites as his next big con?"

"Maybe. Although it doesn't explain the mystery behind the expensive book."

"Atlantic Coast Guide." Reid waved to someone behind me. "Here comes your brother."

"Hey, guys." Fingers circled my elbow. "Kate, you got a minute?"

I met Paul's gaze. "Absolutely. Do you want me to go through Ben's office with you?"

"Yeah. The crime scene guys have finished."

Reid said, "Paul, are you positive a golf club was the murder weapon?"

"Yep. Just between the three of us, it was a fairway club. There were markings on the skin to prove it."

"Ouch. It's easy to see how that was deadly." I rubbed my arms. "Can Reid come to the office with us?"

Paul looked from me to Reid. "Not sure how I can justify it."

Reid cocked his head. "I was in the office the day of the murder. It's possible I'll notice something out of place."

"That works. Come on."

We followed my brother to Ben's office.

The room had been trashed. Papers were strewn about, couch cushions had been haphazardly tossed, the file cabinet had been tipped over, desk drawers were open, books had been flung everywhere, and there was disaster and confusion all around. On top of that, black fingerprint powder covered various surfaces. "Oh, Paul. This is horrible. I can't imagine how helpful I can be."

He handed me a pair of disposable gloves. "I don't know where to start either. It's hard to say if the culprit found what they needed and left the mess to confuse us. Or were they frustrated because they didn't find anything useful?"

I slipped my hands into the nitrile gloves. "Do you have any idea what time this happened? Are there security cameras nearby?"

"Unfortunately, the security cameras were about to be updated." Paul tossed another pair of gloves to Reid. "We questioned the staff at the front desk. There were two women in their thirties, and they seemed to be very reliable. One was on the phone, dealing with an irate guest. The other person had stepped outside to run off some teens who had snuck into the pool area. This happened around two this morning. As we talked, they believe that's the only time someone could've gotten past them."

"It seems like a mighty big coincidence that both women were distracted at the same time." I reached for a file with papers spilling out. "If it happened at two, there would've been enough time for the thug who threatened me to get here and ransack the office."

Reid walked along the bookshelves, looking up. "We don't believe in coincidences, and you're right about the timeline."

"Paul, who was the irate guest? Has that person been questioned?"

"I'll double-check. Be right back."

"Can we touch anything in here?" I straightened the pages in my hand.

"As long as you wear gloves." Paul walked out of Ben's office.

"I'm going to gather the pages first. If we have a system, the task will be easier." I glanced at Reid. "I'll understand if you want to go back to your work."

He smiled at me. "That's a tempting offer, but no. What if I start with a few big things like righting the furniture?"

"Great idea. It'll improve our frame of mind not to be in the center of quite so much disorder." I gathered files and papers. There were so many bent and crumpled pages, and I did my best to straighten them. If they were near an empty file folder, I put them in the folder. Everything went on the coffee table.

Reid whistled, and soon, the office looked somewhat fit to work in. He straightened pictures on the walls. The artwork was modern and not related to the beach or golf. Reid gathered books and placed them on a shelf. "You know, most of these books are about the history of Georgia and pirate treasure. There are a couple of biographies of successful businessmen."

"I think Ben craved to be rich and successful, so the books on successful people don't surprise me. On the other hand, I find it interesting that he has local history books."

Reid opened one of the biographies. "This one has lots of highlights. Do you mind if I skim through this?"

"No, and you should make yourself comfortable." I pointed to the couch.

Reid eased himself onto the couch and began to read.

I gathered more papers, but I wasn't going to clean. Seaside Hideaway had a staff to handle the dirt and grime.

A shimmer caught my eye.

Still wearing my gloves, I picked up the shiny item. It was a divot repair tool. The instrument was compact. Golfers would hold the red end in their hand and use the dual prongs to repair the ball marks on the putting green. The thing was retractable, making it easy for golfers to carry in their pockets. I placed it on the desk and took a picture. "Reid, have you seen one of these before?"

He stuck his finger in the book to hold his place. "Yes. Don't golfers use them to patch up marks they leave on the green?"

"That's exactly what this does. I'm curious why Ben had one in his office. It seems like it should be in his golf bag or maybe on a keychain."

"Well, Ben did own the resort." He grinned at me. "Or did he?"

Chapter Twenty-Three

"What do you mean?" I looked at Reid. "Wait a minute. I need to text Paul real quick."

Reid waited patiently.

Was there a divot repair tool in Ben's golf bag? I sent the message to my brother.

"Now, please explain. What do you mean Ben may not have owned the golf course? And how did reading a book lead you to that conclusion?"

"Not only are some sections highlighted, the man featured in this biography traveled overseas extensively. Have you heard of Whit Dupree?"

"I believe he's been interviewed on the national news. He resembles Gary Cole." I took in Reid's blank look. "He's an actor on a crime show."

"In the book, Mr. Dupree goes into how much he travels. He stayed in so many hotels, that he decided to buy one. But before that, he tried the plan that you were talking about."

"He owned a room in the hotel?"

"Yes. The author says it's not a timeshare. This is different. Hotel room co-ownership generates income, and it can gain value over time. As an investor, you'll get a monthly income from the room, and it's registered as property in your name. Hotel maintenance costs are projected before the sale, and the owner pays the hotel once."

"One and done?"

"Something like that. I think Ben was probably trying this business model here. In the book, they strongly encourage trying the venture if you trust the owner of the hotel or resort."

"Hmph. I don't believe many people trusted Ben. Let's find Paul, and maybe we can borrow that book or at least copy some of the pages."

"I was thinking the same thing."

A young man and a woman with gray hair were working at the check-in desk. After I explained who I was, they allowed us in the business office to make copies.

"What are you two doing?" Paul entered the room on my deaf side and startled me so bad that I jumped.

"Sorry." I took a calming breath. "I'm a little on edge."

He rubbed my shoulder. "No need to apologize. To answer your question, there was a divot repair tool in Ben's bag. We took a complete inventory."

Reid gathered the printed pages and paperclipped them together.

"Come with us." I led the way to Ben's office and pointed to the red object on the desk. "Did it look like this?"

Paul nodded. "They're exactly alike. Where'd you find it?"

"On the floor. I know it wasn't there before the murder, but it could've been in a desk drawer. I worked in the cabinets and with files on the shelves. I brought over the file cabinet, but Ben wouldn't have had time to use it before his death."

"How do you know?"

"Well, because Ethan helped me get it here and situated in the office. Not long after that. I found Ben's body."

Paul pulled a plastic bag from his pocket. "This thing could be a clue or a diversion. Still, I will check it out. Are your fingerprints on it?"

"No, I haven't taken off my gloves."

"The place looks better. Have you found anything?"

Reid showed the book to Paul. "There might be something in here. Do you mind if I borrow it? It's okay if you say no because I copied some of the pages."

"Will it be helpful to have the entire book? Can we get you another copy?"

"The benefit of having this copy is that Ben highlighted sections and jotted down a few notes. It'll help us understand him better and maybe get a feel for why he was murdered."

"Keep it for now, but don't let anyone know you've got it."

I said, "It'll probably fit in my purse, and we can sneak it out."

"After last night, I don't want anyone, especially the killer, to know you two are working on the case and might have evidence."

"Paul, what about the note? The creep wants my evidence by tonight at the lighthouse parking lot. It's supposed to be there before midnight." Panic rose, and I felt lightheaded.

"I didn't forget. Lucky for us, there's a festival starting tonight. I've already reached out to other law enforcement agencies, making it a challenge for the killer to look for you or your information."

Reid frowned. "What's your plan? I don't want Katie to be in more danger."

"Me, either. I'm going to have a policewoman leave a package in the parking lot. If the killer should show up, we'll nab him, or her."

My hopes sank. "If the killer realizes it's not me, he'll be furious. There's no telling what will happen then."

"Calm down. We'll pick a person who resembles you and dress her like your style."

"No, it's got to be me. You asked for my help. I'll leave the package. What are we going to put in it?"

"Nothing important. The goal is to nab the killer." Paul frowned. "Are you sure you want to make the drop?"

"No." Reid's chest puffed out. "It's too dangerous."

"The place will be crawling with cops. She'll probably be safer making the drop than if she stayed home alone." My brother leaned forward. "Kate's my sister, and I won't let her get hurt."

"You can't make promises like that—"

"Guys, I appreciate you both, but I'm a grown woman. It's my decision, and if you're confident there will be plenty of cops around, I'll make the drop."

Reid's eyes narrowed.

Paul said, "I promise."

"Thanks, Paul." I shifted my gaze to Reid. "Hey, I never want to disappoint you, but I've got to do this."

"You were always ready for a challenge. I want to go with you tonight."

"Thanks." I squeezed his hand. Somewhere along the way, I'd lost my gutsiness. My life had centered on my husband and child. Then after David died, I'd focused on what was best for Ethan. That was normal. Probably the closest I'd come to being brave was when I'd dug for clues to prove David was unfaithful. Before I took the information to an attorney, I'd been diagnosed with the tumor and had to turn my attention to surgery and recovery.

Paul looked up from his phone. "This weekend is a simple arts and crafts fair. There are a good number of vendors, and they're beginning to set up around the lighthouse and the adjoining grounds. I imagine your visitor last night didn't realize it when he left the note. However, we'll work it to our advantage. If he doesn't pick up the package, at least he'll believe you're acting in good faith."

"Fox Island Arts and Crafts Fair? I wonder if our town could set a record for hosting events?"

"They bring in the tourists. Visitors help our economy."

"That makes sense." I sighed. "What time should we come?"

"Eight o'clock. It should be crowded then. You and Reid can show up, leave the package, and take off. My people will take over then." He wrote in his little notebook. "Drive the Wagoneer in case they're watching. No need to give them a reason to doubt you're following their demands."

"Okay, but what about Ethan? He knows about the note."

"There's a slight chance the killer wants to get you away from your apartment so he can search it. I'll assign Drake to guard your place with Ethan. They've already met and should be comfortable together." Paul rubbed his hands together. "I think we've got our bases covered."

I wasn't convinced, but what could I do? I was committed to helping Paul catch the killer. "At least you didn't ask us what could go wrong."

Chapter Twenty-Four

Reid walked to the beach in search of his dad.

I headed to the spa to talk to Sue. When I spotted her folding towels, I walked over. "Hi, Sue. Do you have a minute? If you can take a break, I'll buy you a cup of coffee."

She glanced at her watch. "It's past time for my morning break. Let me tell the others. The manager likes to keep us on schedule."

Soon we were drinking healthy drinks in place of coffee. Instead of sitting in the shade, we were walking along a path that took us past the golf course.

Perspiration beaded my hairline, but I didn't ask her to slow her stride. "Sue, I thought you came to Fox Island to confront Ben. Now that he's gone, will you leave?"

"Yeah, but it wouldn't be fair to Lauren to just leave. She's the manager of the spa, and she's been nice. I'll give her a two-week notice."

"That's the decent thing to do. I talked to Craig Hauser and can't decide about him. Can you think of anyone else I should question?" I stopped as a woman was about to tee off. After she sliced the ball, we continued our walk and conversation.

"Not really."

"You said that your brother and Ben played golf together. Did your brother have a divot repair tool?"

"Yeah, he carried one on his keyring. It had the college mascot on one side."

The one I'd found in Ben's office didn't have a mascot on it. Paul claimed it matched Ben's, meaning they didn't match Eli Stewart's device. "Is there any possible chance you know where Ben got his divot repair tool?"

"I'm afraid not." We took a turn along the side of the main building. "Where are you living, Sue?"

"Ben was decent enough to provide temporary housing to resort staff. He deducted an agreed-upon amount from our paychecks. They are smaller rooms, and they haven't been renovated, but considering the price of real estate on the island, it's a bargain. I need to get back to work. See you later." And just like that, she disappeared.

I checked my phone for messages, but there weren't any. I continued wandering around the resort until I spotted Craig and possibly Zeke McCarthy. They were sitting at the bar near the pool, and I headed to them before the opportunity passed me by to meet Zeke.

"Hi, Craig. How are you this morning?"

"Oh, hi Kate. I'm good, but we're about to go to a meeting."

I took a deep breath, hoping to gather courage. I looked at the other man. He was blonde with a lean frame, and he wore khakis, a green shirt, and a tie. "Is there any chance you're Zeke McCarthy?"

"Yes, ma'am. I'm afraid you've got the advantage. Who are you?" He held out a hand to shake with me.

I admired his firm grip. It was a trait I'd instilled in Ethan. "I'm Kate Sloan. I'm a professional organizer and was working on Ben's office."

"Good to meet you."

"I understand it's possible you'll be taking over Seaside Hideaway, and I was curious if you'd like me to continue working on the office. I'm willing to create another plan to suit your needs—"

"Let me stop you right there. Until this afternoon, we won't know who'll inherit the resort. We also don't have a clue about the financial health of this place. With Ben, you just never know." Zeke grimaced.

"It seems as if you know from personal experience. I've heard other people also had unfortunate experiences with Ben." I paused for his reply.

"That doesn't surprise me."

"Do you own another hotel, Zeke?"

He leaned against the polished bar. "No, I'm a car salesman. If you're in the market for a new set of wheels, I'm your guy. I can sell you a brand-spanking new Ford, Jeep, or Nissan. If you prefer a used vehicle, I'll do my best to find whatever your heart desires."

I smiled. "You wouldn't be the first man to question my vehicle. I drive a 1991 Jeep Wagoneer."

He whistled. "That's a classic."

"That's what I told my son. Where do you work?"

"Atlanta, but it would be easy enough to work a deal from a distance." He handed me his business card. It had his name and phone number, but the dealership information was missing.

"I'll keep you in mind, but I'm currently not in the market." I almost put the card in my purse until I remembered the book hiding in there. Instead of taking a chance on him seeing Whit Dupree's biography, I put the card in my pocket. "Zeke, are you here on vacation?"

"Uh, I came to play some golf. My boss insisted I use my days off or lose them. How'd you guess?" His posture stiffened.

"I thought maybe you came to play golf with Ben. When did you arrive in Fox Island?"

"That sounds like a cop question. Ben and I went way back." He didn't smile. "It's hard to believe he's gone."

"Did you two play golf together in college? Or were you two business partners? I understand Ben had his fingers in different businesses."

Craig wore a black suit that fit his muscular frame perfectly. He clapped Zeke on the shoulder. "We don't want to be late. Kate, it's always a pleasure to see you in action."

"Good luck today, gentlemen." I guessed they were heading to the attorney's office.

I watched them walk away. Zeke had been friendly, but his smile never reached his eyes. He also hadn't answered my question about working with Ben. I needed to find my notes on what Ethan heard at Shrimp and Grits before the murder. I also needed to add what I'd learned this morning.

It was time to find Reid and go over everything related to Ben's death.

Chapter Twenty-Five

I stood at Seaside Hideaway's outside bar, musing over my conversation with Zeke and Craig.

Fast footsteps pounded on the concrete. Paul and Officer Diaz ran past me. They exited the pool area and ran down the path to the beach.

What happened? Instead of waiting, I trailed behind them.

When I reached the beach, it was easy to see that they were heading to Reid and his father. Both Barrett men were tall. Reid had a few strands of gray hair, but his dad had a full head of white hair. The older man was on the frail side, probably from years of living on the streets. Until recently, he'd been homeless. He'd finally been able to find a counselor and pull himself together. At that point, he returned to Fox Island. It'd been about a month, and Reid's mom was beside herself with happiness to have Sam back in her life. Reid had been cautious.

Now, both men were working together to solve a murder. It'd be weird to know Ben's murder healed Reid's relationship with his dad. Time would tell.

Paul held a golf club in his hand.

When I reached the foursome, Sam pointed to the club. "I don't rightly know if it's the club you're looking for, but I found it and thought you should know."

Paul took his eyes off the club and looked at Reid's dad. "We appreciate your help, Mr. Barrett."

"Call me Sam. I'm happy to continue looking, in case this isn't the right club."

"It's a fairway wood. Powerful enough to do the job." Officer Diaz leaned close to the club in question. "It couldn't hurt to keep searching. I don't play much, but I've seen golfers hurl their clubs after a particularly bad hit. Ha, even after a semi-bad shot. Depends on their personality."

I'd seen plenty of golfers do the same. "If Mr. Barrett finds more than one club on the beach, how can we prove which one is the murder weapon?"

Reid's dad said, "You need to call me Sam, too. My old man was Mr. Barrett."

"Okay, Sam." I smiled at the older man.

Paul turned the wood in his gloved hands. "This could be a blood stain. The lab guys will test it, and if it's Ben's blood, we'll have the murder weapon."

Reid moved close to me. "But we won't have the killer."

Paul said, "Buddy, we'll be one step closer to catching him. Emerson, will you take this to the lab?"

"Yes, sir." He took the club in gloved hands and left us on the beach.

"Pop, you did good today. Have you had lunch?"

"No, but I best keep at it."

I elbowed Reid, but he couldn't read my mind. "Sir, what if we just grab a quick lunch at the resort?"

He hesitated.

Reid said, "My treat. Let's go, Pop. They have great burgers and fries."

Sam wiped his eyes with the back of his wrist. "You haven't called me Pop in a long time. You know, a burger and fries sound good."

Reid, Sam, and I found a table on the restaurant's patio area. We mostly chatted about the weather during lunch.

Sam finished his burger and fries. Not a speck was left on his plate. He propped his arms on the table and leaned forward. "I've spent a lot of years observing people. I listen, too. That Ben Hauser, he got around."

My brain shifted gears. "What do you mean, and do you mind if I take notes?"

He nodded, and I removed my notebook.

"Pop, you've only been back around a month. Are you saying you knew Ben?"

"We weren't friends, but I saw him here and there. He was up to no good. If you ask me, his brother had STP syndrome."

"That sounds like a motor oil company." I jotted the letters next to Craig's name.

"Not in this case. It stands for something to prove." He cleared his throat. "The kid had something to prove to his brother."

I took a deep breath. "Even though Ben was crooked?"

"Yes, ma'am."

I considered the possibility. "You may be right. Ben was involved in some big deals and had a lot of money. But he also had a knack for separating people from their money. Maybe Craig was jealous of all the attention his brother got."

Reid rubbed his chin. "Bad attention is still attention. In a warped way, it makes sense. What else do you know?"

"Ben was pursuing investors for this place." Sam pointed to the building behind us. "He told anyone who'd listen that it was going to be Fox Island's premiere resort, and to his credit, the place has a lot of amenities. Ben offered investors the moon. Some believed his promises. Others walked away."

"Pop, how do you know so much?"

"Years of being homeless taught me the art of invisibility. It's easier not to be seen than it is to see pity, or disgust, in peoples' expressions." He pressed his lips together.

His words pierced my heart. Every person had a story to tell. That went for homeless individuals as well as scam victims. "You guys know all those files I wanted Ben to organize? Maybe we can find the names of some of his investors in them."

Sam clapped his hands and stood. "I believe we've all got our marching orders. I'm going back to the beach with my metal detector. You two do your thing. I'll let you know if I find anything else. Carry on."

"Bye." Reid turned his attention from his dad to me. "Well, that was abrupt, but he is being supportive. Do you want to look at Ben's files now?"

"I can't wait. Let's go."

After three hours in Ben's office, I'd found numerous business deals. "Ben was involved in so much. How did he never get arrested?"

Reid stretched. "He was always on the move. Tell me about some of his business ventures."

I rattled off a few scams and the names I'd found on contracts. "So far, none of our suspects are listed in any of the papers I've read. That worries me. If we consider every person ever burned by Ben, the list could be endless. Technically, not endless, but it's a lot of people."

"With a Ponzi, the beginning investors make money. Down the line, it crumbles, and the last investors lose the most." Reid took a deep breath. "Some of Ben's scams seem like Ponzi schemes to me instead of deals going bad."

"According to Craig, his family lost everything. How do you treat your loved ones like that?"

"You know how bad my dad hurt us. It seems like those closest to us are the ones we hurt the worst. Does that make sense?"

"Yeah. So, the question is, does opening yourself up to love make you an easy target?"

"It's possible, but Ben stole from friends and strangers too. He was a smooth talker." He raised the biography in his hands. "Whit Dupree seems like a legitimate businessman. He cares about his employees, and he gives back to the community and the world. Lots of charitable foundations have been created by Dupree. It seems like a real shame that Ben couldn't model himself after this guy instead of running scams."

"So, has the book been helpful?"

"In relation to Ben, the thing that strikes me is the hotel. Dupree has businesses all over the world, and he's in favor of the hotel room co-ownership model."

My phone vibrated, and a message appeared. *Can't get into Ben's computer. Any updates there?*

I met Reid's gaze. "Let's go to Paul's office."

"What about the information you found? How will we know the office is secure?" Reid stood and paced. "It's already been broken into once. There could be some incriminating evidence the killer missed, and we're not seeing it either."

"Good point. Let me call Paul." We needed to make some progress on the murder case before something else happened. I couldn't pinpoint it, but a sense of doom hung over this office.

Chapter Twenty-Six

Paul had assigned a police officer to guard Ben's office. Meanwhile, Paul, Reid, and I sat at Reid's dining table. The guys looked at my notes and the paperwork I'd brought from Ben's office. I worked on trying to hack into Ben's computer.

"Thank goodness there's no obvious limit to log-in attempts." I wrote down another failed password. I'd tried his name, the name of the resort, the island, and the names of his schools. "Oh, maybe Whit Dupree will work." I typed the name as one word. "Ugh. Another failed attempt. Paul, were there any sticky notes under Ben's laptop?"

"No, but the computer was hidden in his golf bag. It could be what the killer was looking for last night. It may also be what the killer thinks you have."

"Then I need to leave a package as big as this laptop tonight." I turned the page in my notebook and wrote down things that interested Ben. The clock was ticking, and it'd sure be nice to catch the killer before I was supposed to make the drop.

After two more attempts, a box flashed on the screen. It asked if I wanted to reset my password.

"Paul, do you have Ben's phone?"

"It's in my car, but we can't get into it either."

"Most phones only need eight digits. If I can open it, then I can change the password on the laptop."

"Be right back." My brother left us alone.

Reid stood. "I rarely sit this much. Would you like something to drink?"

"I'm good. Thanks."

"How'd you learn to hack computers and phones?"

"Years ago, when I came across some credit card bills for things David hadn't told me about, I became suspicious. There were charges for dinners, hotels, and ladies' clothing he hadn't given me. I learned to get into his computer so I could prove an affair. It was easier, though, because I knew him better, and he was lazy with his passwords. He tended to recycle them."

"Oh, Katie. I'm sorry you had to go through all that."

"Thanks, but you know what? The hurt is gone. It's only a puzzle piece in my life. If it hadn't happened, we might not be together now."

Paul returned. "Here's the phone and a cord to charge it."

I plugged in the phone and checked my notes. Ben's date of birth was the first thing I tried, and it opened right up. "Success. Now to change the computer password."

"That was easier than I expected. Good job, sis. The next time we need to get into a computer, I'll come to you instead of the tech guys at work."

I turned my attention to the laptop and requested to change the password.

Reid placed a hand on his chest. "No offense, Paul, but it'd prolong my life if you wouldn't drag your sister into another murder case."

"She can always say no." He shrugged.

"You and Ethan are her weak spots. She'll do anything you guys need."

"Hey, y'all. I'm sitting right here. For the record, Reid, you're my greatest weakness. But you're also right about Paul and Ethan. If they need me, I'll always try to help."

Reid leaned down and kissed me. "That's one of the many things I love about you."

Paul said, "I'll try not to take advantage, but you do have a knack for sifting through clues."

Ben's phone dinged.

"Here we go." I continued the process of changing the computer password, and soon I had it open. "What do you want to look for?"

"First, what did you use for the new password?"

"Golf resort, all one word, then the digits for one, two, three." I wrote it down for him, and I also added it to my notes.

"Can you search the documents for our main suspects?"

"Yes, but do we have the same list? Rory Ledger, Madison Ledger, Craigh Hauser, and I've added Zeke McCarthy. Phoenix Sue Stewart Porter is off my radar. Is there anyone else you'd like me to search for?"

"Zeke and Craig are at the top of my list. Rory has a sketchy history, but it's harder to imagine his niece did it. Still, I haven't ruled her out. See what you can find. I need to shove off and go over tonight's plans with my officers and the others who are coming to help. Don't go to the lighthouse until I've talked to you. How do you feel about wearing a bulletproof vest?"

"Like under my clothes? I'm not sure I have a top that's loose enough to conceal it."

Reid held up a finger. "I'll loan you a T-shirt. Mine are extra-large and should work."

"I'm always happy when a plan comes together." Paul left with a big smile.

Reid's phone vibrated, and he looked at it. "How long will it take you to search for those names?"

"It depends on how many times they're in Ben's documents. Why?"

"There's a problem with the refrigerator at your new house. Do you feel safe here?"

"Yes, you should go. But there's something we need to discuss." I stood in front of Reid and placed my hands on his shoulders.

He took a deep breath. "What?"

"This is serious. I haven't had time to train for the Memorial Day Triathlon. Can we skip competing in it?"

He laughed and hugged me hard. "Katie, girl. The triathlon is the least of my worries. Consider it forgotten."

I kissed him and felt a huge sense of relief. Me and my unharnessed big mouth had challenged Reid, and there was no chance I'd have been able to keep up with him, much less beat him. "That's very good to know. Thank you."

"Yep, there'll be another race over Labor Day weekend." He laughed and left me alone.

I couldn't stop smiling, but I returned to searching Ben's laptop. If there were no connections to my four suspects, I'd have to begin all over again.

Chapter Twenty-Seven

In Reid's quiet house, I got to work. Luckily, I'd found all four of my suspects mentioned in Ben's files. I created a new document highlighting each person's connection to Ben. Then I logged into my email on Ben's laptop. I forwarded my new document to Paul, Reid, and myself. Afterwards, I erased all traces of being on Ben's computer.

I hadn't slept much the night before, and I moved to Reid's couch. I managed to fall asleep until I felt a touch on my shoulder. My heart raced. My good ear was on the throw pillow, and I couldn't hear. Should I open my eyes or act like I was sleeping? Open my eyes. Definitely. Maybe I'd catch the intruder by surprise.

A hand rubbed my arm. "Katie."

The sound was muffled, but it sounded like Reid.

I opened my eyes. "Oh, hi. Sorry, I fell asleep."

"After last night, you probably needed the rest. I got your email. Good work."

"Thanks. Do you think we should return the laptop and phone to Paul before going to the lighthouse?"

"I've got a safe. We'll lock them in there."

"Cool." I gathered the items and followed Reid to the upstairs loft.

He removed a painting of a coastal landscape hanging on the wall and placed it on the floor before spinning the safe.

"Well, aren't you just hoity-toity? A wall safe is pretty snazzy."

With ease, he slid the items into the safe and locked it before returning the picture to the wall. "A pretentious person would have a swivel picture frame to conceal a wall safe. I'm just cautious."

"Well, I think you're smart." I glanced at my watch. "We've got time to question another suspect. I'm leaning toward Madison Ledger. What do you think?"

"Honestly, I'd like to stop by the bookstore. I'm not crazy about my mother working with a potential killer."

"I know Joy likes smoothies. Why don't we get one for her and Madison? We'll take them to the bookstore, and maybe we can casually question Madison."

"Let me text Mom and confirm she's there."

While he dealt with Joy, I tidied up the dining area and Reid's couch.

"She's at the store. Let's roll."

Thirty minutes later, Joy opened FUN's door for Reid and me. She led us to a table designated for book clubs or after-school activities.

I pointed to the drinks. "You've got a choice of coconut mango, blueberry, strawberry, or peach."

"Coconut mango for me. Let me check with Madison." She left us alone.

I looked around the bookstore. "The shelves and display tables are fuller than when I was here the other day."

"I'm glad you noticed." Madison appeared. "Joy said you came bearing smoothies. Thanks. Which one is mine?"

"You can choose." I explained her options, and she reached for the blueberry. I took the peach, leaving strawberry for Reid, because I knew he was hoping to get that one. "Madison, you don't need to worry that I'm trying to bribe you for a look at *Atlantic Coast Guide*. I was able to get my hands on a copy."

Her eyes grew wide. "Did you pay twelve hundred dollars for it? I would've given you a discount."

"No, like I told you before, that's not in my budget. I borrowed one from a friend." Thank goodness for Darby Meadows loaning me her copy. "I can't figure out why Ben was interested in obtaining a copy. Can you remember if he said anything about why he wanted it?"

"Not really. Oh, I think somebody's at the front." She walked away.

I hadn't heard a knock or buzz, but the entrance was to my right. I reached for the peach smoothie.

"Hey, Mom. I saw you and Reid pull in and decided to stop and see if y'all needed me to pitch in with anything." Ethan turned his attention to the others. "Hi, Reid. Mrs. Joy, how are you today?"

"I'm good, and you know, Madison and I have a project for a strong young man like yourself. Don't we, Madison? Why don't you take Ethan to the storage room to get the ladder?"

Her chin jutted up. "I planned to carry it out here myself."

Joy's long earrings tinkled when she shook her head. "Nonsense. I'm sure Ethan won't mind."

Madison looked at my son. "I guess if you don't mind, come on."

"That's why I stopped. I really thought maybe you'd hired my mother. While I'm looking for a job and a place to live, I want to help her as much as possible."

After they disappeared, I glanced at Reid. "Well, we haven't learned much yet. Ethan probably won't appreciate me questioning Madison."

"She was surprised you had a copy of *Atlantic Coast Guide*."

Joy slurped her drink. "This is yummy. Reid's right. Madison is disappointed you don't want to buy the book. She finally heard back from the person who sold it to her, and they won't take it back. All sales are final. They won't even swap it for another book or books."

"That's too bad." I did feel bad for the young woman, but she'd figure out a way to sell it.

Ethan carried a ladder into the salesroom. With directions from Madison and Joy, he placed big stuffed animals on a top shelf in the children's section. They were propped up and holding books. In the adult area, he arranged a display featuring Georgia authors and framed landscapes of Fox Island. Ethan said, "These pictures are good. Who's the artist?"

"Thanks." Madison laughed. "I took those. This is a beautiful island."

"I bet they sell out. You should also sell stuffed foxes. Maybe they can be reading books or something."

"Oh, that's a great idea." Madison smiled at Ethan.

I sat in a comfy chair for customers and sipped on my smoothie while watching my son with the young, dark-haired woman.

Joy put Reid to work breaking down empty boxes and carrying them to the commercial recycling bin behind the store.

Back on the floor, Ethan pointed to the table where Darby Meadows would sign books. "I met her this week. She's cool."

Madison's mouth formed a circle. "Oh, do you read her books?"

"No, I'm more into thrillers and mysteries, but it was nice to meet her. She even loaned Mom a book."

Uh, oh.

Madison's nostrils flared. "Don't tell me. *Atlantic Coast Guide?*"

I stood. "It's my fault, Madison. I was hired to organize her office, and I noticed the book. She has a copy for research, and I asked if I could borrow it. She agreed for a short time only. Please, don't be upset with her."

Her shoulders slumped. "It's my fault. I was paranoid something would happen to prevent me from returning it. Turns out, I can't send it back for a refund anyway."

"I'm sorry about that."

"Thanks." Madison ran her hands through her thick, dark hair and held it off her neck for a moment. "I looked at the book last night. You know, really studied it, and it's about tides, moons, and safe places for sailors to stop. There was also a map with markings, and you'd think that made it less valuable unless it'd been owned by a president, the governor of Georgia, or someone famous. I'm not good with maps and always rely on my phone apps to get me places."

How did a person survive if they only used apps for directions? "We still don't know what's so special about *Atlantic Coast Guide.* Ben had some history books with pirates, but the one he stuck you with isn't about pirates."

Ethan said, "If I wash my hands, can I see the book? Maybe pirates are mentioned."

Madison agreed, and soon Ethan sat at a table studying the book.

Joy and Reid returned, and Joy had another project for her son. He shot me a grin and did what his mom requested.

"Guys, you won't believe it. This map includes Fox Island, and the markings are on our island. There seems to be a secret code to decipher what the words and symbols mean, though."

Madison leaned over his shoulder. "There's writing on the next page. I can make copies for all of us, and maybe we'll solve the puzzle."

I shook my head. "Before you do that, you should know what happened to me last night. Whether you decide to make us copies or not, we don't want word to get out about this. It might put you in danger."

"Danger? I never considered that. Should I stay with Uncle Rory?"

I stepped closer. "Madison, I don't mean any offense, but how well do you know your uncle?"

Chapter Twenty-Eight

adison gasped at my question.

"Mom." Ethan frowned.

"I'm sorry, but Madison's safety was my main concern."

Joy patted Madison's shoulder and handed her the blueberry smoothie. "This will make you feel better. Drink up."

Madison sipped the drink and glared at me at the same time.

"Truly, I didn't mean to upset you. But just because Rory is your uncle, it doesn't mean his trailer is the safest place to stay."

Joy said, "I have a spare room."

Reid choked. "No, you don't. I need it tonight."

I bit back a smile, knowing he was trying to protect his mom in case Madison was the killer.

"That doesn't make sense, hon. You have your own place."

"I'll explain later, but let's focus on Madison. Where else would you feel safe?"

She chunked her empty cup into the trash can behind the counter. "What's the problem with Uncle Rory?"

I sighed. "There was some bad blood between Rory and Ben. In fact, Ben owed him money. You might be able to tell us something that'll prove your uncle is innocent. He was at the resort the day of the murder, and you were, too. Can you provide an alibi for Rory?"

"I'll provide an alibi." She lifted her chin defiantly.

"That's not what I mean. Don't just say he was with you, if he wasn't. At least be honest with yourself. Is it safe for you to stay with your uncle?"

She rocked from one foot to the other. "I don't know that much about him. For years, he wasn't part of our lives. A couple of years ago, he had a heart attack and reached out to my dad. We lived in North Carolina at the time, and Uncle Rory came to live with us for a few months. He found a job during the week as a maintenance man for the library. He began disappearing on the weekends, and my mom was conflicted by his time away."

I said, "What do you mean?"

"Uncle Rory has always been nice to me, but he knows how to get on my mom's nerves, and he does. But that's another story. Mom couldn't decide if my uncle had a girlfriend or what. Sometimes, he'd reappear and hand her a few hundred dollars in cash to pitch in with expenses. Other weeks, he'd return in a foul mood. Mom began to suspect he was gambling, and when a friend mentioned that she'd seen Rory at a casino, we had our answer. Mom blew a gasket and insisted Dad find a nice way to get him out of the house."

"Is that when he came to Fox Island?"

"No, he worked for a golf course in Myrtle Beach before coming to Georgia. When he left us, he admitted to my dad that he struggles with gambling. He apologized and agreed it was time to go. Uncle Rory left on good terms, and eventually, I landed here, too. Unfortunately, he introduced me to Ben. He was mad as a hornet when Ben refused to pay for the book." She lifted her hand. "Don't ask. Mad, yes. Murderous, no. Deep down, Uncle Rory is kindhearted."

I nodded. "I saw him consoling Sue Porter after she'd seen Ben."

"The staff stick together. Ben could be the life of the party, but at times he wasn't rational. Uncle Rory believes he was under enormous pressure to make Seaside Hideaway succeed." She sighed. "It's easy to relate. I feel pressure to make FUN succeed."

I nodded. "And I've just started a new business. We're all under pressure to do well."

Reid said, "Did Ben have business partners? Maybe silent ones?"

"Evidently, there were a slew of people who'd meet with Ben, but they didn't stay at the resort. Maybe they were business associates."

Reid rubbed his chin. "How do you feel about Sue Porter?"

"She was always crying on Uncle Rory's shoulder about something. As far as I know, they were only friends. She considered him more like a father figure than a boyfriend."

Interesting observation, and I agreed. "There is quite an age gap between them, and she might need a father figure in her life. Have you met Craig Hauser or Zeke McCarthy?"

"I know Craig is Ben's brother, but I don't believe Ben introduced me to Zeke."

"How much contact did you have with Ben?"

"Ben was flirty, and if he focused on you, it was like nobody else was in the room. I've met guys like him before. They're not long haulers."

Joy laughed. "Long haulers. I like that phrase. At least one of my husbands wasn't a long hauler. Too bad I didn't realize the truth before we married."

Madison hadn't really answered my question. "So, nothing romantic. Did you spend much time with Ben?"

"The few times we were together, we focused on books."

It was like a bell went off in my head. "Madison, what were the other books Ben wanted you to find for him?"

"Let me see." She went behind the checkout counter and retrieved her tablet. "Here we go. Would you like me to print it out for you? I can do it while making copies of *Atlantic Coast Guide*."

"That would be amazing."

She tapped the screen and soon presented me with a list of books. "Be right back. The copier is in my office."

Ethan stepped closer to me. "Mom, I can't believe you asked her about Rory."

"What if he is the killer? Do you want to take a chance Madison would be his next victim?"

"No. You're right, but I'm glad she understands your intention."

Madison returned and handed pages to each one of us.

"Thanks. Are you familiar with the books Ben wanted?" I gave the page a quick glance but didn't study it.

"Most are non-fiction about life on the coast of Georgia."

CHAPTER TWENTY-EIGHT

Reid said, "Don't forget the book on pirates in his office."

Madison pointed to my list. "I believe he requested three with a pirate theme. They're old and hard to find. He wasn't interested in ebooks. He only wanted books he could hold, and now that we know he's the kind of person who writes in books, that makes sense."

"Are you judging him?" Reid laughed.

"Possibly. Books are treasures and should be treated with the utmost care, especially old books."

Ethan reached for the list. "It's a good thing you never saw my college textbooks. Of course, they weren't antiques. I liked buying used textbooks that were highlighted and written in. It gave me a clue on the important points to remember."

"Oh, honey, that could be a good clue." I glanced over Ethan's shoulder at the list. "Suppose Ben did the same thing? Maybe he made notes in the books to remember the important stuff."

Reid paced. "The problem is we don't have his books; they're in his office."

Madison looked at Joy. "We're practically finished. Why don't we go with them and see what Ben had? If we all work together, it'll be faster."

What was happening? Madison was a suspect, and now she wanted to assist in my investigation. I needed to come up with an appropriate response, because I didn't want to offend her again. "Um, it sounds like a good plan, but we won't be allowed to remove the books from Ben's office. And the police probably won't allow us to take pictures."

"Not a problem, Mom." Ethan looked at the owner of FUN. "Madison, would you like to ride over with me?"

I'd never told Ethan he couldn't date a girl, but I didn't like the mushy look he gave Madison. It'd be a good idea to keep an eye on her for more than one reason. Was she a killer? Was she protecting a killer? And would she end up breaking Ethan's heart?

Chapter Twenty-Nine

Our little group was like a bunch of unchaperoned preschoolers when we reached Seaside Hideaway.

Reid and I arrived first but stood in the shade and waited for the others. I'd talked to Paul on our way over, and he'd told Officer Troy Merrick to allow us into the office.

After Joy parked, she adjusted her scarf. "Reid, I'm going to see if Sam is still at the beach. He might need a drink or something. I'll join you in a bit."

"Okay." He waited until she entered the lobby. "Let's see what the others decide to do."

Ethan parked his SUV and opened the door for Madison. When they joined us, Ethan said, "Madison's going to check on Rory, and I'm going to grab something to drink. Do you want anything?"

"Nothing for me, honey."

Reid lifted his hand. "I'm good, but thanks for offering."

Ethan and Madison left us standing alone in the parking lot.

Reid chuckled. "That didn't take long. Are you up to going through the books?"

"Definitely. It'll be worth it if we find a clue. Would you rather make sure your mom is okay?"

Reid drew in a slow, deep breath. "She's a grown woman, and since my dad returned, she's told me that numerous times. So, I'm sticking with you."

Officer Merrick requested to see our identification before allowing us in. "Is there anything I can do to help?"

"No, but thanks. Are you, by any chance, the K-9 handler?"

"Yes, ma'am. My partner, Cody, is getting a physical today. I hardly know how to act without him."

Reid said, "I believe Chief Wright mentioned Cody is trained to find drugs and cadavers."

"Mostly drugs, sir."

"We'll quit distracting you, but thanks for all you do."

Reid headed for the bookshelves. "What first?"

"Let's start with Georgia history books." I wiped the desk with a damp cleaning cloth just to make sure there was no lingering fingerprint dust on the surface. I took notes of anything of interest. Reid stood and flipped through books. He was moving at least three times quicker than I was. "How can you go so fast?"

"It's kinda like speed-reading. I focus on looking for handwriting or highlights. You're probably slowing down for chapter titles or section headings." He placed another book to the side. "If I remember correctly, you flunked speed-reading in high school."

I did a double-take. "How rude. I didn't flunk the class. I got a B. The teacher said it was because I loved to read so much that there was no way I could go faster."

"Sounds like a gentleman's B to me."

I couldn't really argue.

Ethan appeared with Officer Merrick behind him. "Mom, that Craig Hauser and the other guy are drinking at the bar. Come on, you might want to hear what they're saying."

"Zeke McCarthy?"

"Yes, ma'am. Rory told me who it was."

"So, you're positive he wasn't the man you saw speak to Ben at Shrimp and Grits?"

"One hundred percent. The man I saw was older."

Reid and I followed Ethan to the pool bar, leaving the policeman to guard the office.

Sure enough, the guys were there, and neither one looked happy.

"Dude, you disappeared on me. Here's your drink." The bartender looked at Ethan and lifted a glass.

"Sorry." My son paid for it and stood there, sipping the drink and watching tennis on one of the televisions."

Reid motioned for me to join him at the bar. We moved to an open spot where my left ear would be toward the men. The bartender asked for our orders.

"I'd like ginger ale, please."

"Same for me." Reid passed him some money.

I didn't want to risk Craig and Zeke leaving, and I tapped Craig's back. "Hey, how'd it go with the attorney?"

Before Craig could answer, Zeke leaned forward. "I'll tell you how it went. Little brother here inherited most everything."

Craig made a negative motion with his hand. "Ain't necessarily a good thing. I also inherited the bills, and there are liens on multiple properties. The attorney said I could turn down the inheritance."

Zeke elbowed Craig. "I'll be happy to help you look at the financials, then that'll give you a better feel for your inheritance."

The bartender gave us our drinks with a cherry on top. Oh, nice. I loved maraschino cherries. Reid dropped his into my glass and winked.

Craig said, "What's the catch?"

"Ben owed me money, and if you can pay off his debt, you should."

"Look, man. I'm not saying he didn't owe you something, but I need you to bring me some paperwork to prove how much."

"You know as well as I do that Ben didn't always work that way."

"Then I can't make you any promises. He stole from my parents, and if I'm going to make his victims whole, I need paperwork and dates. In fact, I should hire my own accounting attorney and come up with a system of who Ben ripped off and how much they are owed. Give me something to work with, Zeke. I want to be fair, but I've got to be fair to everyone, not just the person complaining the loudest."

Zeke muttered something I couldn't decipher and stormed away.

Craig ordered a double shot of whiskey, then turned to us. "This is going to be a nightmare. Even in death, Ben is tormenting me."

CHAPTER TWENTY-NINE

How long had Craig been drinking? "Let's order you a burger or something."

"Good idea."

Rory appeared and spun Craig around. Rory was average-sized, but he was no match for Craig. "When are you going to pay me back what your brother stole from me?"

"Gather up documents to show how much he owed you, and I'll see what can be done."

"Listen, sonny, that's not how Ben worked." He spit out a dollar amount that made me cringe. "That's what he owes for the resort golf carts. This place can't run without a golf course, and that won't survive without carts that work."

"True, but I need some kind of proof. How do I know that's the right cost? What if Ben already paid you? I'm not going to get scammed."

Rory's nostrils flared. One hand fisted. Tense seconds ticked by. "You'll be hearing from my lawyer."

Craig clenched his jaw. "Get in line."

Rory drew his fist back and swung for Craig's handsome face.

Craig ducked.

Rory missed his intended target.

Instead, his fist came straight at me.

Chapter Thirty

"Katie." Reid slung me away from Rory's punch.

I stumbled into a body but kept my gaze glued on Reid and Rory.

Reid grabbed him by the wrist and wrangled Rory to the ground. "Somebody, call the police."

"You're safe." A gravelly version of Reid's voice spoke, and hands held my upper arms.

Joy screamed and turned in a circle.

"Mom, are you okay?" Ethan vaulted to Sam and me.

"Yes, I'm—"

"Kate, I'm so sorry. I'm going to call the cops." Craig swiped his phone.

"Thanks." I met Sam's gaze. "Take care of Joy."

"Yeah, it takes a lot to fluster her." He moved toward his ex-wife. "Joy, calm down. Reid and Kate are safe."

A laugh escaped Ethan, and he hugged me. "Wow, just wow. I thought you were going to get slugged for sure. I don't know how Reid saved you. That guy could've broken your nose or your jaw. Shoot, he could've broken your entire face."

Officer Merrick raced onto the scene and handcuffed Rory, who loudly proclaimed it was a misunderstanding.

Ethan released me.

Madison ran out of the main building. "Uncle Rory, what happened?"

"It's all a big misunderstanding."

The K-9 officer led Rory away.

Madison's eyes were huge. "Ethan, tell me the truth. What's going on?"

He reached for her hand. "Craig Hauser made your uncle mad. Rory took a swing at him, but Craig ducked. My mom was sitting on the other side of Craig, and if Reid hadn't pushed her out of the way, Rory would've decked her. It was scary. Mom's okay, and Reid restrained your uncle until the police arrived."

She groaned. "I don't have money to bail him out of jail. I need to call my dad. Can you take me to the bookstore?"

"No problem."

Madison looked at me. "I'm sorry about my uncle, Kate."

"It's not your fault."

It wasn't long before the crowd disappeared.

Reid slung his arm over my shoulders, and I leaned into him.

Craig straightened the barstools. "I believe the smartest thing for me to do is walk away from this. Only a fool would try to untangle all the financial disasters. Ben always wanted to make quick money, and he didn't care if his schemes hurt others. He always looked out for number one. I came to Fox Island to convince Ben to make things right with the family. If I accept what he left me, can I restore what people lost? Make them whole? What if I try and fail? What if I lose everything and more? Would it be fair to make sure my family is at the top of the list? Probably not. What am I going to do? I've got to try. Right?"

I felt sorry for Craig. Was it possible he was innocent? "You might consider hiring a forensic accountant to help you sort through Ben's mess."

Reid said, "I can give you the names of some respectable attorneys in this area if you need one."

"Thanks, guys. Kate, sorry I ducked. It was instinct, and it didn't occur to me you could've gotten hurt." Craig took his burger. "Think I'll eat in my room."

"Instinct." My pulse accelerated.

"What?" Reid leaned close.

"Craig ducked on instinct when Rory took a swing at him. Rory was mad and wanted to deck him. Are we digging too hard to find the killer? What if it wasn't planned? The killer and Ben might have had a heated discussion. The argument got out of hand, and the killer swung a club at Ben, killing him in the process."

"Yes, but what were they arguing about?"

"Right. And we also need to know where the murder took place."

"Do we? Why?"

I shrugged. "It's one of the basic murder questions. Who, what, where, and why?"

Sam interrupted our conversation. "Excuse me, but I'll take your momma home."

"Thanks, Pop."

I reached for my phone to check the time, but my pocket was empty. "I must have dropped my phone in the skirmish."

I dropped to my hands and knees and crawled around the bar area.

"Katie, it's to your right." Reid pointed. Soon, it lit up with Reid's picture.

I picked it up and swiped to answer. "Thank you." The light from my phone reflected on a flat object.

I reached out and touched a hard object. On closer inspection, it was easy to see a divot repair tool. "Reid, hand me a napkin."

He did as I asked. "Did you find something?"

I scooted my way to him. "Yes. It's a divot repair tool. Now we've got to figure out who it belongs to. Craig or Zeke?"

"To be fair, it could belong to someone else."

"Yes, but we don't believe in coincidences. It matches the one we found in Ben's office."

Reid quirked an eyebrow. "It's red, like the one Ben owned."

"I'll text Paul so he can fingerprint it."

"You know what else? Both of our suspects disappeared. It's possible one of them left the threatening note at my apartment."

"Actually, all the suspects are unaccounted for. Rory's probably at the jail."

"If someone shows up for the drop, it could be Craig or Zeke."

"Don't forget Madison."

"I'll encourage Ethan to stay with her. Then she'll have a reliable alibi.

Wait, I don't want to put Ethan in danger."

"Why don't you let it play out? Trust Ethan's judgment when it comes to Madison. In the meantime, we need to get you fitted for a bulletproof vest."

Chapter Thirty-One

People filled the grounds around Foxy Lady Lighthouse. Vendor tents and food trucks were organized in an efficient manner. In a field to the side, a small stage was set up, and a group of high school students played country music.

According to Paul, there were undercover cops in addition to the local police force in their uniforms.

Reid walked beside me in the grass. "Hungry?"

"I hadn't given food a thought until just now, but yeah. The church youth group is grilling hotdogs. What do you think?"

"I haven't eaten a hotdog in weeks, and my doctor probably won't be happy, but let's do it."

I laughed. "Why is it now that we're in our fifties, we have so many doctor appointments? For years I've prepared healthy meals, so would you rather visit the food trucks and look for nutritious options?"

"Not now. Thanks to you, I'm craving a hotdog." He wrapped his arm around my shoulders, and we ambled to the youth group's concession area. It would have been so much more fun, if I wasn't concerned about making the drop.

The minister of Fox Island Community Church greeted people who walked by the area where they'd set up. Tom and I hadn't started off on friendly terms, but Bess adored the man. I had to try to get along with him. "Hi, Tom. How are you tonight?"

His thick moustache twitched. "Good, Kate. I hope you're not here to accuse me of committing Fox Island's latest murder."

Some people didn't make it easy. "No, I'm just here for a hotdog. I want to do my part to support the youth."

"Pardon my bad manners. The hotdogs are amazing, especially if you like them a little charred. Be sure to order the icy cold lemonade. It's homemade and spectacular as long as you're not a diabetic. There's something about dissolving sugar in boiling water that makes it better. Seems like a lot of trouble when you can buy a gallon at the grocery store, but it's worth the price."

I truly didn't know how to take the man, so I moved to the parents running the concession stand. I ordered two hotdogs and two lemonades. While Reid continued chatting with Tom, I paid and headed to a table set up with disposable red-and-white tablecloths. After sitting in a rickety aluminum chair, I looked around. Was Ben's killer here? Was he watching me now?

Woof!

A fuzzy golden creature jumped in my lap and lunged for the hotdogs I'd placed on the table, knocking over the lemonade in the process.

"Katie!" Reid jogged over to the table, and the golden-haired dog bounded away.

I threw napkins at the mess, but the yellow liquid flowed over the edge of the table, landing on my jeans. I leapt out of my chair before getting completely soaked. "Brr, that's cold."

Tom and one of the parents ran over and helped blot up the sticky mess. The pastor said, "Man, blame this on me. I encouraged you to order lemonade."

"Yeah, but it's the dog's fault." There was no way I'd ever blame Tom for the accident. "It all happened so fast. I don't know if the mutt wore a collar, but there was no leash."

Tom said, "The least we can do is replace your order, and I'll get some of the youth to search for the dog. I got a glimpse of it. Looked like a goldendoodle."

"I think you're right." My cold, wet jeans clung to my thighs. Ten degrees warmer outside, and I probably wouldn't care. "Reid, I saw a booth selling sweatpants. I'll be right back."

"Wait, I'm not letting you out of my sight tonight." He walked beside me.

"Thanks. Did Tom say more bad things about me trying to pin Ben's murder on him? As far as I know, they were strangers."

"Turns out they weren't strangers. Tom told me that Ben asked if he'd like to invest in the hotel room co-ownership program at Seaside Hideaway."

"Did Tom give him money? No wonder he joked about me accusing him of murder."

"He planned to invest a sizable chunk."

"But?"

"Tom could never catch Ben at his office. It appeared legit to him. Tom said that he had the money and was prepared to write a check. After three failed attempts to meet, Tom thought it might be a sign. Tom is around our age, and he's nowhere near ready to retire, but he's spent a lot of money on rehab for his son through the years. He doesn't have much saved for retirement."

I nodded. "I remember Brandon. I hope it works out for him this time, but go on with your story."

"Tom thought Ben's plan sounded promising."

"It's interesting he'd approach a well-respected member of the community." I veered to the booth. They were selling different colors of sweatpants and shirts. I found a gray pair with polka dots stitched on the legs. The lady even held the back curtain to form a private area for me to change clothes. After putting on the dry clothes, I paid the woman and found Reid. He stood at the corner of the booth, watching the diminishing crowd.

He chuckled when he saw me. "Now, that's an outfit I never imagined you'd wear, but it's, er, well, it's cute. Yeah. Cute."

"Thanks." I laughed with him. "At least I'm warm, and I think there's still time for us to eat."

"I believe I need a footlong chili dog now, with cheese and mustard."

The knot of anxiety in my stomach warned me to stick with something simple. "I'll go with a plain hotdog and mustard."

The youth concession stand was still open, and we placed our order.

The woman handed the hotdogs and drinks to us. "No charge."

"It's not your fault the dog stole our first supper." I stuffed the money in the tip jar. "Will you let me know if the dog is found? Pastor Tom knows how to reach me. I hope the poor creature has a family."

"Sure will. Have a good evening."

Reid and I found a table where we could stand and eat. He devoured his food. "I can't figure out why there are more loose dogs these days. A couple of years ago, it was unheard of, but we've seen two stray dogs this week."

"Do you think vacationers lose them while here? Vacation is over, and they go home without their family pet?" I adjusted my purse.

"I guess. Would you like me to hold your purse while you finish eating?"

"Yes. I'm afraid to put it down. Do you think the killer is watching us?" I scanned the people around us.

"If the killer is Craig, Zeke, Rory, or Madison, the answer is no. Unless they're wearing a good disguise. If the person isn't known to us, it makes sense for them to watch. They'd want to make sure this isn't a setup. They'll watch to see if we talk to the cops. So, yeah, it makes sense to watch us."

"That's what I was afraid of." I chewed my hotdog and glanced toward the outskirts.

"It's ten o'clock now, and soon there will hardly be anyone here. The good thing is we'll be able to watch for the goon while he's watching for us."

"He or she."

"Yep. Do you prefer to stand here or move around?" Reid tossed our trash into the nearest garbage can and sank it.

"Nice shot." His antics relaxed me for a moment. "If you hear water when you're lost in the woods, you hike to it. Then you follow the water. Ben was focused on making money, no matter what. It makes sense to follow the money to catch the killer, except in the case of Sue Porter. She wanted revenge."

"That's what she told us, and you decided she's innocent." Reid's eyebrows lifted.

"Ben left his estate to Craig. Zeke and Rory are mad because Ben died owing them money, but they can't prove it. Unless they can convince Craig what Ben owed them, they won't get their money back."

"I'd say Rory was more than mad since he took a swing at Craig."

Tom joined us. "Last call for food. Are you interested in seconds?"

Reid nodded. "Katie, can I get you something?"

"I'm good."

"Tom, don't leave her alone." Reid patted his shoulder and took off.

I met Tom's gaze. "Well, this is nice and awkward. How are you doing?"

"Fine, but are you in danger? Why does Reid want me to stick with you? Should I call the police?"

"No, they're here." I pointed to Officer Diaz. "Where were you when Ben approached you about his hotel room proposition?"

"He came to me at Marsh View Brew. It's a new coffee shop in town."

"I haven't tried it yet."

"They serve decent a cup of coffee, but the pastries are nothing compared to the coffee shop that used to be at the art gallery. I heard the bookstore isn't going to open the coffee shop."

"Not yet, but maybe one day. So, you were sitting there minding your own business, and Ben asked if you'd like to invest with him?"

Tom fingered his moustache. "I was reading a Dave Ramsey book. He's the guy who has a radio show and writes books about investing wisely."

"I've heard of him." The first time I'd ever seen Tom, he'd been reading in a coffee shop. I believed his story.

"I guess by reading the book, Ben decided I was a prime target. He was probably right, and the resort was local. I did my research and thought it could work. I guess you're investigating his death. Why?"

"I found Ben's body." There was no need to confide that my brother asked for my assistance in solving the case.

"Am I a suspect?" This time, his tone was serious.

"You have not been on my radar. Now that Ben's passed, and looking back on your conversations with him, can you think of anything hinky?"

"Ben was a likable guy, and I thought he had my best interest at heart."

"Did he explain how he could fairly assign your room to guests?"

"He had a rotating system. It was all supposed to be fair between him, me, and the other investors."

CHAPTER THIRTY-ONE

"No red flags?"

"The only problem was not being able to meet with him after I decided to invest. I guess Reid told you I went to see him three different times. He was never in the office."

"And that worried you?"

"Yes, for a couple of reasons. First, how can you run a business, if you're never around?"

"That makes sense." His words made me feel a little guilty. "Second?"

"I believe in signs. Three strikes, and you're out. I went to see Ben three times with no luck. I decided it was time to back out of the deal before I handed over my money and signed a contract."

"I have one more question. Was Ben going to present you with a contract?"

"Yes. It wouldn't make sense for me to go into business with Ben and not have a binding contract."

"Interesting. It's my understanding some of his investors have no documentation of their investments."

Reid returned with another hotdog. "I convinced the youth leader to donate the leftovers to a homeless shelter."

"That's impressive." I was proud of Reid. He was often on the lookout for ways to help others.

Tom put his hands in his pockets. "I best help shut down the booth. You two have a good night."

"You, too." I turned my gaze to my handsome boyfriend. My heart swelled with love for him. I was ashamed for hesitating when he brought up our relationship on the beach the other day. If I lived through this night, I'd be sure to tell him I was crazy about him.

Chapter Thirty-Two

My anxiety increased. There were a few stragglers left at the lighthouse festival. Most of the people milling around were vendors packing their products and food trucks cleaning their space for the evening.

Reid and I stood beside the ticket booth. On a sunny summer day, there'd be a line of people paying to tour the lighthouse and spend time on the property. We faced the parking lot full of dark shadows. "I guess this is it. I'm just so nervous."

"It's going to be fine. We picked a good time. There are people still around, but nobody is paying attention to you."

I placed my mouth next to his ear. "Well, nobody except you and the police."

He turned his head and snuck a kiss. "Where are you going to put the package?"

I gave him a quick kiss in return, then studied the almost deserted parking area. Sand, grass, and blacktop. Concrete wheel stops marked the parking places. "I think the last parking spot will work. It should be visible to the bad guy."

Reid gave me another kiss. "Be careful, and I'm right here."

Woof. Woof.

A goldendoodle dashed across the parking lot. It had to be the same dog from earlier. He raced in the opposite direction from us.

My neck pulsed. "Do you think I'm safe?"

"You don't have to do this. We can go home right now." Reid squeezed my hand.

"This could be our best shot to catch the killer. If he strikes again, and I could've prevented it, I'm not sure I could live with myself." I released Reid's hand and walked to the destination. The only sound I heard was my own breathing. One step after another. Step by step, I moved toward my goal. At last, I reached the shadowy parking spot. My labored breathing and racing heart made me feel like I'd run a race. I placed the manila envelope on the concrete wheel stop and backed away.

The dog barked from a distance.

The hairs on my neck popped up.

A man yelped.

Because of my hearing loss, I couldn't decipher what direction the sounds were coming from. I spun, and my ankle twisted on gravel. *Ow.*

The dog growled.

"Let go." A man's angry tone reached me, but again, from where?

"Katie, get down."

I ducked my head and limped to the ticket booth and Reid.

He met me in the middle. "It sounds like the dog took a bite out of our suspect. Hurry."

"Can you tell where they are?"

Reid wrapped his arm around my shoulders. "Behind a trailer over there."

The dog growled again, then barked.

The suspect screamed.

A shove knocked me to the ground.

A shot rang out.

The sound echoed over the ocean.

Had the killer shot the dog? Why had Reid knocked me to the ground? Why was it even harder to breathe than before? I couldn't get a full breath, and my chest hurt.

"Katie, honey, are you okay?"

I tried to nod, but it was too much effort. I closed my eyes and focused on breathing.

Chapter Thirty-Three

A female EMT sat in the back of an ambulance with me. "Take a deep breath, baby. I'll be as careful as possible getting the vest off. Did Chief Wright remove the bullet?"

"Yes." I'd thought the bulletproof vest hadn't been necessary, but it'd probably saved my life. "I'm Kate Sloan. What's your name?"

"I'm Allison Brooke Cameron. My coworkers call me ABC because I'm all 'bout caring for people. You can call me Allie."

"Nice to meet you, Allie. Did the police catch the shooter?"

"I believe all they've caught so far is the dog. That dog may be the hero of the night." She unstrapped one side of my vest. "I call this the side door entry and exit. Can you raise your arm?"

I pushed myself to lift it. "Ow, ow, ow. Sorry. I'm usually not a baby."

"Now there's nothing to worry about. Put your arm down." The EMT went about unfastening every possible strap and removed the vest without inflicting any pain. "I should've done that first."

"Do you know what happened to Reid's shirt? It was over the vest."

"The chief cut it off."

"Whoa. Then it's a good thing I was wearing another T-shirt under the vest. That could've proved embarrassing."

Woof. Woof.

I peeked around her shoulder and spotted the goldendoodle. Our gazes connected. "It's like the dog is checking on me." A tear ran down my face.

"It sure enough wouldn't be the first time." She glanced back before her attention returned to me. "Let's have a look at your ribs. You can take off your shirt one arm at a time."

One arm at a time was exactly how I slipped out of my shirt, and it still hurt.

The woman frowned. "You've got a welt here. It's beginning to bruise, but in time it'll heal. I don't believe you broke or cracked a rib, but would you like to go to the emergency room for X-rays?"

"No. If the pain gets worse, I'll ask for x-rays." I just wanted to find Reid and go home.

"You can put on your shirt. I also heard you rolled your ankle." She pointed to my foot.

"Reid's the only person who knew that, but it feels okay."

"Do you mind if I take a look at it?"

I had wriggled back into my shirt and felt stronger. Sitting in an ambulance not fully clothed was demoralizing, but at least I was alive. "Okay. It'd be silly to refuse your offer. Thanks for being so nice to me."

"Of course." She removed my tennis shoe and sock. "It might be a tiny bit swollen. Let me know if I hurt you."

"Ha, I don't like pain. You'll be the first to know if something hurts." In the past, I would've held in the pain. I'd always done my best not to show weakness, especially around my husband. It amazed me how my life had changed in the last few months.

Allie chuckled. With a tender touch, she felt my foot and ankle. "You may have a slight sprain. Prop it up and apply ice—"

"Oh, I know this one. Rice." Ethan had suffered from more than one injury growing up, and we'd used this protocol a few times.

"Yes. Rest, ice, compression, and elevation. Would you like me to wrap it?" The lady could wrap more syllables into a word than anyone I'd met.

"Sure."

Woof. Woof.

"Your dog is certainly devoted."

"It's not my dog, but if he doesn't have a family, I may adopt him. It's possible he saved my life tonight."

"You're probably right." Her attention was focused on my ankle. "I also suspect the dog has adopted you."

"I like that."

It only took a few minutes before the EMT finished wrapping the ankle and put my shoe on me. She opened the door and hopped out. "Are you ready?"

"Definitely."

She gave me her hand, and I stepped down gingerly.

"Hey, there." I touched Reid's arm.

Reid stood near the ambulance with his head bent, and the dog was at his side. "Oh, Katie. You gave me quite a scare."

"I scared myself a little bit too, but I only have a welt."

The EMT jerked her head my way and frowned. "And?"

"And mild bruising." I pointed at the young woman. "This is Allison Brooke Cameron. She took good care of me and even wrapped my ankle. But I'm good."

"That makes me very happy." He wrapped his arms around me. "Allison, thanks for taking care of Katie."

"It was my pleasure. See y'all around." She strode away with determined steps.

Woof. Woof.

"The dog may be your guardian angel. If not for her, the killer might have gotten a closer shot at you."

So, the dog was a female. I reached down for the goldendoodle to sniff me, then I rubbed her head. "I don't know where you came from, but thanks for watching out for me."

"Animal control is on the way to take the dog."

"No. Reid. They can't take her. If this little lady doesn't have a home, I'll adopt her." I felt her soft ears, then worked my way down to her neck. "No collar."

"They'll check for a chip, but I figured you'd want her. So, they've been warned."

The tightness left my shoulders. "Good. What about the shooter?"

"He got away, and before you ask, there's a shoe print. And it's big."

"Some women—"

"Please don't argue. The police believe it's a man's shoe print. How about if we move Rory and Madison down the list?"

"I don't mind. If it's a toss-up between Craig and Zeke, which way do you lean?"

"Craig. He inherited everything. No matter how much he complains about the complications it'll cause, he's still got the money, the resort, the Corvette, and who knows what all?"

Paul joined us. "You and Ethan should spend the night with Susie and me."

"I'm too tired to pack an overnight bag."

"Then I'm sending an officer to your place."

I hadn't joked about being too tired. I couldn't summon up the energy to argue. "Fine. I mean, thanks."

Paul's shoulders drooped. "I regret asking for your help with this case. Can you drop it now?"

"Even if I did, the killer thinks I have something they need. So, I'm in too deep. I can't quit my investigation. Why do you think I got shot at tonight?"

"I'm noodling on a couple of ideas. One thought is that it was always his intention to shoot you in case you had discovered something that would incriminate him."

I shivered. "I don't like your idea that the drop-off was a play to kill me. It seems like he'd want to keep me alive until he knew I handed over the evidence."

"Sis, you don't have any evidence."

"True, but the killer thinks I do."

Reid raised his hands. "Guys, we need to get somewhere safe until the shooter is caught. Paul, can you handle the dog?"

"Yes, but Susie won't be thrilled if I adopt another dog."

"I thought she liked Chloe." The West Highland Terrier had belonged to a previous victim.

"Yes, but it's been an adjustment. If nobody claims this pooch, she's all yours."

"She saved my life, so I'm happy to adopt her." An idea hit me. "Maybe the killer planned to get the package, but when the dog went after him, he decided to shoot me."

My brother stared at me a moment as if processing my statement. "That's one theory. We should regroup tomorrow when we're thinking clearly."

"Okay. Goodnight." I gave him a hug, then we left Paul and headed home.

Reid leaned forward as he drove. Both hands gripped the steering wheel.

"Do you think I'll be a good dog mom?" I hoped to lessen the tension.

"Katie, I believe you'll succeed at anything you put your mind to, including dog ownership."

"Can we swing by Seaside Hideaway?"

"It's almost midnight."

"Yes, but I want to see if Craig and Zeke have their cars parked in the lot. It also wouldn't hurt to see if the front desk staff saw either of them come and leave."

"You know, they might also be able to tell us if Rory is out of jail." He sighed. "Against my better judgment, maybe we'll learn something that will help catch the killer. If I sense danger, will you agree to leave immediately?"

"Of course." I'd be as cautious as possible, but I wanted the shooter caught.

Chapter Thirty-Four

Reid circled the Seaside Hideaway parking lot.

"Craig drives a white Ford Escape. Zeke drives a gray Camry, and if you happen to see a black Corvette, it belonged to Ben."

He chuckled. "I forgot how good you are at naming car makes and models. It's nice to see some things never change."

"Look. There's a Camry. I want to feel the hood." I reached for the seatbelt.

"I'll go. Why don't you record the license plate?" He was out before I could answer.

The parking lot was well-lit, making it easy to read the car tag. I wrote it down with Zeke's name. It was the newest model Camry and looked sporty. It made sense that Zeke would want a nice, flashy vehicle, because he was a car salesman.

Reid waved at me and pointed to a white Escape. He jogged to it.

I couldn't read the plate, so I waited. I texted Ethan in case he was concerned. *Be home soon. I'm with Reid.*

His reply was immediate. *I'm at the resort with Madison and her uncle.*

I glanced around the lot. *Don't see your Range Rover.*

My phone rang. It was Ethan. "What do you mean you don't see my vehicle?"

"I am in the resort's parking lot. Where exactly are you?"

"In the pro shop, but the door's locked. Why are you here?"

"It's a long story, but we're coming inside soon. Bye." I pushed the circle to end the call.

Reid got inside the truck. "Neither hood feels warm, but that makes sense in one way. It'd be easier to avoid getting spotted if you walked or rode a bike to the lighthouse." He shifted the gears.

"I wasn't able to see Craig's license plate."

We rolled up to the car in question, and Reid lowered the window.

I recorded the series of numbers and letters. "You won't guess who's here."

"Rory?"

"Well, yes, but Ethan and Madison are with him."

He backed into a parking space and shut off the truck. "I believe your son is sweet on Madison."

"I'm afraid you may be right. If she or Rory murdered Ben, it'll be awkward." I'd feel better if Ethan was interested in the EMT who'd taken care of me, but I'd never tell him who to date.

"That about sums it up."

I ran a brush through my hair and secured it in a band. A glance in the visor mirror startled me. Pale complexion, wide eyes, and a pained expression. Whoa. I applied lipstick and pinched my cheeks to add some color. "Let's go."

We walked into the resort's lobby.

"Ethan said they're in the pro shop." I hobbled to the front desk. "Good evening. I'm Kate Sloan."

The woman bore an amazing resemblance to Jennifer Aniston. People probably told her that all the time, but I refrained. She typed on the computer. "I don't see a reservation under your name."

"I'm here for another reason. Can you tell me if Craig Hauser or Zeke McCarthy left the hotel tonight?"

"I really don't know. One day, we'll have valet service, but it's not available yet." Her southern drawl indicated she might be from Georgia.

Reid propped his arm on the desk. "Any chance they rented bikes?"

The woman pursed her lips. "I don't share information about our guests. Why do y'all want to know?"

"It's related to Ben Hauser's murder." Reid's face remained neutral.

Her mouth dropped open. "Are y'all with the police?"

I said, "Unofficially, I'm helping gather clues, but I'm not an employee of the Fox Island Police Department."

"There's really not much I can share."

Reid said, "Is it worth asking Chief Wright to come over and question you?"

She looked both ways. "I don't need the hassle. Yesterday, Mr. McCarthy rented an electric bike for the week. I can't tell you if he has ridden it or not. But we have a bike rack on the deck behind the bar. There's also a path that leads to the beach."

"Is there a way to distinguish one bike from another?" Reid shot her a smile that would've made my knees weak. Who was I kidding? I was weak-kneed even though he smiled at the other lady.

She typed on her computer. "Mr. McCarthy's bike should have the number thirty-seven painted on the seat tube. That's a fancy word, meaning it's the bar the seat is on. Of course, it could be on the down tube. I'm sure you'll figure it out."

I was tired and added the number to my phone app for notes. "Thanks for your help."

Her gaze remained fixed on Reid. "You're welcome."

I bit back a laugh. Who could blame her?

We left through the back door. The pool bar was open, and a man played the blues on a guitar. He was good, and his tip jar overflowed. Yay for him.

Reid waved to the bartender. It was the same person as earlier in the day, but we didn't slow to chat. We hurried to our destination.

Reid got there first. "Here's the rack. Can you shine your light over here?"

"Happy to." I used my phone's flashlight and angled it so Reid could inspect the bikes. There were nine bikes, and he looked at each one. "Do you want to write down the numbers?"

"Good idea." I opened my app again and typed in the numbers as Reid called them out.

He stretched his back. "There's no thirty-seven, but don't jump to conclusions. It's low tide, and there's a full moon. It's a nice evening for a bike ride."

"You make a good point. Can we sit by the pool for a while and see if Zeke shows up?"

"I thought you were tired."

"Yeah, but I can't walk away from a potential clue."

He heaved a mighty sigh. "Lead the way."

"Thanks, Reid."

At the bar, we ordered decaf coffee and carried it to a table.

I felt movement, and a shiver slithered up my spine. I turned and saw Ethan pull up chairs for Rory, Madison, and himself.

"Hey, Mom. Mr. Ledger would like to say something to you."

With his fingers on the wide-brim sun hat, he spun it in his hands. "I'm right sorry about what happened this afternoon. I would never hit a woman, and hope you can accept my apology for what happened earlier."

His words touched me. "Technically, you didn't punch me. There was a lot of confusion, but why'd you get so upset with Craig?"

"Mom, it's late. We can discuss it tomorrow." Ethan propped one foot on top of his other leg. "You didn't tell me why you're here."

"That's another conversation that can wait until tomorrow."

Reid tapped my arm, then pointed to the path we'd just been on. "I hear someone coming."

I was almost too tired to get excited. It seemed like every time we were close to adding a clue, it was a dead end.

The bartender approached with a basket of sliders and a plate of nachos.

Ethan and the Ledgers started eating.

My eyes remained glued on the path.

I could hear voices, too. Please, oh, please, let it be Zeke McCarthy.

Chapter Thirty-Five

"Oh, good grief." Reid rolled his head back.

From around the corner, Sam and Joy Barrett came into focus. Joy's fingers were curled around one of Sam's scrawny arms. In his opposite hand, he held a golf club.

Madison stood. "Is that what I think it is? Is he carrying the murder weapon?"

"Um, I'm not for sure." I sent Paul a quick text. *Sam is at the pool carrying a different golf club.*

Sam and Joy walked to our table.

"Hey, y'all." Reid rose to his feet. "Pop, this is Madison Ledger. Mom works for her at the bookstore. And her uncle, Rory Ledger, runs the resort's pro shop."

The guitar player quit playing. The bartender turned down the sound on the TV. People grew quiet. It felt like everybody was watching us.

Sam looked in all directions. "Nice to meet you both."

"Were you practicing your sand shots on the beach tonight?" The look Reid gave his father pierced my heart. It was like he begged him to do the right thing.

Sam gave Reid a slight nod. "Something like that, but it's late. Might be best to take your mother home."

Crisis averted. Maybe.

My phone vibrated. *On the way.*

"Reid, why don't we walk your parents to their car?"

I showed him the phone screen.

He glanced at it, then nodded. "Good idea."

Madison propped her fists on her hips. "Wait. How do we know Ben wasn't killed with that golf club? It could be evidence."

Ethan stood. "Mr. Barrett didn't even know Ben. There's no reason for him to kill the guy."

A person appeared wearing a thin hoodie and a fishing face mask. The person slipped past Sam and Joy and disappeared into the darkness around one corner of the resort. I wanted to race after him, but I couldn't leave the altercation.

"But he's carrying a golf club." Madison's voice rose.

Rory leaned toward Sam. "It's not a sand wedge. Thought you claimed to be working on your sand shots."

Madison frowned. "I'm calling the police."

"No need. I'm Chief Paul Wright." My brother's appearance deflated Madison's hysteria.

"I'm glad you're here. Mr. Barrett has a golf club, and it could be the murder weapon." Madison sank into her chair.

Paul said, "Mr. Barrett, will you come with me?"

"Why, sure. What about Joy?"

"She can come too."

And what about the masked stranger? He'd gotten past us.

I looked at Reid. "Go with your parents. I need to check the bikes one more time."

"Take Ethan with you. I'll be back." Reid jogged away.

I moved to my son and used my sternest mother's voice. This was not time for a debate. "You need to come with me for a minute."

"Yes, ma'am."

I led the way to the backside of the bar.

"Mom, are you limping?"

"Yeah. It's a simple sprain."

"How did you sprain your ankle, and where are we going?"

"To check on a bike." I gave him a quick update on the night's events.

"Shot? You got shot?" His voice held a note of panic.

"Shh. I don't want everybody to find out."

"The shooter knows he shot at you. If you'd told me six months ago that moving to Fox Island meant you'd put your life in danger to solve murders, I never would've believed it."

"It's hard for me to believe, too." I stopped at the bike rack and turned on my phone flashlight. "We're looking for thirty-seven. I need you to call out the numbers, and I'll put them in my notes."

"You know, I always just thought of you as Mom. You raised me, you had the surgery to remove your tumor, you lost your hearing, you became a widow, and you started a career in real estate. To me, these were normal things a mother does. Until now, it never occurred to me how much courage it took. Now, you're in your fifties, you've moved to another state, started a new career, and you're solving murders. That's impressive, Mom."

His words warmed my heart. "Before I get a big head, I've technically only solved one murder."

"So far. What specifically are we hoping to find."

"I want to see if bike number thirty-seven is the only one that's been returned since I was down here with Reid. If so, I think it's safe to assume Zeke came back."

"Meaning what exactly?"

"He's likely to be the person who shot me tonight."

Ethan shook his head but gave me the number on each bike, including thirty-seven. "Okay, that's the numbers for all twelve electric bicycles."

"That's too bad. There were only nine here earlier, and I thought maybe if there were ten bikes, and if the new bike was the one Zeke rented, then there was a good probability he planned the drop tonight."

"Let's go home. It's been a long day, and you need to rest your foot."

"You're probably right." We made our way back to the others.

Ethan said, "I'll take Madison back, then go to the apartment. Do you want to ride with us?"

Reid joined us. "Your mom can ride with me."

Soon, we all split up. Reid took me home and insisted I prop up my foot. He even fixed an ice pack for me. We watched a show about flipping houses until Ethan and Officer Collins arrived. I was so exhausted that I headed to bed while the men discussed the case.

Chapter Thirty-Six

Friday morning. Yawn. I stretched in bed. *Ow.* My chest was sore. I gently rubbed the area over my left breast, but it didn't help much. Time to get on with my day. I swung my feet out from the covers and stood on the throw rug beside my bed. Nice. The ankle didn't hurt.

There was a soft knock on the bedroom door. "Mom, are you awake?"

"Yes." I opened the door. "You look nice."

He tucked his solid blue polo into khaki slacks. "Thanks. Coffee's ready, and I got called for a second interview with the park department. Drake went home to get some sleep. He reported nothing suspicious through the night. Reid's on the way over."

I squealed. "I must look dreadful."

Ethan looked over his shoulder. "That must be him at the door. Hop in the shower, and I'll make sure he's situated with coffee and the morning sports show. Bye."

I grabbed a change of clothes and scurried to the bathroom. While waiting for the water to get warm, I looked at the area where I'd been hit with a bullet. It was bruised and tender, but you wouldn't hear me complain. I was alive.

Life was good.

It didn't take long to shower and dress. I wound my wet hair into a messy bun and wandered to the main room. "Good morning."

"Morning." Reid's voice was gravelly, and there were dark circles under his eyes. "How'd you sleep?"

"Like a rock." I moved into the kitchenette and poured myself a cup of coffee. "Do you need a refill?"

"I believe so." He moved to the refrigerator and pulled out two yogurt parfaits. "These are from the smoothie shop. Fresh strawberries, homemade granola, local honey, and Greek yogurt."

"Yum. Do you want to eat on the deck?"

"If you don't mind, I'd rather discuss last night. Let's not take a chance someone will walk by and hear us."

"We won't have to worry about people overhearing us when I move into the house." I pulled my notebook out of my purse, and we sat at the little table. "What's the story on your dad and the golf club?"

"He found it on the beach. There were no obvious signs of blood, but your brother is going to have the lab examine it." He sipped his coffee.

"Don't forget some players get mad and chuck their golf clubs."

"Chuck? I didn't expect you to use that word." Reid grinned.

"It seems to fit the situation."

"True. So, I guess you saw the person sneak by us last night when Madison flared up over the golf club."

"I sure did; that's why I wanted to check out the bikes. Zeke's had been returned, but so had two others."

"There were twelve bikes?"

"Yes." I spooned up a bite of the parfait. It was cold, fresh, and delicious. "Yum."

"I know." We ate in silence. "Let's check on the progress at your house. If you don't mind, I'm going to hire a security company to wire it for your protection."

"Is it affordable?"

"At the rate you're going, you can't afford to be without a home security system. Besides, I have a friend who owns a security company. I often recommend him and use him in home improvement jobs. I'm sure he'll give me a discount."

"Okay. Thanks." If it was too expensive, I'd cut back somewhere else. The house didn't have to be completely furnished right away. I wanted the place to feel like a beach home, and I wanted to decorate it with comfortable furniture. I'd shoot for a relaxed vibe and incorporate natural elements where I could.

"Should I follow you over?"

"Nah, I took the day off. At least, mostly. After we check the house, we can go to Let's Get Organized. I can deal with messages and bids from there."

And just like that, we were off and running.

Later in the morning, I sat at my work desk. Bess left us alone and went to speak to young mothers at the library. Reid had taken over her desk with his laptop. He put on his readers and declared he had hundreds of emails to sort through.

I couldn't focus on work and decided to review my murder notes. Once again, it was clear I didn't know enough about Ben.

I searched online and found Benjamin Cole Hauser. Most of the links related to his golf career, but there were some random police reports that popped up. I took notes of the accusations. In one town, he pretended to be a CPA and stole money from people who thought they were friends. Another time, he ran an online dating scam. He convinced women he was a stock broker. Instead of investing their money, he stole it. When one woman threatened to turn him in to the police, he blackmailed her. By the time she reported the crime, he'd vanished.

According to notes from a crime podcast, Ben ran a mix-mingle scam. "Reid, have you ever heard of a mix-mingle scam?"

"Is it a dating thing?"

I smiled. "Good guess. Ben mixed legitimate high-end purses with knockoffs."

"Like pocketbooks?"

"Yes. He was going by the name Cole Benjamin, and he dyed his hair blond for the scam. By mixing some legitimate high-end purses with knockoffs, he sold thousands of purses. Again, he escaped going to prison. How?"

"I don't know, but it sounds like he was a serial conman."

I made a note to reach out to the podcaster, who was an authority on cons.

"Katie, you've got a customer."

Either I was too deep in thought, or I needed to move my desk to hear customers enter the store.

A man with his back to me looked at some of our brochures.

"Good morning. How can I help you?"

Craig Hauser turned. His gaze connected with mine, and it wasn't friendly. "Hi, Kate. Can we discuss the work you did for Ben?"

"Yes. Have a seat." I pointed to the consultation table and grabbed a fresh notepad.

Reid stood. "Can I do anything for you?"

This time, my back was to Craig. I whispered, "Don't leave me alone with him, please."

"No problem. I might even check in with your brother."

I joined Craig. "What would you like to discuss?"

"I decided to take over Ben's business. My attorney has a plan to deal with the liens, but I need to know something."

"What?"

"There are some business files missing from my brother's office. Do you have them?"

"No. How do you know some are missing?" My heart beat faster.

"Because I was part of one of my brother's ventures, and I can't find the records. The police gave me permission to go into Ben's office. Technically, it's my office now. I've spent hours looking for what I need."

"I was only hired to organize the office. I didn't deal with files. Not physical files or computer files. Don't forget, his office was ransacked. Maybe that person has the paperwork you're looking for."

Craig rolled his shoulders. "Why couldn't he have kept everything on a thumb drive? He never listened to me about the dangers of physical paperwork. It's bulky and easy to steal."

"Sorry, I can't help you."

"Me, too." Craig pushed his chair back with a screech and left the store.

Reid joined me at the table and massaged my shoulder.

"Do you think it's strange that he asked me for the missing file?"

"I prefer it to you being threatened. I do find it interesting that he needs it."

"Yeah, it seems urgent. So, if he doesn't have the file, and I don't have the file, who does?"

Chapter Thirty-Seven

I'd come up with a plan to talk to Zeke, and Reid reluctantly agreed to go along with me. Zeke was a car salesman, and we'd see if I could use that to my advantage. I locked the store, and we took off in Reid's truck.

"Zeke asked me to meet him in his hotel room."

"He what?" Reid's reaction was so severe that he jerked the steering wheel, causing us to swerve.

"Yeah, and I was offended. There's no way I'd meet any man in his hotel room, especially a murder suspect. He claims the WiFi connection is better in his room than anywhere else on the island."

"Baloney." His face reddened. "Why are we going to Seaside Hideaway?"

He made me giggle. "I convinced Zeke to meet me in the resort's restaurant. He agreed, but he's not expecting you. I figure we'll say you had to give me a ride."

"You can tell him anything you want, but I'm not going to leave you alone with that slimeball. Who asks a woman they barely know to their hotel room?" His mouth continued moving, but I couldn't hear well enough to understand.

"Reid, calm down. Even if you and I weren't dating, I'm smart enough not to go to a man's hotel room by myself."

"Sorry. I know you're smart, but Zeke probably gets some women to go along with his ploy." Reid took a deep breath. "What's your goal from this meeting?"

"Yesterday, he said something that seemed off. I can't quite figure out what, but maybe it'll come to me when we chat."

"Seems like a vague goal."

"Maybe you can mention riding bikes. Where did he go last night?"

"I'll do my best." Reid pulled into the parking lot right as my phone rang. "This is Ethan."

"Go ahead." He backed into a shady spot.

"Hi, honey. What's up?"

"I got the job, Mom."

"You don't sound thrilled."

"No, I'm happy. We took a golf cart and rode around parts of the island where locals live. I've got a better feel for what I'm working with. They'd like me to start tomorrow, but I need to square things with my other company. I can't leave them hanging."

"Good for you, but I feel like you're leaving something out."

"Yeah. We went to eat an early lunch at Shrimp and Grits, and you won't guess who I spotted."

"Who?"

"Craig Hauser, and he was with the same man I saw Ben with the other day." He inhaled loudly. "My new boss said the other man is Pastor Tom Cross."

My ears rang, and I tried to make sense of Ethan's statement. "You mean to tell me that Ben saw Tom right before he was murdered?" What had happened to Tom's declaration he'd tried to find Ben and backed out?

"Yes."

"Didn't you say he was mad?"

"Yes, they argued then left together."

"What was the mood like between Pastor Cross and Craig Hauser?"

"Civilized."

"That's interesting. You need to tell Paul as soon as you can. Thanks for letting me know, and congratulations on the new job. We'll have to celebrate."

"Sounds good. See you later."

"Bye." I swiped my phone. "Tom Cross is the man Ethan saw arguing with

Ben at Shrimp and Grits the day Ben was murdered."

Reid shook his head. "From what I could tell from your side of the conversation, I was afraid you were going to say that."

I repeated what Ethan had told me. "It seems like Tom lied to us about trying to invest three times."

"I can't believe it."

"Why do you suppose he was so angry?"

"We'll ask him." He removed his sunglasses and rubbed his eyes. "What else?"

"Today, Craig and Tom had lunch together."

Reid's face turned red. "We need to unpack that, but I'm ready to eat."

I'd give him time to digest the news about his friend. "Good thing we're meeting Zeke in a place that serves food."

It was a quiet walk to the resort's restaurant.

Zeke smiled and stood when he spotted me. "Kate, thanks for coming."

Reid appeared. "Hiya, Zeke."

The other man's smile froze. "Reid, I didn't expect to see you."

"Kate needed a ride, and I was happy to bring her." Happy didn't describe the look on Reid's face.

"I could have come to your apartment or your workplace. You shouldn't have troubled Reid."

I opened my mouth, but Reid spoke first. "Spending time with Kate is always the highlight of my day." He held the right chair out for me, before he sat on my left. For a man who hadn't lived with me when I'd lost my hearing, he was always considerate to make sure I could hear better.

Zeke said, "I ordered grouper bites for an appetizer. They should be here soon."

Reid looked over the menu.

I pointed to a stack of papers beside Zeke. "Are those vehicles you'd like to sell me?"

"Yes. These are a few options available. I need to know what you'd like in a new car. Jeep has brought back the Wagoneer, and it's getting great reviews."

"Wagoneer? Why are you suggesting that?"

He grinned. "Everyone on the island knows what you drive. It's a classic."

"True. I want something safe, comfortable, and affordable." I was happy with my current vehicle, but I wanted to give Zeke something to talk about.

A waitress brought the appetizer and took our order.

"Zeke, have you always sold cars?" I squeezed a lemon slice into my water.

"Not always, but it's a living."

"What would you like to do?"

He laughed. "The big dream is to make so much money that I spend all day handling my investments."

Reid popped a grouper bite in his mouth and chewed.

"Wouldn't you get bored?" My stomach began to growl, and I reached for a piece of grouper, too.

"Never, but we're here to discuss you." He pulled out a listing for a used Corvette. It was black. A Stingray.

I looked closer. "Isn't that Ben's car?"

Zeke's head jerked back.

Reid laughed, then coughed, trying to cover the laugh. He'd never make it as an actor.

"Zeke? Why are you selling Ben's car?" I couldn't let it go.

He tugged on the collar of his bright red polo with bulldogs on it. "Craig doesn't need it, and Ben's gone."

Did he think that Craig would just let him sell the ultra-sleek sports car? "That may be true, but maybe Craig wants it. I'm not going to get into anything between you two. What else do you have?"

Zeke showed me two more prospective vehicles before our lunch arrived.

We ate lunch and discussed golf. I finished my salad and leaned back. "Zeke, have you considered working in the golf industry?"

His eyes sparkled. "That would sure enough be my dream job."

Reid's mood had improved. He said, "Have you applied for jobs in that field?"

"I reached out to a couple of country clubs recently, but they didn't reply."

I wondered how hard he'd tried. "Atlanta has a lot of country clubs and golf courses. Do you have a family?"

"No." His answer was clipped.

I'd hit a nerve with the family question. "You're younger than me, so you probably know about websites for job seekers. Have you tried them?"

"Listen, we're here to help you find a car. Let me worry about my career." His smile was strained.

"Oops, I didn't mean to offend you. Sorry."

Reid looked at his watch with exaggerated movements. "Oh, my. Look at the time. Kate, I'm sorry, but we need to get to another meeting."

Zeke stood. "Are you going to see another car dealer? I guarantee they won't be able to match my prices."

"It never hurts to comparison shop, but no, we've got to meet somebody else this afternoon. To be clear, I don't plan to buy a vehicle without test-driving it first."

"Since the beginning of the pandemic, people buy cars all the time without taking them for a spin."

"You must have forgotten one of my top criteria. It needs to be comfortable, and I can't tell that without a test drive."

"But you can know if it's safe and affordable without a test run."

I stood. "Thanks, Zeke. I'll keep that in mind."

We left before he could try another tactic to sell me a car.

Outside, Reid looked at me. "Did it feel like he was desperate to sell you a vehicle?"

"Yes, and I'm curious about Ben's Corvette. If I wasn't afraid of running into Zeke again, I'd look for Craig. I'd like to find out about his time with Tom."

"Hey, there's Ben's car. Let's see if there's any indication it's for sale."

The car was parked diagonally in a corner spot. We walked around it. "I don't see a sign, but it's in a different spot than yesterday."

"Yeah, so somebody has driven it today." Reid clenched his hands. "Oh, man. Last night, I felt the hoods of Craig and Zeke's cars. It never occurred to me to check the Vette."

"One thing we know is Zeke was out on an electric bike."

"You're right. It's Friday, and it wouldn't surprise me if Tom is at the arts and crafts fair, setting up the youth concession stand."

"Let's see if we can find him."

Chapter Thirty-Eight

The first people we saw at the Fox Island Arts and Crafts Festival were Ethan and Madison. She was handing out flyers, inviting people to drop by FUN on Saturday. There was information on what she carried, a coupon for a purchase, and information on the book signing by Darby Meadows.

"Hey, guys." Reid shook hands with Ethan and Madison.

I gave them hugs even though Madison was a little stiff. "How's it going?"

"Good." Ethan reached around me and handed out another information sheet to a woman with a child. "This event is impressive. I can't get over how many people are here."

"Fox Island knows how to hold a festival. Are you going to be here all day? Should we celebrate your job later?"

"That sounds like a good idea, Mom."

Reid said, "We'll be on our way then, and let you two continue your work."

"Bye, honey." I gave him another quick hug. My heart felt lighter, knowing Ethan was going to live so close. I glanced at Madison. "Of course, you're invited to celebrate with us if you have time."

"Thanks."

Reid held my hand, and we walked to the church's concession stand. "I'd say you've got a happy momma's heart."

"Most definitely." I leaned into him, and a slight pain rippled across my chest.

"What's wrong?"

"There's some bruising near the welt from getting shot." I laughed. "Do you know how weird it is to say that?"

"The main thing I know is you're alive, and that's a miracle. You wore a bulletproof vest, and the bullet hit the vest."

"Yes, I'm very thankful." I squeezed his hand.

He kissed my cheek, and we wound our way to the concession stand. "Look, they've already opened the concession stand."

"What if I order two lemonades, and you try to get Tom into a conversation? He'll probably be more relaxed with you." A big sign indicated new flavors. "Would you like to try lavender lemonade?"

"I'd prefer strawberry."

"Coming right up." I got in line to place our order.

The same lady was working as the night before, and two students filled glasses with ice. When it was my turn, the woman recognized me. "I'm happy to see you're back. Guess what?"

"New flavors?" I smiled.

"Well, yeah, but we found cups with lids. I'm so sorry again."

"You need to forget about the spill. It wasn't your fault." I placed my order and waited. What had happened to the goldendoodle? The dog had probably saved my life, and I wanted to take care of her. Once I had the drinks, I found Reid. He and Tom were deep in conversation. I took a big breath and walked over to them.

Reid took his drink and smiled. "Tom heard the dog is at the vet clinic, and she's up for adoption."

That wasn't the news I had expected to hear, but I'd roll with the flow. "Oh, I want to adopt her. What's the vet's name?"

The full power of Tom's smile hit me. No wonder Bess had a crush on the man. "Dr. Noah Arkin. Should I let him know you're interested?"

"Yeah, but how did you find out?"

"Noah's a good friend, and we are in a Friday morning Bible study together. I've been trying to get Reid to join us for years."

"I'm usually at a worksite by the time y'all meet."

Tom clapped Reid's shoulder. "It's all about priorities, my friend."

Wow. That was rude. Or was it the action of a man holding his friend accountable? My emotions toward Tom see-sawed back and forth. "So, Tom, did you have lunch today with Craig Hauser?"

His smile dimmed. "As a matter of fact, I did."

At least he didn't lie. "If you didn't invest with Ben, why'd you meet him at Shrimp and Grits the day he was murdered?"

Tom frowned. "Ben texted me. He accused me of backing out of our deal. He went so far as to say he'd already planned how to use the funds I wanted to invest. He threatened to sue me. I couldn't allow that to happen."

Reid set his drink on an empty table beside us. "I can understand how that would make you angry, Tom."

"Now, hold on. Yes, I was angry. I was not murderous, though." His nostrils flared.

I wasn't sure what to think. "You may have been the last person to see Ben alive."

He shook his head. "Except for the murderer, which was not me."

"I hear ya, but did you maybe see anyone else approach Ben? Or did he mention going to meet someone?"

"Not that I can remember."

Reid said, "Why did you leave the restaurant with Ben?"

"We needed to finish our conversation, and I wanted him to understand why I was not going to invest with him. We walked to his sports car and finished our conversation, standing on the sidewalk. He drove away, and I went to my office at the church. That was the last time I saw Ben."

If he wanted nothing to do with Ben, what was going on with him and Craig? "Okay, so that takes us back to my original question. Why did you have lunch with Craig today?"

"I wanted to get to know Craig. Ben's gone, but the resort is still here. I was curious if there would still be an opportunity to invest in the business."

"You lost faith in Ben." Reid put his fists on his hips. "Do you trust Craig?"

"Haven't decided. Then again, Craig hasn't decided how he plans to run Seaside Hideaway. I gave him my contact information in case he decides to sell individual rooms. You know what I found interesting?"

"What?" I tipped my head to hear his answer better.

"Craig didn't know Ben was doing that. He couldn't find a file on the computer or a paper file. He asked me if I had any information. I agreed to bring him what Ben had given me."

A knot formed in my belly. "Please, make a copy for Craig. Don't give him the originals in case it's linked to the murder."

"If you don't mind, would you make an extra copy for Kate and me?"

Tom shook his head. "I can't believe you two, but yeah, I'll make a copy. After you helped solve Carissa Ruffalo's murder, I feel good about you tackling this one."

"Why?" The last murder had put me at odds with the pastor.

"If any of my dealings with Ben are misconstrued, you two will confirm my innocence."

"But you didn't give Ben your money. Right?"

"True, but I was aggravated. I went to a lot of trouble researching his business model. Then it took time to organize my money to invest it."

Reid rubbed his chin. "You would've been angrier if you'd lost your money. When can we get a copy of your contract?"

"I've committed to cooking hotdogs and pitching in for the rest of the day, but maybe tomorrow."

I didn't want to wait so long. "I've got an idea. What if Reid cooks the hotdogs, and I'll help the crew while you go make copies?"

Tom challenged me with his gaze. "Do you want me to also go see Craig, or just bring a copy to you?"

Selfishly, I only cared about myself. "Why don't you do whatever you think is best? I can stay until you return."

"Okay, folks. I'll do it."

I reached for the pastor's arm to stop him. "Just one more thing. Be careful."

"Why?"

"We don't know why Ben was murdered. What if it has something to do with the resort? You may be the only person to have proof about the hotel room co-ownership deal."

"Got it. I won't tell anyone why I'm leaving, and I'll watch my back."

"Perfect."

Tom told the others we were going to fill in for him, then he left.

Reid chuckled. "I'm not sure who hoodwinked who, but at least we'll get a look at one of Ben's plans."

"Yeah, you're right, but he's pretty slick for a pastor."

Chapter Thirty-Nine

Woof. Woof.

I smiled at the familiar sound and tried to decide where the bark came from.

"Katie, over there." Reid pointed to Tom and Bess. My favorite goldendoodle tugged on the leash Bess held.

I left my workstation and joined them. "What's going on?"

The dog jumped on me.

"Hiya, girl. I'm so happy to see you." I knelt and hugged her.

She licked me, and we all laughed.

Bess passed the leash to me. "Dr. Arkin said there was no chip, no collar, and no alerts for a missing dog. She's yours unless an owner mysteriously appears. What are you going to name her?"

"Hmm, what do you want to be called? Angel?"

The dog panted.

"How about Bella? Goldy? Hazel? Cookie?"

Her gaze connected with mine.

"Lady?"

She barked.

"Lady, it is." I tightly gripped the leash and stood, hoping she wouldn't try to run away.

Bess said, "That was easy enough."

"Easier than naming my car."

"I'm voting on The Beast." Bess laughed.

Lady remained at my side.

Reid joined us and held out a bite of a hot dog. "Hey, girl. We need to be friends, too, if Katie's going to be your person."

Lady's tail wagged, and she gobbled the food.

Reid gave her another bite before looking at the rest of us. "I thought she'd go for that after stealing our food last night. So where are we? Tom, did you see Craig?"

"Yes. He was in his office, and I gave him a copy of the papers, like you suggested. He questioned me why it wasn't the original, and I explained I wanted to keep it. Craig asked for time to study the document, and he asked if Ben had mentioned others who might have invested in the own-a-room plan."

Good question. Why hadn't I asked Tom that? "Do you know?"

"No, but Ben said others had invested. It might have been a ploy. You know what I mean? Like, there are only two left. Invest before it's too late."

Bess patted Tom's arm. "I think they got the point. Don't you have something to give Kate?"

"Of course." He handed me a Manila envelope. "Here you go. I best take over the grill."

I remembered his warning about youth burning the hotdogs. "Yeah, you can't serve burnt dogs."

He laughed but remained next to my best friend.

Bess pointed to my new goldendoodle. "Do you plan on bringing her to work?"

"I haven't put any thought into it yet. I just got her."

"Until the killer is caught, it might be best to keep her close. She saved your life once, and it might be a good idea to keep her around."

"I expected resistance from you, but you make a decent point. The only flaw in your plan is I'd never want Lady to get hurt while protecting me."

Reid rubbed the dog's head. "She's already attacked one person while trying to save you. It may be out of your control."

"You're right." My body stilled. Lady had gone after last night's shooter. "I wonder if she took a bite out of the bad buy? Do you remember what he yelled? I feel like she may have bitten him, or at least she ripped his clothing when he was trying to shoot me."

Reid snapped his fingers. "If she bit the shooter, the culprit might be limping today."

"Or have a bandage on their wounds."

Bess laughed. "There they go, Tom. Let's get to work while they try to solve the mystery."

"Thanks for bringing Lady to me. How did you two get together?"

Tom lifted his hands. "We ran into each other in town, and I offered Bess a ride."

My best friend didn't duck her head. Instead, she looked straight at Tom Cross. "And I accepted."

It was time to have a heart-to-heart with my best friend. Did she realize she was in love with Tom? It made sense not to date him while they both worked at the church. But she was my business partner. What was she waiting for?

"Katie?" Reid nudged me.

"Sorry. Did you say something?"

"Should we find a quiet place to look at the papers Tom gave us?"

"Yes, but first, can we walk around the area where we think the shooter was? I know the police probably looked, but Lady might lead us to a clue."

"It couldn't hurt to look." We weaved through the crowd to the parking lot.

I shivered and didn't want to continue, but this could be more important than my fears.

Reid stopped. "Are you up to this?"

"Yes. Let's replay last night. I left the envelope here." I walked to the spot, and Lady stayed with me.

A car drove past, and I waited.

"Then you turned and came back to me. The shot came from over there." He pointed to a small clump of trees and bushes.

"Let's see if we can find anything." I kept a grip on the leash and was impressed with Lady's behavior. She didn't race ahead or pull on the leash.

We walked off the sandy pavement, across a bit of grass, and to the trees.

"Man, it's tight." Reid stopped at the perimeter.

I stepped closer. "Here's a path."

He looked over my shoulder. "Watch out for poison oak."

"Thankfully, I didn't wear sandals. Would you stay here with Lady? I can look easier, if I'm not worried about her."

"As long as you don't get out of my sight." He took the leash and the copy of Tom's contract with Ben.

Lady barked.

"I'll be right back." I watched the ground as I walked through the small wooded area. Limbs, dirt, and sand. I kept going around pine trees and oaks. It was cooler in the shade but not cold. I stopped. Ahead of me, the ground appeared disturbed. I crouched and moved forward. There. A round, shiny object, and I suspected it was a shell casing, possibly from the bullet that hit me last night.

I took a picture and sent it to Paul along with a pin for my exact position.

He replied with a text. *Get out of there. I'm on the way. Talk later.*

I rejoined Reid. "I think I found a shell casing. Paul told me to leave. How about going to Let's Get Organized? We can make another copy of Tom's papers and read them at the same time." "Let's roll. You can tell me more on the way."

Lady barked and wagged her tail.

"Looks like we're all in agreement."

Chapter Forty

Reid and I sat at the consultation table in Let's Get Organized, and Lady snoozed beside me. Their calmness helped soothe my nerves. Reid highlighted sections as he read his copy of Tom's contract with Ben. "Tom said he was ready to go into business with Ben. I'm better at drawing house plans and renovating old homes than I am at reading contracts. Katie, with your background in real estate, does anything jump out at you?"

"We've got Ben's purchase price of the resort. There are no disclosures."

"What would that have meant to Tom?"

"Well, let's see. Would Ben have charged Tom, or anyone buying into the resort rooms, for beach renourishment? What if the place needs to be painted? Would Tom have had to help pay for updates on the property? Or was he solely responsible for the room he was going to buy?" I glanced at the notes I'd taken. "Also, what if Ben and Tom had a dispute? Would Tom sell the room back to Ben, and would the price be fair to both parties?"

"Knowing Ben, Tom would take the financial hit."

"I agree. My main concern remains. How could Ben guarantee he'd be fair about renting rooms. For instance, if business is slow, there'd be the temptation to always rent out your own rooms. Forget your investors."

Reid flipped through his copy of the contract. "Nothing addresses that in here. Do we agree that Tom is innocent of committing the murder?"

"I suppose, but it'd be easier if he hadn't been involved with Ben."

"He didn't sign the contract, so they only discussed a business proposition." I tapped the table. "Unless, Tom was so excited about the deal—"

"Stop."

"Yeah, you're right." My attitude concerning the pastor needed a true adjustment. "Do you think he and Bess might get together?"

"Even in the deep south, biracial relationships are acceptable these days. You've missed out on painful years of watching the two of them. They care about each other, but is it romantic on both sides? Hard to say. I only hope Tom doesn't break Bess's heart.

Chills raced up my spine. The time wasn't perfect. The store wasn't romantic. There were a lot of better ways to go about this. But last night, I'd been shot. It'd be a crying shame to die without ever telling Reid my feelings. He deserved to know the truth.

I reached for his hand. "Thanks for waiting for me."

His eyes narrowed. "I'll always wait for you, Katie."

Lady circled the table.

I ignored the lump forming in my throat. "I love you, Reid. I always have."

He stood and pulled me to him. "It's always been you for me, Katie."

"Aw, Reid. How did we—"

"Shh. We're together now." He kissed me, and I wrapped myself around him.

When the kiss ended, I smiled. "Maybe it's time to have a serious discussion about our future."

"I'm all for that. We've wasted too much time, and life is precious."

The door swooshed open, and Joy appeared.

Lady barked and wagged her tail. My new dog probably sensed Reid's mother was friendly.

"Mom? What are you doing here?"

"We took a chance that you might be here because the light is on. Sam's looking for a parking spot. My, but the bars are hopping tonight." Her chatter stopped. "What is going on in here? You two look mighty cozy. Would you prefer privacy?"

My face grew warm, and I waited for Reid to answer his mom. I didn't want to overshare, if he wasn't ready.

Joy leaned over and petted Lady's head. "Who is this sweet girl?"

"She's my new dog and possibly my guardian angel. Her name is Lady."

"I'd say she's a lucky lady if you adopted her."

Sam entered the store. "It took me three blocks to find a legal place to park. It must be summertime in Fox Island."

Joy linked her arm through Sam's. "Honey, meet Lady. Kate just adopted her."

"Hi, Sam. I'm going to lock the front door." I must have been distracted to have left it unlocked after closing. I flipped the bolt and turned back to the others.

"Nice dog you got there." Sam pulled a dog treat from his pocket and tossed it to Lady. She jumped and caught it in the air. "Good girl."

"That's impressive. I can't wait to see what else she can do."

"Pop, how did you happen to have a dog treat in your pocket?"

"When I was homeless, carrying dog treats was a luxury and a necessity. It'd break your heart if you knew how many stray dogs there are."

"I'm pretty sure Reid inherited his tender heart from you, Sam."

Joy laughed. "And his romantic side from me. So, what did we interrupt?"

Reid took my hand in his. "I guess witnesses won't hurt what I'm about to do."

My heart skipped a beat.

Reid knelt on one knee. "Katie, will you marry me?"

Tears filled my eyes. I took his face in my hands. "Yes."

He jumped up and swung me around. "Whoo-hoo! This is the best day ever."

Lady barked and ran circles around us.

Happiness flooded through me. Reid and I were going to get married. I kissed him.

Joy squealed. "It's about time."

We all hugged each other.

"I'm real happy for you two. We should probably let you celebrate." Sam's voice held a note of emotion.

"Thanks, y'all." I touched Sam's arm. "Wait, was there a reason for your visit?"

The mood in the room turned somber.

Sam ran a hand through his thick white hair. "I hate to discuss murder—"

Reid lifted his hand to stop his dad. "The sooner the killer is stopped, the sooner we can plan a wedding. What do you know?"

"I had decided to continue looking around the resort with my metal detector, because I don't think the club from last night is the murder weapon. Most likely, it's the first one I found." Sam spoke with slow deliberation. "But that's as good an area as any to spend my time hunting for treasure. This morning, I saw a person on the dunes. It's illegal because, well you know why, got to protect the land and all. So, I was going to warn the person he might get a ticket if he was caught."

I refrained from hurrying him, but it wasn't easy.

"Why didn't you?" Joy gave her ex-husband a tender smile. When she was with Sam, her eyes lit up.

"He wore a hoodie and one of those fancy face masks that fishermen wear. It occurred to me that he was up to no good, and I ambled on down the beach. I don't go looking for conflict."

"Did you report the guy, Pop?"

Sam crossed his arms much the same way Reid often did. "I've spent years avoiding the police, so I'm telling you."

"Thanks, Sam. I'll let Paul know." Life was moving at warp speed, and I had to think about the past few days. Had Sam met Paul? Yes. It'd been when Sam found the first club.

"Then we'll shove off. Congratulations on your engagement." Sam's low voice was so deep, it was often hard for me to distinguish his words.

"Thanks."

The two of them left us alone.

Reid took my hands in his. "My proposal may have seemed impromptu, but I've got a ring at my house, and I already asked Ethan for his blessing."

"Just when I think I can't love you more. I wish we didn't need to tell Paul about the man your dad saw."

"What if we call your brother then swing by my house and let me give you the ring."

"That sounds amazing, but you know I don't need a ring." I'd quit wearing the rings from my first marriage when I left Kentucky. There'd been some good times, but the bad outweighed the good. I knew Reid would never treat me the way David had. "I only need you."

"That's good to hear, because I plan to spend the rest of my life loving you." His lips touched mine, and thoughts of calling Paul vanished.

Chapter Forty-One

Paul showed up at my apartment early Saturday morning, carrying three cups of coffee from Island Perk. Lady and I greeted him and walked into the tiny kitchen.

"Good morning. How'd the first night go with a new dog?" He set the cups on the counter.

"She's just the best dog ever. Somebody trained her, and it breaks my heart to consider how much they must miss her."

"Your Georgia accent is coming back."

"Arg. It's time for me to move out." Ethan rolled off the couch and disappeared into the bathroom.

I chuckled. "He never was a morning person."

"I heard that." My son returned and made up the couch. "Nobody should be up this early on a Saturday morning."

"Time loses meaning when you're trying to catch a murderer. Even when you think you know who it is, you've got to be sneaky." Paul handed a cup to me. "Mocha latte for you."

"Thanks, but sneaky?" I sipped the drink and could feel my brain waking up.

"Which one's mine?"

"I couldn't remember what you preferred, so I ordered strong black coffee. It's the tropical island blend."

"Perfect. Thanks." He looked at the newest addition to my family. "I'll take Lady for a walk and drink my coffee in peace. No offense."

"If you don't have bags to pick up dog poop, there's a dispenser near the path to the pier."

"Thanks for the heads up. That wasn't on my mind at all."

"I can take her out, honey."

"Nope. I've got this." Ethan attached the leash to Lady's collar and left us alone.

"Would you like a bagel, Paul?"

"I'm good. Let's make sure we're on the same page for the investigation."

"Sam Barrett saw, but didn't report, a man wearing a hoodie on a dune near Seaside Hideaway yesterday." I shared Sam's story. "What do you mean about being sneaky?"

"I need to be careful how I get information from suspects. I don't want them to lawyer up, but I need enough evidence to get an arrest warrant." Paul propped his arms on the counter and stretched his back.

"What do you think about Rory Ledger?"

"He's a gambler and a hothead. He gambled on Ben and probably lost money on this venture."

"From what he told me, he most definitely lost money. After he took a swing at Craig, I agree to your theory that he's a hot head. But is he a killer?"

"Possibly. What if he grabbed a club and took a swing at Ben? He hit him in the head. Ben collapsed. Then Rory panicked. It could have happened that way."

"Yeah, but Ben seemed bigger and stronger than Rory. Craig ducked, so why wouldn't Ben have protected himself?" I sipped my mocha latte.

"Element of surprise?" He did some squats.

"Okay. So, what's the best way I can help you today?"

"Phoenix Sue Stewart Porter is still in town. Would you try to talk to her again?"

"I think she's innocent."

"Me, too. But she's living and working on the resort property. She may be aware of something that she doesn't even realize."

"Okay. If I can make an appointment at the spa, maybe it'll look innocent. Why are you stretching and everything?"

"I didn't get much sleep, and I need to work out the kinks and wake up."

Ethan returned with Lady. "Mom, your dog is a good way for me to meet women. Who knew?"

"I thought you might be interested in a certain bookshop owner?"

"We get along, and we've got a lot in common, but she's focused on starting her business. One day, we might be more than friends, but not yet."

Lady looked up at me expectantly.

"Let me get you some water, and you're probably hungry. Let's see what we've got."

Paul said, "You need to buy dog food."

I opened the refrigerator. "You're right. Oh, chicken and rice."

"Mom, what's on your hand?" Ethan crossed the room in three steps. "Did—"

I put the container of food on the counter and waved my hand around. "Yes, Reid proposed."

Paul whooped. "That either didn't take long, or it took over thirty years. Congrats, sis."

My gaze darted to Ethan. Did he realize how rocky my marriage had been?

"Mom, I'm happy for you and Reid. He's a real cool hand Luke, and he seems perfect for you."

"Thanks, guys." I hugged them.

"Y'all, I need to go, and don't forget to get your dog some food." Paul left with his coffee in one hand and making a call with his other hand.

"Reid said he got your blessing."

"Yeah. I respect that he came to me first, and he told me he's loved you since high school. He also explained how he married his first wife to help her through cancer treatments."

"Evidently, she didn't have family to turn to. It wasn't insurance fraud or anything. They got married and lived together. They were good friends, and he hoped she'd survive."

"I never gave insurance fraud a thought."

"Oh, good. I'm excited for you and Reid to get to know each other."

"Me, too. Do you remember the mission trip I took in high school? I was on the house-building team. Do you suppose Reid would let me help with your place so you can get out of here sooner? This place is tight."

"I never imagined having so much company when I signed the lease, but ask him. I'm ready to get out, too."

"Will you guys live in your house after you get married?"

"That's a very good question. We've got time to figure it out."

"Cool. I need to get ready for the bookstore's opening. I told Madison I'd help."

"It's not even seven."

"True, but I'm picking up an order from the bakery. Cookies and pastries and unhealthy treats that attract people."

"Okay. I'll warm up the food for Lady just enough to knock off the chill. Take as much time as you need in the bathroom." I put a portion of the chicken and rice in the microwave and hit thirty seconds. I looked at my goldendoodle. "You are so patient with me. We need dog food, a bed, dog dishes, shampoo, and toys. I don't know if there's a pet store on the island. We may need to drive to Savannah."

The microwave beeped, and I tested the temperature. It seemed perfect, but I blew on it just in case before giving it to Lady. "There you go."

Her tail wagged, and she dug into the food.

I opened my phone and booked an appointment at the resort spa. Before I had finished my mocha, my phone vibrated with a text. It was from Sue. *We need to talk. Can you meet?*

I called her. "Sure. When and where?"

"Not here, and someone may be watching your place."

I didn't want to suggest my store or the bookstore. It was too early for the library to be open. "Where do you suggest?"

"Marsh View Brew is new and usually not crowded. Try to make sure you're not followed."

This would be a good time to own a nondescript car. "Okay. I may park in back or a block away. Give me a few minutes to get dressed."

"Be careful." Her voice shook.

"Sue, you need to be careful too. I'll see you soon." The call ended. I changed clothes while my son finished in the bathroom. One he was done, I freshened up.

Ethan had gone, but Lady stood at the door looking at me.

"How could I forget you?" I left a note for Ethan, so somebody would know where I was. I stuffed my murder notes and everything I'd copied in my green backpack with navy polka dots. It all seemed safer with me. I grabbed Lady's leash and gave her a smile. "Here we go."

Chapter Forty-Two

Fluffy white clouds provided some shade from the rising sun. Because of Lady, Sue and I found a secluded spot on the back patio at Marsh View Brew. I placed my bag under my legs with my foot on the strap. Nobody would steal it without me noticing. The barista brought our drinks, muffins, and a dog treat for Lady.

I had ordered decaf tea, and I added honey from a small crock and stirred it with a wooden spoon. "Sue, I'm glad you called me. What's up? Are you okay?"

"Yes, ma'am. But yesterday I overheard something between Rory and Craig. I kept debating whether to tell the police, because Rory's always been kind to me. After a sleepless night, I decided to tell you. I don't want to be the next person to die."

"What was it?" I scooted my chair closer to the table and leaned toward her. "Sorry, but I'm deaf in my right ear. You don't need to shout or anything, but I don't want to miss what you're about to tell me."

Sue looked both ways. "I was on my way to Ben's office. Craig has taken over the space, and technically, it's his office now. Rory was in there, and I heard them talking. It's not like I was eavesdropping, but they were loud. Rory wanted his cut from a scam he and Ben were running."

"What kind of scam?"

Lady sat beside me and held her head high. She watched a couple take a seat at another table, and she remained alert.

"Good girl." I patted her side.

Sue said, "You know how people buy knockoff purses, sunglasses, and other stuff? I thought it only happened in New York City, but it turns out you can buy fake stuff no matter where you live. It's even available online."

"I know what you're talking about, but that doesn't sound like something Rory would be involved with. Maybe Ben, but not Rory. Right?" From what I'd learned, Rory was more into gambling.

"What about counterfeit golf clubs? Do you know there's a market for them?"

"You're kidding me, but I can see how it might be popular. You have no idea the amount of money I've spent through the years on sports. So, if people are willing to buy fake purses, why not golf clubs? I wonder if there were others involved besides Rory and Ben. How did Craig sound?"

"Exasperated. In fact, he also asked who else was tangled up in the scheme. I couldn't hear specific names, but it sounded like at least a couple of others who work at pro shops were participating in the con."

I flashbacked to when I tried on golf shoes and noticed the cheap golf clubs at Rory's shop. "I don't get it. If they work, or own, pro golf stores, wouldn't they make a bigger commission selling the real clubs?"

"You would think so, but what do I know? If you talk to Rory or Craig, please don't tell them it was me who blabbed."

I patted her hand. "Trust me. I'll protect you, but are you safe here? When are you going to leave town?"

"Lauren asked me to give her a two-week notice, and I respect her enough to do that. You're on today's schedule for a couples massage, but you can't bring your dog." Lady whimpered, and Sue laughed. "But she is adorable."

"Thanks, I'll figure out something."

With jerky movements, Sue gathered her red hair and stuffed it in a ball cap. "I need to go. Be careful, Kate."

"You, too. Call the police, or me, if you feel like you're in danger. I don't want anything bad to happen to you." I squeezed her hand. "I'll wait a few minutes before leaving, so nobody suspects we've been together."

Her stiff posture relaxed. "I appreciate that."

I started to text Reid, but decided to call instead.

"Good morning, fiancée. Are you calling to plan a wedding?"

I laughed and looked at my antique rose-cut diamond ring. It was gorgeous without being ostentatious. "No, but Paul and Ethan know we're engaged now."

"Want to meet for breakfast?"

I updated Reid on my morning and offered to bring breakfast to him. We made a plan to meet at my apartment and plot out our day.

I left a new message with Sue and requested a couples massage; then I ordered coffee and a breakfast sandwich for Reid. Once we were married, I'd make him healthy breakfasts, and we could eat together in my new house. Although, he might want us to live in his place. It didn't matter as long as we were together. I couldn't wait.

First, I needed to help catch Ben's killer. "Let's go, Lady."

Chapter Forty-Three

Reid and I entered the lobby of Seaside Hideaway. I made a production of looking at my watch. "Oh, dear. We're early."

"In that case, I'd like to check out the pro shop. There's a wedge I might be interested in buying."

"Sure." I followed Reid into the shop. "Hi, Rory."

The man's eyes widened. "Hi, guys. Did you change your mind about the golf shoes?"

Yesterday, he'd seemed sincere when we'd spoken. Today, I couldn't decide, especially after hearing about the golf club scam.

"I'd like to look at a wedge for someone my height." Reid stood over six feet tall.

Rory turned and began grabbing clubs. "You're tall, but not so tall you'd need me to place a special order for you."

Reid looked at the prices on the clubs Rory handed him. He let out a long, low whistle. "This is more than I wanted to spend. I'm just a beginner and not positive I'll like the game."

"Why start at your age?"

"Katie and her son both enjoy golf, and it seems like a good idea to give it a shot." He gave a little swing with one of the clubs. "Do you have anything less expensive?"

"It's possible—wait a minute. Are you setting me up?" Rory jammed his hands into the pockets of his loose khakis.

I widened my eyes, hoping to look innocent. "Set you up? What do you mean? I saw some reasonably priced clubs yesterday."

Rory brushed past me and locked the doors to his business. He turned and faced me with an angry, red face. "You know, don't you?"

Reid dropped the pitching wedge and stepped between Rory and me. "You've already taken one swing at Kate. Don't even think about trying to hurt her again."

Rory looked Reid up and down. Reid was muscular in the way that people who use their bodies every day for years are muscular. "Don't plan to hurt a lady."

"Do you want to tell us about selling fake golf clubs? Or shall we call the police?" Reid held up his phone.

"Nah, I've seen enough of them this week." Rory looked at me, and his shoulders sagged. "Ben got a hold of some cheap golf clubs, and we marketed them as originals. It took a little work, but people always want a bargain. If you ask me, most of the buyers knew the clubs weren't authentic. As long they have the brand name on them, they didn't care. It was a status symbol. Occasionally a buyer claimed the club didn't work like advertised. If they came to me, I'd give a refund."

I asked, "What about the other buyers?"

"It wasn't just me working with Ben. He had a sales team. He advertised on social media, and people contacted him online or by phone. It was ridiculously easy. Until it wasn't."

"What happened?"

"I began to get complaints. The people I talked into buying Ben's clubs knew me. I wasn't an unseen face on the telephone, and they knew where to find me. I wanted to make it right for them, but Ben could be stubborn."

"Which came first, the golf club scam or Ben not paying you for the golf carts?" I took notes on my phone.

"Golf clubs were first." He shook his head. "Don't ask why I trusted him on the golf carts. Maybe I wanted to believe I was different. Special, you know. When he approached me about the golf carts, he said it'd be a way to make up for my losses with the golf clubs. You see, I refunded people who complained until I ran out of money. That's when I skipped town."

"My chest tightened. "Ben hadn't been here very long before he was murdered."

"Nobody ever accused me of being smart. I believed Ben had also turned honest, until he stiffed me for the golf carts."

"Wait, you had some fake golf clubs for sale in this pro shop."

Rory hung his head. "Yes, I did. Most of the customers were only here for a week. Nobody demanded a refund for the fakes. Selling those clubs helps me stay open, especially after losing money on the golf carts."

A tap on the door ended the conversation.

Rory opened it for Sue. "Do you need a Coke?" He looked at me again. "She's not supposed to drink soft drinks when the public might see her because the spa frowns on soft drinks."

"Thanks, but I'm here for those two. They have an appointment, and they're five minutes late."

I had more questions for Rory, but they'd keep. I didn't want to make it look like Sue was behind my recent questions. I reached for Reid's hand. "Let's go honey. This will be our first activity as an engaged couple."

"I can think of other things I'd rather do."

Sue said, "I don't think you'll be disappointed. Come on."

We left Rory standing alone in his empty shop. How much was baloney? Had he ever intended to turn over a new leaf?

Craig and Zeke were standing by the corner of the front desk with their backs to us. Their heads were bent over a piece of paper big enough to be a drawing.

I elbowed Reid. "When we're finished at the spa, maybe you can talk to Craig about your bid on remodeling one of the suites."

"Or I could go now, and you get a massage."

I smiled. "It's for couples. Don't let me down."

"Ouch. How can you imagine I'd ever let you down? I even found someone to dog sit while we're here."

Chapter Forty-Four

I found myself more relaxed after our massages, but I wasn't walking away from my investigation. Reid and I searched for Craig and found him in his office.

"Hi, guys. Do you have an update on Ben's murder for me?"

"We're not the police. I'm just curious because of finding Ben's body. His death hit me hard." I studied the bookshelves. "Your brother seemed to have an interest in the history of this area."

"No doubt to take advantage of someone, but I don't know how."

"Do you mind if I write down the titles of some of his books? I've recently returned to the island, and I'd like to refresh my memory on our history."

"Sure, but I don't want to loan them to you."

"I understand, and I'd never ask. Do you have much to remember Ben by?"

"Do you mean besides the resort and a mountain of debt? Then no. Those books are pretty much it."

Reid said, "I heard you might want to sell his Corvette."

Craig pounded the desk with his fist. "Who told you that? No, let me guess. Zeke?"

"Yes, he asked Kate if she was interested in buying it."

"Well, it's not for sale. What can I do for you?"

Reid stepped closer to the desk. "Ben planned to remodel some of the suites, and he asked me to give him a bid. I'm a business owner, and if you plan to use me for that project, I'll take on fewer jobs. I never want to get so busy, that I can't give my attention to projects I take on. If you're interested,

I'll email my bid to you."

"Ah, you're a real hands-on type of person. I respect that. Send me the bid, then give me forty-eight hours to get back with you."

Reid opened his wallet and removed a card. "Here's my business card. If I don't answer, leave a message."

Craig put it in the desk drawer, then handed his card to Reid. He stood and they shook hands. "I'll be in touch."

"Thanks."

As Reid and I left Craig, we passed a woman in the hall. According to the nametag on her chest, she was head of housekeeping. She entered Craig's office and closed the door.

"Reid, I want to see if I can hear what they're saying." I returned to the office and leaned close to the door. I motioned for him to join me.

He walked with slow, deliberate steps until he reached my spot.

Secret room. Those were the only clear words I could understand.

"Come on." Reid grabbed my hand, and we hurried to the entrance. He pulled me close and kissed me.

The housekeeping lady breezed past us, and the kiss ended. "Nice. As much as I'd enjoy more kissing, it's not going to solve the murder. What's next on your list?"

"Honestly, I don't know."

"Let's clear our minds and go to the bookstore. Do you think Ethan is still there?"

"He acted like he'd be at FUN all day. Why?"

"A friend of mine is ready to sell his mother's beach bungalow. It could be something Ethan's interested in."

"Should I pick up Lady first?"

"Nah, she's fine with my friend. What do you think?"

"Okay, the bookstore it is." On the drive over, I got up the courage to ask the question that'd been nagging me. "Where do you want to live when we get married? My place, yours, or somewhere completely different?"

He hummed along to a Darius Rucker song on the truck's radio. "I've lived in and flipped quite a few homes on the island. There's not a sentimental attachment to my current house, except for the pantry where the town's new professional organizer put her touch. You haven't even had the opportunity to move into your new house. Can you envision sharing it with me?"

"I'd be thrilled for us to live there together. Ethan even offered to help you with construction if it'll get me out of the apartment sooner." I detailed my son's work experience.

"Ethan and I should discuss it." Reid parked on a side street by FUN Bookstore. "It looks like a nice turnout. Mom was a little worried that Madison hadn't advertised enough. Most of it was on social media."

Cars filled the parking lot, and people streamed into the store from different directions. "Bess and I need to hire Madison's social media expert. This is an amazing turnout."

We approached the front door, and Reid held it for a young mother with three children.

Strains of guitar music floated out the door. There was a table set up with the refreshments. It was probably the food Ethan had picked up earlier. A woman I didn't recognize served lemonade and water.

There was a line of people waiting to get their books autographed by Darby Meadows. It appeared as if romance fiction was alive and doing well.

"Mom, it was nice of you to come by. Hey, Reid. Congratulations on the engagement." He man-hugged my fiancé.

"I'm glad she said yes."

I did a doubletake. Had my handsome Reid Calhoun Barrett been worried I'd say no? Maybe my reaction on the beach the other day when I hadn't given him a positive response caused the worry. Shame on me. I'd make it up to him over time. "Of course, I said yes. Ethan, do you have a minute? Reid wants to talk to you, and I'll be sure to buy a book to support Madison."

"Yeah. Reid, why don't we step outside where we can hear better?"

I made my way to the Georgia history shelves. Madison carried two of the same books I'd seen sitting on Ben's shelves. I took them and found a cozy mystery from one of my favorite authors.

Madison approached. "Hi, Kate. Would you like me to hold those for you?"

I shouldn't buy any more books, but it'd be a shame not to support a local author. Plus, she'd hired Let's Get Organized to handle her home library. I handed the books to Kate along with my credit card. "I'm also going to buy Darby's new book. Do you want me to pay first?"

"I'll ring you up while you stand in Darby's line."

"Great." It didn't take long to reach the front of the line.

"Well, if it isn't my favorite organizer. How are you, Kate?" Her red hair was styled perfectly, and her lipstick hadn't faded a bit.

"Good. I'd like a copy of your new book. This is a great turnout. Congrats."

"Thanks, but the credit goes to Madison. She really got the word out." She signed my book with a flourish. "Enjoy."

"Thanks, and I'll get the *Atlantic Coast Guide* back to you this week. It was super helpful." I moved away so the next reader could speak to Darby. I looked for Madison. When I didn't see her among the crowd of people, I moved in the direction of the offices.

"You're skipping town again? Why can't you ever stay in one place?"

My pulse accelerated. Was Rory leaving Fox Island? I stood still in the hall. This was turning into a week of eavesdropping in hallways.

"If you're innocent, there's nothing to fear." Madison's voice held a note of angst.

There was a long pause.

"Bye, Uncle Rory." She exited her office. With her head hanging, she walked toward me.

"Madison, are you okay?"

"I need a tissue." She opened the door to another one of the offices and went inside. "This is your fault."

I followed her. "If your uncle is leaving, it's not my fault."

She plucked a tissue from a box on a table beside a suitcase. Clothes had been tossed haphazardly on the furniture and floor. There was a pillow and blanket on the couch.

"Um, Madison, do you live here?"

"Yes, I haven't found a place to live yet. This works for now."

"But there's no shower."

"Uncle Rory lets me shower at his trailer. It's nice enough. Maybe I should ask if I can live there before he takes off, but I can't leave FUN. Everything I have is invested in this place. I'm staying in Fox Island." She blew her nose again.

I could sell houses, write contracts, throw parties, and organize. I'd never had to run a cash register, but the nice thing to do would be offering to help. "I don't mind to pitch in here at the store, if you want to catch Rory."

"No. The store is my responsibility, and he's a grown man. I'll come up with better living conditions after today." She lifted her chin. "Your package is at the front register. Thanks for coming to my grand opening."

"You're welcome. I wish you the best of luck with FUN." I gripped the autographed book in my hand and retrieved my purchase. After exiting the crowded shop, I sat on a bench and waited for Reid. Poor, Madison.

Had Rory's decision to move to Fox Island started a chain of events? He moved, so Ben moved, then Madison moved? Had she somehow felt like her uncle needed looking after? And the poor girl needed a real place to live.

Fox Island was a small island, and there wasn't much room for expansion. At least there weren't many affordable options for regular people. I didn't know what she could afford, but maybe Reid and I could help her find a decent place to live.

Would it be more affordable to turn an office into an apartment?

No, that would probably require zoning changes.

Maybe she could catch Rory before he skipped town. The admirable thing would be for him to let her live in his trailer.

I texted Paul. *Rory Ledger is planning to leave town.*

Chapter Forty-Five

After a light lunch, Reid and I walked through my new home. He pointed out what still needed to be accomplished before moving in. "Technically, the upstairs is good to go, but I don't want you to move in while there are workmen coming and going. Plus, the main bedroom is on the first floor. Ethan volunteered to paint the walls and ceiling of the owners' suite and the ensuite. That'll save a little money and get you in sooner. How does the place look to you?"

"Amazing, and it smells like a new home. I can't wait to move in, so it's time to buy furniture." I'd sold most of my dark furniture before moving to Georgia. "I prefer whites and neutrals. What furniture do you want to move in here? Your recliner? Couch? Our home should be comfortable."

He propped his fists on his hips. "There are a few pieces I'd like to keep. The dining room table was the first piece of furniture I built, and it's sentimental to me. It can go anywhere, though."

"You built it? I'm impressed, and it won't just go anywhere. It's going to be a prominent piece on the main floor. We'll eat there every day."

He hugged me. "You're the best. I wasn't sure if it'd meet your standards."

I remained in his arms. "Of course, I want it here. This will be our home, and we'll treat it as such."

"When Ben's murder is solved, I want us to look at our schedules and come up with a wedding date. I suppose you want a big wedding?"

"Do you?" I'd already had one big wedding, and it took a lot of time and work. I didn't want to delay our big day.

"As long as you're there, it doesn't matter." He kissed my forehead.

"I'll be there. The problem is once you start inviting people, it's hard to know where to draw the line. You're right, though. Let's help the police solve the murder so we can relax and plan the wedding."

"Perfect. Madison told you that Rory plans to leave town. Where's your notebook?"

I went to my purse and bag of new books on the kitchen counter. "Where's your card table?"

"In the laundry room. By the way, I got a discount on the washer and dryer you like, so I ordered them." He disappeared and returned with the table in one hand, and two chairs gripped under his opposite arm. I took the chairs and opened them while he set up the table.

Reid sat on my left, and I opened the notebook. "There are things missing because I don't think everyone is comfortable with me taking notes. I also bought two books at FUN that Ben had on his shelves about Georgia history."

"Ben appears to have a motive for everything he does. He likes money, and he finds ways to separate victims from their life savings, IRAs, 401Ks, probably even cryptocurrency. He plays golf and runs a scam on golf clubs. It doesn't seem likely that he reads history for the fun of it. There's got to be a purpose."

Purpose. Every move Ben made appeared to be calculated. Purpose had become a popular word this week. "Was he looking for buried treasure? There were battles here during the American Revolution and the Civil War."

"Don't forget pirates."

"Oh, I wish I had Darby's copy of *Atlantic Coast Guide* with me. There was a map and a chapter on pirate treasure."

Reid propped his ankle on the opposite thigh. "This area is full of ghost stories and tales of people hiding family heirlooms from the enemy. Lots of times, homeowners buried their silver and jewelry. After the war, they'd forgotten where they hid their valuables. Or the head of the family had died, and nobody else knew the exact spot."

"That's sad."

"Yeah. What about the pages Madison copied for us out of her copy of *Atlantic Coast Guide*? We never solved the secret code, unless you're holding out on me?"

"I've got an idea. Let me organize my notes and study the code."

"And what will I do?"

"What if you pay a visit to our favorite riverboat captain?"

"Good idea." Reid pulled out his cell phone. "Jimmy Morgan might be able to shed light on the book, and he might have other information for us. If he can meet me, I'll go see him, then pick up Lady and meet you back here."

"That should give me enough time to make sense of my notes, but is this a crazy idea? Was Ben interested in pirate treasure?"

"Ethan pointed out the markings in Madison's copy of *Atlantic Coast Guide* on Fox Island. What if it's the reason Ben bought Seaside Hideaway?"

"I guess it's no crazier than selling fake golf clubs or running a Ponzi scheme."

"Don't forget the hotel room co-ownership plan."

"Right. If Ben thought there was pirate treasure on the resort property, why didn't he buy the book from Madison? If he found a cheaper copy of the book, it wasn't in his office."

"I don't have an answer for you." Reid tapped on his phone. "Do you feel safe here by yourself?"

"I'll lock the door, and we left Vinny at my apartment. Ugh, I'm still getting used to naming my Wagoneer, not sure I like it. If the killer is looking for me, he'll probably look there. Now I'm rambling. I'll lock the door and be perfectly safe."

Reid glanced at his phone. "Jimmy is at the bookstore. He says Darby Meadows is a dear friend. I'm going to meet him at Shrimp and Grits because he needs a stiff shot of whiskey."

I laughed. "It's hard to imagine him needing much of anything. Here's my copy of the map."

"Perfect." He kissed me, then walked to the door. "Call if you need me."

"Absolutely. Tell Jimmy hi for me."

"Will do." Reid locked the door behind him, and I looked at my notes.

The secret code was with the pages I'd given Reid, so I'd use this time to transfer notes from my phone to the notebook. Then, I'd read over everything and see what I'd left out. Maybe I'd have figured out a new clue by the time Reid returned.

Music would've been nice, but in case the killer looked for me here, I wanted to hear him coming. I glanced around the room. Without curtains or blinds, it would be no problem for anyone to see me.

I dragged the table and a chair to the kitchen, where I'd be out of sight. Not that I was paranoid, but with a killer on the loose, it made sense to use extra caution.

Chapter Forty-Six

oof. Woof.

My heart leapt with happiness, and I hurried to the front door of my future home.

Reid stood near a tree with my leashed goldendoodle, who sniffed around. "How about a walk?"

"Sounds heavenly. Do you have the house key?"

He patted his pocket. "Yeah, go ahead and lock up."

I grabbed my sunglasses and locked the door behind me. It didn't take long to reach the beach, and I took the leash from Reid. "Too bad it's not low tide, but it'll still be good to exercise. Did you learn anything from Jimmy?"

"Yeah. I think he's got a crush on Darby. He asked her to dinner, and when she said yes, he didn't know what to do."

"Is that when he started drinking?"

"Not exactly. He nursed one whiskey. Neat. Their date is tonight. He needed courage, but he wanted to be sober. We moved from the bar to a table in back, and I showed him the map. It's no surprise he recognized Fox Island. He said Blackbeard buried treasure on Cumberland Island. It wouldn't surprise him if we have buried treasure here."

"Has your dad ever found anything that could be considered pirate treasure?"

"Not that I know of, but maybe."

The breeze blew my hair, and I juggled, securing it with a ponytail holder while holding the leash. "I should add a ball to my list for Lady. She might enjoy playing fetch."

"Good idea."

"Reid, is the thought of pirate treasure throwing us off track from solving the murder?"

"We can't know for sure. The treasure could be the motive behind Ben's murder." Reid stopped and watched a wave crash on the beach. "Remember when Pop saw the person on the sand dune? We believed the guy was looking for the murder weapon, but what if he was searching for pirate treasure?"

My pulse picked up speed. "Or what if there's no treasure? What if Ben convinced people there was treasure on the resort property? He gives them the opportunity to invest, and they'll share the treasure?"

Reid's gaze met mine. "Knowing Ben, that's entirely possible. What do you want to do?"

"Let's keep walking, and tell me what else Jimmy said."

"When the map was made, the island was not the thriving metropolis it is now."

I laughed. "No doubt." Fox Island was a small town. In fact, it was so small there wasn't a superstore and maybe not a pet store. I needed to find out soon about the latter.

"It'll be easier to explain with the map, but here goes nothing. Some symbols indicate holes, caves, and large rocks. Jimmy is clueless about the writing that looks like gibberish. He doesn't think it's French or Spanish."

A man wearing a bright orange T-shirt and sculpted running pants ran toward us. Orange earbuds stuck out, and he didn't look threatening.

"Is that Zeke?"

"I think so."

Lady growled, then barked.

"No, Lady." I tightened my grip on the leash.

She fought me.

"Katie, get her under control."

"I'll go this way, and you talk to Zeke."

"What about?"

I couldn't answer. My attention was on getting my goldendoodle off the beach before she hurt someone.

A skinny red fox ran in front of us and toward a nearby dune. Thank goodness, it wasn't close to the turtle nest. I needed to alert the turtle patrol in case the animal had disturbed the nest.

"Is that what upset you, Lady?" From what I remembered, foxes liked mice, snakes, and birds. I felt like we were safe, but Lady wasn't happy. "Let's go to the house."

We beat Reid there, and I rinsed the dog's paws in the outdoor shower. "This will be so wonderful when we live here. Beach walks and showers."

Lady gave a happy bark.

"Yay for happy barks and happy dogs. You're a good girl." I led her to the front steps, and we waited for Reid. I loved on my goldendoodle. What had distressed her on the walk?

Had it been the fox? Or was the sight of Zeke enough to throw her in a tizzy?

Chapter Forty-Seven

Reid drove us to an independent pet store. Island Pet was owned by a retired veteran, Sandy Potts. If I had to guess, Sandy was around my age with sandy blond hair and freckles. She didn't wear makeup, and she wore jeans and a T-shirt advertising her business.

Reid moseyed around the store, humming an unfamiliar song.

Sandy said, "I've got a list of items new dog owners might want to invest in. How old is your dog?"

"I don't know, but she's been trained. In a short time, she's become a blessing to me." I glanced at the list. "But her family must be worried. The veterinarian doesn't know who she belongs to, but he posted her picture on his website."

"Dr. Arkin?"

"Yes. Do you have something like that on your store website?"

Reid returned. "Katie, there are big tubs here for bathing dogs. Would you like me to give Lady a bath while you shop?"

"I hate for you to do that."

"It's no problem, and it'll be easier for me to do it here than for you to give her a bath in your apartment."

Rinsing her off in the outdoor shower had only gotten her paws clean. I passed the leash to him. "Okay, thanks."

"We get lots of people who regularly bathe their dogs here." Sandy nodded. "Grab a buggy. I won't push you to buy more than you need, so why don't we begin with food, treats, and dental care."

"And dog shampoo." I reached for the nearest buggy and met her at the dog food aisle.

"Got it. I never answered your question. When I first opened, I had a bad experience with a lost dog. That's not right. A friend had found a French bulldog. She took care of it, and we posted on my website and social media while protecting my friend's identity. A man came into the store claiming it was his dog."

"But it wasn't?"

Sally handed me a box of treats, a dog toothbrush, and toothpaste. "No, but we fell for his story. We turned the dog over to him, and a couple of hours later, a family appeared asking about their dog. I was crushed, but we called the police. Our security cameras in the store and parking lot recorded the guy and his car. The police were terrific and tracked him down before the day was over. After that experience, I only post pictures of lost dogs online. I can take a picture of Lady for my private files in case her owner comes in looking for her."

"That sounds safe. Was the first guy trying to run a scam?" I laughed. "That's kinda a theme on my mind these days. Like was he going to sell the dog to someone? Or hold the dog for ransom?"

"French bulldogs fetch big prices, and I think the scumbag was going to sell him." She pointed to two different options of dog food. "Lady looks underweight to me. This one is more expensive, but it might help her to get healthy. You can transition to less expensive food down the road."

We discussed the pros and cons, and I selected the pricey food. "She probably saved my life the other night, and at some point, you may have to tell me not to spoil her. Let's see what else you have on the list."

Sandy didn't take advantage, and I was paying for my purchase by the time Reid had dried my dog.

On the way home, I held Lady. "You smell so good."

"She behaved while I gave her a bath. Her family must be worried."

"I know." I looked at Reid. "I believe we may have found a con artist more despicable than Ben. Sandy had an experience with a guy who came to her claiming a dog was his when it wasn't." I gave him a few more details, and he parked in front of my apartment.

"That's despicable."

"I forgot to ask about your conversation with Zeke."

"He wasn't cool with Lady's barking. I saw the fox and said something along the lines of the dog was trying to protect us from the fox."

I reached for Reid's hand. "Zeke is a loose cannon, and it's possible he murdered Ben."

"What about Rory?"

"Another loose cannon."

His gaze searched mine. "And Tom?"

"He's on the back burner for now. Bess won't be happy if I point to the pastor again as a murder suspect."

"So, Zeke?"

"Yeah, and Craig is my number two suspect. Is it time to quit thinking about the motive and dig into their alibis?"

"How do you suggest we go about that?"

"Hear me out. Let's go to Seaside Hideaway's restaurant and have a fancy dinner to celebrate our engagement. It'll be a pretend celebration, and we'll really celebrate later."

"Is the goal to find out more about Zeke and Craig?"

"Bingo. If that doesn't work, we'll set a trap."

"I really don't like the sound of that. I'll help you get all the dog supplies inside; then I want to get dressed for our big dinner. How do you feel about asking another couple to go and keep an eye on the situation?"

"Do you think we'll be in danger?"

"Maybe, but I think it might be good to have someone watch for reactions. For instance, if Zeke is around and making frantic calls. He could be out of our line of vision, or something like that."

"Next question is who will we ask? Bess is helping the youth group at the craft fair tonight. Madison is upset about her uncle, so that leaves her and Ethan out. Not that they're a couple. Paul and Susie would be suspicious. There's no way Bobby and Lois would agree." My brother Bobby loved me, but he would never stoop to going undercover, especially to solve a murder.

Reid shook his head. "You want me to ask Mom and Pop?"

"They are our best option since this is last minute." But could Sam afford it? "It'll be my treat."

"Hmm. I'll call them on my way home, and we can discuss who pays later." Reid helped me move the dog supplies into the apartment, then took off.

Lady snoozed on her new, soft dog bed. Between the dog sitter, the beach walk, and a bath at the pet store, she seemed worn out.

I showered and styled my hair, using a product to help with beach frizz. Then I slipped into a new little black dress I'd been saving for a special occasion. It'd never occurred to me, I'd wear it to celebrate my engagement to Reid.

Chapter Forty-Eight

A quartet played soft jazz music in Seaside Hideaway's restaurant. The wall of windows had been opened, and a soft breeze wafted through the place. White tablecloths, napkins, and candles adorned every table.

Reid wore a light gray suit and a blue necktie that matched his eyes.

A tuxedoed host led us to a table for two and set fancy menus in front of us. "Your waiter will be with you directly."

"You look beautiful, Katie." Reid squeezed my hand.

My cheeks grew warm. "Thanks, and you look very handsome." Handsome didn't begin to describe Reid. Swoon-worthy came close.

"My parents are already eating their salads. They're at a table close to the doors."

Without moving my head, I glanced around the room. "Whoa, your dad went all out."

"Yeah, Pop did good tonight."

I squeezed Reid's hand. "Try not to worry about him hurting your mom."

"Easier said than done, but I'm trying."

A waiter came, described the daily specials, and took our drink order.

Reid patted his stomach. "In the old days, I would've gone for a steak. Tonight, I'm ordering salmon."

"Oh, that sounds good to me too." A hand touched my shoulder, and I looked at Captain Jimmy Morgan. "Hi, Captain Morgan."

"Jimmy, please. It's nice to see you." He shook my hand, then did the same with Reid. "I believe you two know Ms. Darby Meadows."

I nodded. "Yes. Hi, Darby."

The four of us talked until the waiter appeared with our drinks and a basket of rolls.

Jimmy said, "We best move along. Maybe we'll see you all on the dance floor."

"Hopefully, Reid will want to dance with me."

"I'm going to dance your feet off." Reid winked.

They dodged the waiter and walked to their table.

We placed our orders; then I reached for a roll. "I'm starved. So, are we really going to dance later?"

"If it means I get to hold you in my arms, you bet we are." He took a roll and swiped butter on it. "After our conversation with Jimmy and Darby, everyone in the restaurant is bound to have spotted us."

"We just have to hope Zeke and Craig are around."

"Brace yourself, here comes Zeke." Reid put his roll on the bread plate and stood to greet Zeke. They chatted a minute about the weather, then Zeke tapped the table. "Kate, I talked to a dealer in Savannah who's willing to work with us. Why don't you go over with me tomorrow morning? We'll get you a new set of wheels before you know it."

What was Zeke up to? There was no way I was getting into a car with him alone. "Um, tomorrow is Sunday, and I'll be at church tomorrow morning."

His mouth dropped open. "Church? Well, we can drive over tomorrow afternoon."

"Zeke, I'm sorry. Reid and I just got engaged, and we're celebrating tonight. I don't want to think about cars right now. Also, I'm sorry if my dog frightened you earlier today. We saw a fox, and I think that spooked her."

He looked from me to Reid. "Congratulations on the engagement, but don't you want your fiancée in a safe vehicle?"

Reid frowned. "Of course I do. Kate's a grown woman, and if she feels like her old Wagoneer is safe, then I trust her judgment."

The waiter appeared with our salads but paused, because Zeke blocked his access to the table.

"Think about it." Zeke glared at Reid, then walked away.

The waiter set our salads on the table. "You two are certainly popular. Except for when I've waited on the boss, well, the old boss, Ben, yeah, except for him, I've never had so much trouble getting to a table. Would you like ground pepper on your salads?"

"No, thanks, and I'm sorry for your loss." He'd opened the door to a conversation I hadn't planned. "Were you and Ben close?"

"He believed in me and gave me a job when others wouldn't."

"I hear a story there."

"It's a long story, and you're here for a nice dinner. Enjoy your salads." He walked away.

Reid laughed. "Good thing I didn't want pepper. You really flustered him."

"Don't you find that often people just need someone to listen to them?"

"Yeah. We all want to be seen and heard, and you have a gift for noticing people."

"Aw, thanks."

We enjoyed our delicious dinner and made it to dessert before Craig entered the restaurant. He wore black slacks and a white shirt. His sleeves were rolled up, and he looked tired.

I waved to him and smiled. "There's Craig."

Reid turned and gave him a one-finger salute. "And here he comes. Shall I take the lead?"

"Go for it." I appreciated my fiancé. He allowed me to make decisions, and he was always supportive.

Reid said, "Hi, Craig. How's it going?"

"It's been a long day. How are you two?"

"We're celebrating our engagement." Reid beamed.

I held my hand out so he could see my ring. Light caught on the diamond, and it sparkled.

"Congratulations, guys. Let more order you some champagne."

Reid shook his head. "That's not necessary, but very nice of you to offer. Thanks."

"Another time, then. Listen, if you swing by my office on Monday, I'll give you my decision on renovating the suites. Quick question. Are you willing to do more than one suite?"

"Probably, but it depends on the timeline. I won't make a promise I don't intend on keeping."

"An honest answer. I respect it." He shook Reid's hand. "See you Monday."

"Wait a second, Craig." Time to be courageous. "Have you had time to reflect on Ben's death?"

"Everything I'm doing is because he's gone."

"Sorry, that's not what I meant. Who do you think killed him?"

"The most likely suspect is probably me, but I'm innocent. I'm counting on the police to catch the killer."

"You haven't come across any paperwork or contracts that have made you pause and wonder if that's why Ben is gone?"

"It's hard to decide." Craig's shoulders slumped. "I'm going to have all the financials audited, because I know Ben wasn't honest with people. Take Seaside Hideaway, for instance. It seems legit. I see signed contracts. Money comes in and goes out. It'd make me happy to think Ben was finally using his business finesse for good, but was he? I don't have any idea. My reason for agreeing to take over Ben's business dealings is to make things right with his victims."

He had discussed his intentions with me. "How will you find the victims?"

"My attorney agreed with your suggestion to hire a forensic accountant. I'm going to follow his advice. But you know the murderer could have had a different motive. It could be a disgruntled employee or a lovers' quarrel. I was mad over how Ben treated me and our family. I imagine there are plenty of other motives besides getting scammed by Ben."

Sue Porter's motive had been avenging her brother's death, but she couldn't go through with hurting Ben. "Did your brother have a girlfriend?"

"He was popular with ladies, and they were always around, but I'm not aware of him being in a relationship."

"Did you know Zeke before this past week?" Both men had been in town the day of the murder.

"No. I didn't meet him until after my brother died."

Reid said, "What did you do before coming to Fox Island?"

Craig's transformation from being uptight to relaxed was visible. His blue-green eyes shone. "Those were the days. Mind you, it was only last week, but I was the manager of three fitness centers. It was awesome. I can already feel my body getting flabby from inactivity. If I stay here long, I need to plan a way to stay in shape."

Nobody could argue that Craig was in good shape. "There's bound to be a learning curve, taking over for your brother. I'm curious. Why quit a job you obviously loved?"

"It's the right thing to do. I haven't exactly quit. I've been good at my job, and my boss is giving me extended time off. I've got six months to decide if this job will work for me. One thing is for sure: I'm going to improve the fitness room. I might even hire a trainer to work with guests and bring in local clients. Our conversation has inspired me to go for a run." He smiled and appeared younger. "Congratulations again on your engagement."

"Thanks."

After Craig walked away, Reid leaned forward. "Mission Accomplished. You talked to Zeke and Craig. Are you any closer to finding an answer?"

The jazz band played one of my favorite songs. "No, but I am ready to dance."

Reid and I spent the next two hours dancing and never once mentioned murder or suspects.

Chapter Forty-Nine

Ethan drove me to church, and we stopped to pick up Madison at the bookstore. I refrained from asking about Rory.

Once inside, we sat with Reid, and soon Bess joined us. She grabbed my hand and examined the rose-cut diamond engagement ring on my finger. "Girl, I can't believe you two are already engaged. This is beautiful." She squealed and gave me a hug.

"Shh." Ethan grinned.

Reid slid his arm around the back of the pew and ran his fingers along my shoulder. "Your son has a point. The praise band can only drown out so much noise. By the time the service is over, the whole island will know about our engagement."

"Do you regret proposing so soon?" I held my breath, waiting for his answer.

"My only regret is not popping the question the minute I found you in my kitchen organizing my pantry."

"Oh, Reid. I love you."

"I love you too."

The music faded, and Pastor Tom greeted the crowd.

An hour later, the service ended, and just like Reid had predicted, people flocked to us. Most of the island was getting adjusted to me being back in town, and Reid was the hometown guy they all loved. Who could blame them?

Ethan and Madison took off before I could ask about Rory. I texted my son. *Will you please ask if Rory has left town?*

Reid leaned against his truck. "It's a beautiful day. Seems like it'd be a waste to look at files or read history books cooped up inside."

"I heard rain is coming our way later, so would you like to go to the Seaside Hideaway and rent two electric bikes?"

"If it means we get to spend time outside, it's all right by me. Have you ridden an e-bike before?"

"Yeah. Bess and I rode bikes on Bald Head Island once." My sundress wouldn't be the best for a bike ride, and Reid wore long khakis. "Can we change clothes first?"

"Absolutely. Let's get a move on. I don't suppose you're hungry?"

I laughed. "How do you feel about peanut butter and jelly sandwiches?"

"Sounds like lunch."

My phone vibrated with a message from Ethan. *Police spoke to Rory before he left. He was asked to remain in town. Lady is with me.*

With the threat of rain later in the day, we hustled and in less than an hour, we were renting bikes at the resort. The teenager working at the resort's rental area perked up when we approached. He gave us a quick rundown on how to ride the bike.

Reid was given a big dark blue bike with fat tires. I got a sweet baby blue bike, and it looked more manageable for me. The tires were fat enough to ride on the beach, but the bike wasn't as big as Reid's. We hopped on and rode them down a path to the beach.

"Low tide will make for a nicer ride. Which way?"

"The lighthouse?"

"Well, well, well." Reid pushed up his sunglasses. "Well played, Katie Sloan."

"Whatever do you mean?" I shifted into my best Georgia accent. If I'd had a colorful hand fan, I would've fanned myself.

"Best guess? We're riding to the craft fair and timing ourselves."

Holding my bike steady, I stood close enough to Reid to get a whiff of his woodsy, clean scent. "Yes. It'll help us decide if Zeke could've ridden his bike to the lighthouse, shot at me, and gotten back here in a reasonable amount of time."

Reid tapped his watch. "Go."

It'd been a long time since I'd ridden an electric bike, and there was a definite learning curve. I laughed and hoped I wouldn't fall. That would be embarrassing, but not totally surprising.

White clouds drifted by, but the sky remained mostly blue. The sun warmed my face, and my ponytail whipped in the wind.

A man was teaching a young boy to surf. Younger children squealed and jumped in small waves, landing on the shore. A jogger waved to us.

I recognized Craig and waved back. He must've been serious about liking to stay fit.

I rode until Reid stopped.

"I think this is the most likely path the shooter took."

"Why don't we walk our bikes in case there's a clue on the ground? The sand could have shifted since Thursday night, and maybe we'll find some evidence."

"All right."

We pushed our bicycles along the sandy trail, and I focused on the ground. At last, we reached the arts and crafts festival.

I looked both ways. There weren't as many vendors, and fewer people milled around. "How long did it take us?"

"Fifteen minutes."

"Even if the bike had been stashed in beach grass, it would have been easy enough to hide, shoot at me, hide again, get the bike, and ride to the resort."

"Don't forget. Three bikes were returned during the commotion around the pool."

"Yes, but one of them was rented by Zeke. So, that's the good news."

"What's the bad news?" He met my gaze.

"We still don't have a solid clue to prove Zeke killed Ben and shot at me. Should we keep moving?" Discussing the shooting while being in the area where it had occurred was making me uncomfortable, and I struggled to take a deep breath.

"Yeah, honey. Standing around probably isn't too smart."

"How about we walk and talk?"

"Sure. The bikes should be safe there." Reid pointed to a bike rack, and we parked them.

I reached for Reid's hand. "It's silly to feel spooked."

"I'd be more worried if reflecting on the shooting didn't affect you."

"Thanks." We walked around the outskirts of the fair. Most of the pop-up tents and canopies remained standing despite the smaller crowd. "How did Lady affect the shooter's getaway? Did he have to hide from the dog and the cops before he got to his bike?"

Reid said, "That would explain how we beat him to the resort. He might have climbed a tree, hidden in a parked car, or snuck into a fenced-in yard."

"You're right. All of those would make good hiding places from a dog and the cops."

"Thanks. Next problem. You know, we're working on the theory Ben's death could've been committed in the heat of the moment. But whoever shot at you intentionally left a threatening note. The person tried to scare you in your SUV, and they wanted you to leave the evidence or something in the parking lot. They brought a gun and shot at you. Correction, they did shoot you—"

"Praise the Lord for bulletproof vests." Anxiety and relief competed for attention in my gut.

"Do you see where I'm going with this?"

"Everything after Ben's murder was done intentionally."

"Yes. Probably to cover up the fact he, or she, killed Ben."

"Self-preservation. I get it, but I don't have anything." I shivered. "There hasn't been another attempt on my life. Do you think the person found what they were looking for when they trashed Ben's office?"

"Maybe, but you've rarely been alone the last couple of days. That could explain why you've stayed safe."

"True." The clouds grew dark. "Maybe we should ride back before it rains."

Reid looked at the sky. "Good idea."

We walked quickly to the electric bikes and pushed them to the beach.

"The wind's picking up." Reid waited for me to get situated.

"Yeah, I might shift this bike from level one to the second level if it begins to rain." There were five levels on the bike, and two would still be safe for me. I started pedaling.

Reid caught up in no time and pointed to a black cloud near the resort. "See that?"

"I'll hurry." I increased my speed. My legs pumped, and I sailed along the beach on the firm sand near the surf's edge. Water misted my face from waves crashing and maybe from the sky.

"Katie, slow down." Reid rode beside me.

I decreased my legs pumping, but the bike didn't slow. Instead, it picked up speed. The LED display showed I'd gone up a level.

I pushed the throttle button, hoping to regain control. It didn't work, and the display indicated I was riding at thirty miles per hour.

Reid yelled, "I can't keep up."

"It won't slow down." I glanced over my shoulder at Reid.

"Use the brakes."

I squeezed the hand brakes. Nothing.

Except for a man surfing, there wasn't anyone on the beach. I skirted around a towel and kept squeezing the brakes on the handlebars.

Thunder rumbled, and lightning danced across the sky. That surfer needed to get out of the water.

My bike shook. The speed had gone up to thirty-five. I pushed my feet backwards to stop the old fashion way. Nothing happened.

I glanced over my shoulder. Reid was a shadow in the mist. The person at the resort had assured us the maximum speed of the bike was twenty-eight miles per hour.

I pushed every button and lever possible to stop. Failure.

Now what? How could I stop this thing?

My heart raced. How bad would it hurt to jump off at, oh my goodness, forty miles per hour? This was bad. Bad, bad, bad.

Chapter Fifty

Forty miles per hour. When I crashed, and I surely would wreck, something was going to break on my fifty-three-year-old body. I didn't want it to be my neck. A broken neck could kill me. No. Fear would not consume me.

Water splashed on my ankle.

I steered away from the tide.

Wait. The water. Was that the solution? If I drove the electric bike into the ocean, it would either stop, or I could swim off without breaking anything.

Except years ago, there was a time when I'd been playing in the surf, and a wave had crashed over me and threw me to the ocean floor. I'd scraped my face, chest, arms, and legs. Was there a better option?

I gripped the handles tightly. Still going forty. According to the display, the battery was full of charge. My arms ached with the exertion from trying to remain steady. I was too tired to stay on the bike until it ran out of power.

Rain pelted me in the face. Black clouds filled the sky. I was fast approaching the resort. Wind gusts challenged me to stay upright, especially at such a high speed.

It was do-or-die time, and I sure hoped it wasn't going to die.

The water seemed like my safest option.

I turned the bike toward the ocean and plunged in. Cold chills covered my body. Small waves turned into bigger waves. Water covered my feet. The electric bike slowed. I lifted my feet off the pedals. Deeper and deeper I went, hoping to avoid pain. My heart raced. At last, I pushed the bike in one direction, and I lunged the other way. I swam away from the dreadful bike, then tread water, and looked back.

It sank in the water.

"Katie!"

I turned to the sound of Reid's voice.

"Baby, it's not that deep. You can stand." Reid was in the ocean, making his way to me.

I put my feet down, feeling silly. "I thought I might die."

He pulled me to him and kissed me. Thunder shook the earth, and Reid pulled back. "I'm going to grab your bike."

"Why? I probably ruined it." The rain grew steady and hard.

"Because somebody must have tampered with it."

The e-bike I rented had been smaller and a lighter color than Reid's. If somebody had watched us, it would've been easy to know which one to tamper with. Once again, I'd been targeted. This had to stop. "I'll help."

The bike had sunk and was partially buried in the sand. Buried. Like pirate treasure? What had Ben suspected about pirate booty around the resort? I'd have to think about it later. For now, I refocused on the electric bike.

The current made it hard to pull the bike out. An enormous wave appeared.

I held my breath and plunged under the cold water until it passed.

I surfaced and spotted Reid, who had one hand on the bike, and with the other, he wiped the salt water off his face. "The bike broke free with the wave."

"I'll help." I swam the short distance through the dark waves.

He ignored me and headed for shore.

"You're not deaf, and I know you heard me." I grabbed a handle. "We need to be able to count on each other."

"Sorry, but I've got it."

I kept holding the handle on my side and aimed for land.

When we reached the beach, Reid turned to me, breathing heavily. "Thanks."

"You're welcome. Is it possible the spa is open for business today? After this experience, I need some pampering." At least candles and a hot bath were in order. "Hey, is it too late to add a soaking tub at my new place?"

Reid shook his head. "We're standing on the beach in a storm. You could have died, and you want a soaking tub? I guess it'll take the rest of my life to figure you out, but if you want a soaking tub, you've got it."

The surfer jogged our way with his surfboard under one arm. He stopped and looked at us. "The waves are cranking today. Looks like your bike got dinged. Big time. Need help?"

I pointed to the e-bike Reid had been riding. "Can you possibly push that bike and carry your board at the same time? We need to get it to the resort, and I'm exhausted."

"No prob." He took charge of the extra bike by riding it and holding his surfboard. He zigged and zagged in the howling wind, but he never fell.

Reid said, "I'm going to try not to be jealous of his moves. Let's get somewhere dry."

I summoned all the strength in me and followed the guys to the resort. At the bike rental area, we thanked the surfer and Reid passed him some wet money.

I said, "Is there any chance you saw somebody follow us on our way to the lighthouse?"

"Afraid not. I was focused on catching waves until I saw you rag-doll."

Paul ran down the path and hugged me so hard I was afraid my ribs would crack. "Sis, I can't believe there's been another attempt on your life. You've got to quit investigating Ben's murder. I'm sorry for dragging you into this mess."

"No, I'm glad you asked me to look at your case. How'd you know about today?

"I do have some sources on the island."

Reid held up his hands. "This overhang is keeping us dry, but we could still get struck by lightning. Paul, this is the bike Katie was riding. It's been to the bottom of the ocean, but maybe you can get something from it."

The three of us walked to the main building and stood in the lobby, dripping on their nice floor. A maintenance man was rolling out rugs and placing signs all around to warn people about wet floors. We moved to a large rug, and Reid apologized to the employee, mopping up the puddle we'd left in our wake.

The lady I'd seen before with the head of housekeeping nametag zipped past us and scampered down the hall leading to Craig's office.

I stood close to Paul. "The bike was fine when we left here. It must have been tampered with when we walked around the lighthouse."

He frowned. "Did you see anybody suspicious?"

My thoughts jumped to Zeke, but we hadn't seen him. "Craig was running on the beach. He was dressed for exercise, and he was coming toward the resort while we rode in the opposite direction."

Paul huffed. "It doesn't mean he didn't turn around."

A police van pulled up and parked under the covered entrance.

"He's here for the bike."

The automatic glass doors opened, and Officer Collins walked through. "Mrs. Kate, I can't believe you had another brush with danger."

"Hi, Drake. It was a close call, but all is good." I shivered. It wouldn't be good to dwell on the experience too long. "I'm sorry you have to work on a Sunday afternoon."

"I'm happy to do it, especially if it helps catch the person who is after you."

Paul gave me a quick hug. "You two lay low for a while. I'll let you know what my team discovers."

Paul and Drake took the bike to the van and wrestled it into the vehicle.

I shivered again.

Reid said, "We need to get in dry clothes and warm you up."

"I couldn't agree more, and maybe some hot coffee will knock off this chill."

We stepped toward the door.

"Guys, hold up." Craig walked toward us at a fast pace. "Whoa, looks like you got caught in the rain."

"Something like that, and we were about to head home." Reid touched my arm. "Can we talk later?"

"Yeah, but we might have a clue to Ben's murder."

As much as I craved warm clothes, I couldn't pass up a possible clue. "I guess a few more minutes in cold, wet clothes will kill me."

Craig stared at us. "You two really are drenched, and I bet you're freezing. The pro shop is closed, but maybe we can find some dry clothes in the spa."

It didn't take long for me to put on a silk robe, and I left some cash for a T-shirt and pajama shorts with the spa's logo. Wearing the combination helped me feel a little more covered up and warm. Reid refused to be seen in public wearing anything so frilly.

Without elaborating on what he wanted to reveal, Craig took us up the elevator to the third floor. "Housekeeping said there has been a sign on this door for a couple of weeks. There was no sign today, and a housekeeper entered the room after checking with the department head."

If there was a dead body, surely the police would have been contacted instead of reaching out to me. Still, I was nervous. "Who's staying here?"

"It's booked under the name of Whit Dupree."

Whit Dupree. Ben's hero. Chills popped up on my arms. This could be big.

Chapter Fifty-One

Craig paused his movements, and the three of us looked at the door. "I highly doubt Mr. Whit Dupree is staying here."

Reid had been the one to study the biography on Ben's shelf. He said, "Your brother had a book about Whit Dupree."

"Yep." Craig held the room card over the door pad, and it unlocked. "There have been no charges to this room, and no payments. There's not even a credit card on file."

"What do you think is going on?"

Craig pushed the door open but blocked our entry with his body. "The police didn't find anything in the room where Ben was supposedly living. I think this may have been his secret man cave slash office. Don't forget, my brother liked paper files."

I met his troubled gaze. "I remember you saying it'd be easier if he'd put it all on a thumb drive."

"Yep. Brace yourselves." Craig waved us into the suite.

On the king bed were stacks of files. The wastebasket overflowed with food wrappers and beer cans. There were no clothes in the closets. Instead, it was full of golf clubs. They were probably more of the knockoff clubs. I walked through the suite. "Here's a laptop and a tablet. Do you have access to gloves, Craig?"

"Yes. What do you think about this place?" His frowned.

I continued surveying the rooms. "Despite the garbage, there are no dirty dishes, no dirty towels or clothes, and the files are somewhat orderly. The police need to know about this, but if you can get me the gloves, I'd like to see if we can get into the laptop."

"There should be a housekeeping cart on this floor. Be right back." Craig left us alone.

Reid rubbed my shoulders. "Feel better?"

"Yeah, but you're probably still cold."

"I can't walk around the entire resort in a spa robe and white cotton slippers." He stepped back and looked around. "This is almost like a war room. There are charts and graphs on the coffee table. I imagine this is where the real work—"

"Or the illegitimate work."

"True. This explains why we didn't find much in Ben's office."

"Here you go, Kate." Craig handed out gloves for all of us. "I can try to get on Ben's tablet, and you try the laptop. Reid, I asked the maid to go to my room and grab shorts and a T-shirt for you, if you don't mind wearing my clothes."

"Thanks, man." Reid gloved up. "If y'all work on tech, I can go through the files on the bed."

I smiled at my fiancé. "It sounds like we have a plan of action."

Would Craig be this helpful, if he murdered his brother? Or was he trying to deflect our investigation from looking at him? "Hey, Craig. Where did you go after your run this afternoon?"

"I came here, of course."

"Can anyone confirm it?"

"I ordered lunch at the pool bar, then went to my room to shower and change. My lunch was delivered. I ate it by myself, then carried the dishes to the kitchen and thanked the staff. After that, I went to work in Ben's office. Excuse me, my office. I've got to get used to that. I was around, but nobody watched me all the time. Why?"

"We rode two of your bikes to the arts and crafts fair at the lighthouse."

"The Foxy Lady, ah yes, I want to go up in it soon. Go ahead with your story."

"Reid and I walked around the lighthouse grounds, and somebody tampered with my bike."

He gasped. "That's terrible. We have a regular maintenance schedule and go over each bike when it's returned. I'll ask the staff if anyone noticed something suspicious."

"It probably didn't happen here. Somebody may have followed us to the lighthouse." I explained my theory.

There was a knock on the door. When Craig opened it, the same lady I'd seen before stood there. The head of housekeeping handed him neatly folded clothes. "Thanks, Camila. Please don't tell anyone we're working in here. I need some privacy."

She nodded. "Si. Your brother liked privacy, too. I never told the others about this room. You can trust me to keep your secret."

I walked to the door. "Did Ben bring other people to this room?"

Her eyes grew wide, and I realized how it must look for me to be wearing a robe in a hotel room with her new boss. "Oh, this isn't what it looks like. I got drenched in the rain, and Mr. Hauser was nice enough to find something for me to wear. Those clothes are for my fiancé, because he got wet too. It's all perfectly innocent."

Reid touched my arm. "Katie, you're making it worse than it is. Take a breath."

Craig handed the dry clothes to Reid and turned back to Camila. "Trust me. This is innocent."

"Yes, sir. I know how to keep things to myself." She walked away, and Craig shut the door.

He looked at us. "Camila is smart and appears to be loyal. We probably won't get much more out of her. On the bright side, she won't spread rumors about the three of us in here."

"Oh, what if you call her back? She'd see we're legitimately working."

Reid rubbed my shoulder. "Give it up, babe."

"You're right." The most important task was to catch a killer. Another time, I could worry about what Camila thought about me.

Chapter Fifty-Two

It was dark, and the rain had ceased by the time we ended our investigation in Ben's secret room. Craig stretched. "I have an early meeting tomorrow, and I'll call the police tonight. I won't lie to them, but I think we did the right thing by going through this stuff."

I had been able to crack the passwords on the laptop and the tablet. We seemed to be playing a cat and mouse game, and I didn't tell Craig everything I'd discovered in case he was using me to find evidence pointing to him as the killer. "Thanks for bringing us here."

"Ben wasn't the best human, but he was my brother. He deserves justice."

Reid shook Craig's hand. "I'll return the clothes later this week. Thanks again."

"You're welcome. I'll wait here for the police."

I texted Paul while we rode the elevator down and alerted him to what we'd found.

The doors opened, and we stepped into the lobby.

Zeke was talking to Sue. His hand gripped her arm, and she frowned.

I moved in their direction.

"Hi, Kate." Sue's voice shook.

Zeke did a double take, and his eyes bulged.

"Hi, Sue. You may recognize my outfit. I got caught in the rain earlier and Craig took me into the spa to borrow the robe. I left some money for, uh, well, I made a purchase. I know you're off today, but since you're here, would you mind ringing me up?"

"I'd be happy to."

"Can it wait? We have something to discuss." Zeke gave her arm a shake.

Reid stepped forward. "You're hurting the lady, and you need to release her."

"Mind—"

"Yes?" The frown on Reid's face would've sent me running for the hills.

Zeke frowned at Sue, then released her arm. "Sorry. I didn't realize what I was doing. I'll wait here for you, and after you handle Kate's purchase, we'll have our little talk."

The redhead backed away from him. "There's nothing else to say."

Reid and I stood on each side of Sue and walked with her to the spa. Once we were inside Seaside Hideaway's spa, she broke down. Tears ran down her face, and her body shook.

With my arm around her, I led her to the waiting area. "Shh, you're safe now."

"I was so scared." Her voice wobbled. "If you two hadn't shown up, there's no telling what would have happened."

"He's not leaving." Reid stood in the shadows of the entryway leading to the lobby. "I'm texting Paul. One of his guys needs to put a little scare into Zeke."

I filled a paper cup with water from a fancy dispenser. "Sue, try to drink this."

Sue gulped it down.

"What did Zeke want?" I refilled the cup.

"He's under the mistaken impression that Ben and I were dating. He also believes Ben gave me something for safekeeping."

"Did he say what it is?"

She leaned back in the seat and blew her nose. "You know what? It must have been multiple things. Zeke wanted me to give *them* to him. You wouldn't say them if you only wanted one thing."

"That's true." Too bad there wasn't more of a clue.

"Once I step out there, he's going to be on me like white on rice. Lauren probably wouldn't mind if I slept in here tonight. Do you think I'll be safe from Zeke?"

Reid joined us. "We need to get you off the resort property. Kate's apartment is small and not the safest place. Would you like to stay with my mother? I think she's off Zeke's radar."

"I can't impose."

"You're not. We want to help, and this may be the best option. Besides, Mom would be furious if I knew you were in trouble and didn't offer to help."

"That's very nice of you to offer, and I accept. I'll speak to Lauren tomorrow. If the police don't care, I think it's time to go home."

I patted her hand. "I think you're right."

Reid returned to the entry area. Almost as soon as he texted his mom, his phone rang. "Hey, Mom. Here's the situation." His voice lowered, and I couldn't hear more.

"Sue, going home is a good idea. Spend time with your family and heal." I gave her a quick hug. "Do you want to ring me up while we wait for Joy to reply?"

She handled my purchase, and I changed into my damp clothes from earlier. Brr. "I'll leave the robe in your laundry room."

"Great. Here's a bag for your loungewear."

Reid joined us. "Paul is talking to Zeke. He took him out to the pool area; then two cops took the elevator upstairs. With a little luck, Zeke didn't see them go to the third floor. And Mom said she'd be delighted for you to stay with her. We can drive you over, and she'll bring you here tomorrow. That way, Zeke will think you're on the resort property. Can you take us out the door leading to the parking lot?"

"Yes, but what's on the third floor? Did anyone else die?"

"No, there was just something we wanted the police to see. Please don't tell anyone the police were here tonight."

"It seems like the less I know, the better. No offense, but I'm ready to leave the resort, and I'm ready to leave Fox Island. I can't wait to get home."

After everything that had happened, who could blame her?

Chapter Fifty-Three

After dropping off Sue at Joy's home, we met Ethan and Lady were at the apartment. Reid hung out with Ethan, while I cleaned up. I took a hot shower and put on dry clothes before joining my two favorite men. Even though it was May, I put on warm yoga pants, a T-shirt, and a sweatshirt.

"We ordered pizza and salads for supper, and they should be here in ten minutes." Ethan poured soft drinks into three glasses of ice.

"Let me get some money."

"Mom, it's my treat. Oh, I haven't told you the status of my job situation. The company in Texas let me go once they heard what I wanted to do. They fully support my desire to work at the parks department, and they believe in my vision. Also, if I hold fundraisers, they want to donate with both money and sports equipment."

"Even though they're in Texas?" I was pleasantly surprised.

"Yes, ma'am." He gave us our soft drinks. "I start my new job this Wednesday, so that gives me two days to figure out where to live and schedule my furniture to arrive."

Reid leaned against the kitchen counter. "So, you're still trying to decide where you want to move?"

"Living in the apartment shown me I want a house. Not an apartment or a condo, but I want a legit house. Reid, if you haven't retracted your offer, I'd like to buy your place."

"It's all yours." He pointed at me. "The only glitch is that your mom decided she wants a soaking tub, and that might delay her moving in by a few days. Then we can plan a wedding. Do you mind sharing the house with me until I can move out?"

He smiled. "It'll be great."

Reid turned serious. "Katie, until the killer is caught, we need to get you somewhere safe. What do you say about the three of us staying at the house? Not my house, but the one I'm fixing for veterans? It's more off the beaten path."

Ethan ran his hands through his hair. "If it keeps Mom safe, I'm all for it. What if they follow us there?"

"Not to worry. I have a plan."

The doorbell rang, and Ethan verified it was our food order.

While we ate, we told Ethan about the electric bike incident and about Ben's secret room at the resort.

"No wonder we need to keep you safe. Are you going to work tomorrow?"

"That's my plan."

Reid refilled his glass. "I'll go with you."

"I won't object to that." I smiled.

"Guys, no offense, but you two were together when somebody tampered with your rental bike. Why do you think you'll be safe together tomorrow? Should we hire a private detective who carries a gun? Or should Uncle Paul put a protection detail on you?"

Reid sat by me and patted my leg. "That's not the worst idea."

I sighed. "Paul and his people are going to be busy for hours at the resort. We can talk to him tomorrow."

"Okay, then let's get out of here. How are we going to do this and not get caught by the killer?"

"How about you leave first? If we're being watched, it won't look suspicious. Then Reid and I will go for a walk on the beach. You can pick us up, and we'll hightail it out of town. Maybe take Lady with you. It'll make it easier for us to sneak into your Land Rover when you drive by us."

"No problem, but what if we're followed?"

Reid said, "There are plenty of back streets between here and the house. It should be easy to lose a tail, and we'll know if we're followed."

I patted Lady and looked around the apartment. "Okay, guys, we need to gather up everything connected to the murder and take it with us. The killer believes I have something, or else he wouldn't keep coming after me. I don't want to take a chance on him breaking in here and finding the unknown evidence."

Ethan grabbed his backpack. "I can put the files in here. That shouldn't look suspicious."

Reid clapped his hands. "It sounds like we've got a plan."

An hour later, we were at the house Reid was renovating for veterans. My brother had hidden out here when the public turned against him weeks earlier. Now, it was my turn. I stood in the large living room and looked around. The walls had been painted, and the floors had been sanded and refinished. "I don't know what my family would do without this place. And the homeless veterans will appreciate it even more."

"Hey, now. Paul did a lot of work on the house. In fact, it's come a long way in the past few weeks. Want a tour?"

"Yes."

Reid took us to the kitchen first. "The local housing authority said that I had to get specific appliances to have so many people live here. It was a hard hit to the budget, but I follow the law."

Reid took us through the public rooms, the bathrooms, and the bedrooms. When we ended up back in the main room, I sat on the leather sofa. "This is nice."

Lady lay at my feet.

"A furniture store over on Tybee Island went out of business. The owner is a friend of mine, and he gave it to me along with most of the beds and the dining table. It's a tax write-off for him and a huge gift to us."

"I'm so proud of you, Reid. This is going to bless so many people."

"Thanks. I hope you're right. I've learned a lot through this process."

Ethan sat in a recliner. "How will veterans find out about this place?"

Reid smiled. "You'll soon learn how small Fox Island is. Word gets around. According to Pop, homeless people often know more than we realize. They blend into the background, but they're alert."

"That's good to know. After I get settled in at my new job, I might want to find out more. It's possible I'll come across people who need shelter."

I said, "Not all homeless people live on the street. Some live out of their cars."

"Right, and I hope to make this place available to veterans no matter what their exact situation." Reid rubbed his chin. "Ethan, my goal is to renovate this place and let somebody else run it. I'm working with an attorney to find a director. This is out of my area of expertise, but when the right person is hired, I'll put them in touch with you."

"All right."

I yawned. "Guys, I need to go to bed."

"I'll take Lady out for her last pit stop of the night." Ethan hugged me. "I'm glad you're safe."

"Me, too. See you in the morning."

"I'll walk you to your room." Reid helped me to my feet and led me to one of the rooms. "Ethan can take the other bed, and I'll crash on the couch."

"Oh, I hate for you to do that."

"I want to be near the points of entry just in case anyone comes here to look for you." He kissed me. "Get some sleep."

"Thanks for having my back again."

"Always."

Chapter Fifty-Four

Zeke was the killer.

It was my first conscious thought. Where was I? I looked around the room. Oh, yeah. I'd spent the night at Reid's place for veterans, and it was Monday morning.

The other bed was rumpled but empty. There was no sign of Lady. It made sense Ethan had taken my goldendoodle for a walk. I'd never seen Ethan come or go, but it was obvious he'd slept at some point.

I'd crashed in my yoga pants and a T-shirt, so I didn't need to get dressed. However, I freshened up before following the aroma of coffee to the kitchen.

Reid sat on a barstool, hunched over an open file. "Good morning." His deep voice sounded wooly.

I wrapped my arms around him from the back. "What are you looking at?"

"Hope you don't mind, but I helped myself to your files. My gut says Zeke is the guy."

"Hey, I woke up thinking the same thing. We have a motive and possible evidence once the crime lab is finished, but we don't have proof."

Reid turned on the stool and faced me, placing his hands on my shoulders. "You've mentioned trapping the killer before, but I'm not thrilled with the idea."

"What do you suggest?"

"How about letting the police solve the murder, and we'll do something fun?" He nuzzled my neck.

I giggled.

The front door opened then slammed shut. "Breakfast is here. Oh, guys. Come on. It's one thing for me to give you my blessing, but I don't want to see you kissing all the time."

I pulled away from my fiancé, but I didn't apologize.

Lady sprinted across the open room and skidded to a stop in front of me. I leaned over and petted her. "Hi there, girl. Did you go for a walk without me?"

Ethan said, "We've been for a walk, and a ride. The woman at the drive-through thought Lady was adorable, and she gave us dog treats."

"Treats for Lady, and what'd you bring us?"

"Everything bagels with eggs, bacon, and avocado slices. There are also fruit cups."

"Yum. Thanks." I poured coffee into clean mugs, and we ate on the back deck. I could see the creek from where I sat, and my body relaxed. Reid's vision for converting this specific house into a haven for veterans astounded me. I could imagine people sitting out here and taking time to breathe and let go of the stress in their lives.

Birds sang their early morning songs, and squirrels chased each other on branches and around the trunks of pine trees. "This will be a peaceful oasis for the people who live here."

Reid sighed. "I hope you're right."

Lady snoozed by my feet, and I ate my bagel and fruit.

Reid said, "Ethan, I can stay with Katie if you need to do things."

"I would like to get organized and make plans with the moving company. I'm not officially starting work until Wednesday, but I'd like to set up my office."

"If you don't have a budget for it, tell me what you need, and I can probably get a discount."

"I had a sleek, modern office in Dallas. This is the complete opposite, but I'm okay with that. Some of the furniture may be older than me, but that means it's durable. If I have kids and teens in my office, I want them to feel comfortable."

"I'm proud of you, honey."

"Thanks. How soon can you two be ready to go?"

"Ten minutes, and I need to go to the apartment first and put on appropriate clothes."

Soon, Lady and I rode in the backseat on the way to the apartment, and Reid rode shotgun.

It would be a struggle to work at Let's Get Organized until the murder was solved. My mind was fixated on Ben's death. "Guys, I got to thinking about something Ethan said earlier. You want to prepare your office before you begin work. You also want it to be comfortable. Let's consider Ben's office."

Reid held up his hand. "You mean the public one?"

"Yes. It's obvious he meant to impress people with it, even though he wasn't very organized. He cheated other people, but he paid me when I insisted. Why? I thought his goal was to make his space orderly. Then Craig showed us the secret room."

Lady nudged me, and I patted her.

"His man cave was all business." Reid rubbed his chin. "The files were organized on the bed, and he wasn't aiming to impress anyone in there."

I leaned forward. "Do you think he left files lying around his office on purpose?"

"Why would he do that?"

"Maybe to give the impression he was laid back or something. Also, you know the resort staff thought he snuck out to golf. He even told me he used the back passage so he could get to the golf course without being slowed down by staff and guests. What if he gave all of us that impression on purpose? We're all thinking he's some kind of playboy, interested in golf and parties. What if he was more focused on his counterfeit business? Or another illegal venture?"

Reid nodded. "Is it possible Ben bought the resort as a decoy?"

Ethan said, "That would be brilliant. His investors are focused on the resort."

Reid twisted around to look at me. "The people in Fox Island have been so excited about the updates that were planned, and new job opportunities, and more money coming into town. Ben gave some people the impression he had turned his life around. Seaside Hideaway made Ben look respectable. While all along, he was still running the golf club scam."

Ethan pulled up in front of the apartment. "Reid, I'd like to make an official offer on your house. After hearing all this talk about fraud and scams, I want our business dealings to be beyond reproach. Is there a real estate agent or attorney you'd like me to contact?"

"I trust you, but what you want to do is admirable. I'll text you the name of my real estate attorney. If you decide to go with someone else, there'll be no hurt feelings." Reid stepped out and held the door open for me. "Katie, don't forget to grab your research."

Lady hopped out and immediately growled.

The hairs on my neck popped up, and I hurried after her. I kept a firm grip on the leash.

Ethan said, "I won't drive away until you're inside."

"Thanks." I slid my arms through the straps of the polka-dot backpack and walked up the wooden steps leading to my apartment. After a quick glance over my shoulder, I inserted the key into the lock.

Reid stood guard.

I kept looking over my shoulder, expecting someone to jump out of the bushes and attack us.

Lady growled.

"Katie, focus on the lock. I'll watch for danger. Here, let me hold the leash."

I passed it to him and concentrated on unlocking the door and getting to safety. At last, it clicked, and the knob turned.

Lady bounded past me and into the apartment.

"Sorry about that. Did she hurt you?"

"No, I'm fine." I walked inside.

No longer was I fine. Papers had been tossed around. The small home had been trashed, and I cried.

Chapter Fifty-Five

Paul allowed me to grab a change of clothes and a minimum of toiletries, before he kicked Reid, Lady, and myself out of the apartment. He promised we'd talk later, but I wasn't positive he had time.

We had decided the store would be a safe place to work, and we walked the short distance to Let's Get Organized.

Bess stood at the coffee maker, staring at it.

"Good morning," I said.

"Morning."

"You know, staring at it won't fill the carafe faster."

"I'm too tired to accomplish anything before my morning coffee. Good to see your dog."

"My place is crawling with police officers, and I couldn't leave her."

She whipped around. "Please, don't tell me somebody else shot at you."

"No, but my apartment was broken into." I gave a short explanation.

"Gracious. Are we safe here?"

"Reid will hang out with us this morning."

Bess eyed him up and down and shot us a saucy smile. "I suppose that's better than nothing."

A laugh burst out of Reid. "Thanks for the vote of confidence."

The coffee maker beeped, and Bess poured coffee into the largest mug we had, then added creamer.

"What does today's schedule look like?" I turned on my computer and looked for the calendar app.

Once the calendar opened, Bess reviewed it with me. "Should I take the appointments off site? You can start drawing up plans and create detailed estimates for these clients, if you like that plan." She handed me four files.

"This will be great."

Lady sniffed the floor by my desk before settling down.

I needed to get her a throw rug or a dog bed for the store.

Reid walked around the store's public space. "Can I go in the back room and make a few calls? I need some privacy."

"Of course. We have a small desk and chair back there."

Bess stood and stared at me.

"What's wrong?"

"I still can't believe you're investigating another murder. At least Tom's not on your suspect list."

I moved around the desk and leaned against it, dangling one leg. "What is the story with you and Tom? Are you two dating?"

"No." She held her arms around her stomach.

"But you love him."

"Yes."

"But?"

"His marriage was a disaster, and he doesn't want to ever get married again. So, all we can be is friends." She looked at the floor.

"You need to distance yourself from Tom, even if it means attending a different church for a while. Date other men, or don't date. See a counselor. Talk to me about your frustrations, and quit protecting him. Life is too short to be miserable, and I know you're miserable."

She didn't argue. "You're a good friend. I'll see you later."

"I hope you have a good day." I hugged her, and she left. I went to the storage room with Lady at my side. "Will you be comfortable here?"

Reid said, "It'll work."

I turned around but paused at the sight of two boxes with Ben's name on them. "Well, what do you know?"

Reid stood beside me. "I didn't think you had anything belonging to Ben."

"I forgot about these, but didn't we decide the important files were in his secret room?" I reached for a box, and Reid grabbed the other one. "Could it be this easy?"

"Maybe."

The store phone rang, and I ignored it. "They can leave a message."

Reid set his box on the little desk and removed the lid. "It looks like random papers, golf magazines, and mail."

"I was going to sort those, then let Ben decide if he wanted to file them."

My box clinked as I placed it next to the other box. I lifted the lid. "Oh, my. Video games, CDs, and tapes. Wasn't Ben too young to have listened to tapes?"

"Maybe one of his cars only played tapes."

"His Corvette was the latest model, and I'd bet money there's no cassette player in it. These cases are for hard rock music." I opened the small plastic case, and a plain cassette fell into my hand.

Lady barked.

I glanced at her. "You have a canny ability to sense trouble."

"Why?" Reid reached for another case.

"Didn't someone mention that Ben blackmailed people?"

"Yeah, I think Rory accused him of that."

"What if these tapes have incriminating information? This could be what the killer has been looking for."

"And it's probably why he's been coming after you. He wants them back." Reid clenched his jaw. "Do you have a cassette player?"

"You mean besides in the Wagoneer?"

"Well, yeah. Unless you want to drive around while you listen to them."

"That would make it a little hard to take notes. Paul's gotten on me about talking on my cell phone while driving. If I try to write and drive, he might go ballistic."

"No doubt."

"Let's see. I think we have a few boxes of items to give to the church yard sale. The owners wanted us to haul off their junk, and I think there was a tape player." I walked to the back door where we'd neatly stacked the boxes and opened the top one. "Do you want to go through this one?"

"You go ahead with that, and I'll take the next one in the stack."

We began to sort through the items.

Lady sat between us, and her head bobbed back and forth as Reid and I took turns pulling out junk.

"Success." Reid held up a cassette player. "And there's a cord. If the tapes contain sensitive information, you should work back here. I'll deal with my business calls out front. We don't want anyone to know what you're doing."

"What about your private conversations?"

"I'll watch the door. If someone comes in, I'll pause my call and come get you. It'll work."

"You're the best. I'll get my notebook and write down anything that sounds blackmail worthy."

With notebook in hand, I sorted through the tapes. Dates had been written on each one, so I started with the oldest.

Two men were talking. Ben's voice was clear. The other man's words were muffled. I strained to follow the conversation. Wife. Kids. Work.

Nothing noteworthy so far. What had Ben hoped to accomplish by taping this conversation? Who was the other man?

Zeke was my primary suspect, but I'd never heard him mention a family.

I knew Ben had blackmailed a woman when he was running an online dating scam. With his long history of fraud, it made sense he wouldn't just blackmail one person.

The tape ended, and I traded it for the next one in chronological order. This time, Ben was talking to a woman. She was irate about the money he'd stolen from her. She mentioned trusting and loving him. He called her Jennifer. I hit the pause button and looked through my notebook.

There she was. Jennifer Smith met Ben through his dating app. According to my notes, she accused him of stealing money from her. She believed he was a CPA and gave him access to her accounts. He blackmailed her to keep quiet. She had been running for mayor of her small town and was embarrassed. By the time she filed a police report, Ben had skipped town.

My notes jibed with what I was hearing on the tape, and I pressed the play button. The conversation ended with her in tears and a door slamming.

I went to the next tape.

By the time I reached the sixth tape, Ben was in another discussion with the man in the first conversation.

This time, I hit paydirt.

Reid appeared. "Hey, you've got a customer. It's Craig."

My heart skipped a beat. "Is he alone?"

"I think so."

"Will you guard this stuff?"

"Yes, but should I call the police?"

"Not yet. I'm not entirely sure what's on them." I moved to the front. "Hi, Craig. How can I help you today?"

"I plan to move into a different room than where Ben was living. The space I'm considering is a large suite, and I wondered if you could help me plan storage. It's not really designed for a person living there. Know what I mean?"

"Storage for your clothes?"

"Yeah, and there's a kitchenette. I can't live off restaurant food. Can you help me make it more efficient, too?" He handed me a blueprint of the suite.

"Absolutely. What's the budget?"

He gave me a reasonable figure.

"Okay. I'll create a plan and review it with you later this week." I made a note on the business calendar and set the blueprint on the desk. "Craig, have you ever been married?"

"I came close once, and it'll happen one day."

"And Craig never married."

"No. He was a love 'em and leave 'em kind of guy." He rolled his head back and sighed. "Ben loved himself more than he cared about any other human."

"Last question. Is Zeke married?"

"Not anymore. His wife left him and took the kids, but I don't know exactly what happened. I need to go, Kate. Got another appointment. Have a good day."

"You, too." After he left, I hustled to the back room. "Reid, I think we're closer to proving the killer is Zeke."

Chapter Fifty-Six

I shared with Reid what I'd heard so far on Ben's tapes, plus what Craig had told me about Zeke.

The next few hours, I lost myself in listening to the recordings Ben had made. There'd been a few interruptions to wait on customers. Reid ordered lunch, and I ate a salad but continued to listen and make notes.

Around three o'clock, I joined Reid. "That was exhausting."

"Did you learn much?"

"Yes. If Ben blackmailed everyone in those tapes, it would've been a full-time job. He was so sneaky. He'd begin a conversation and somehow lead people to admit stuff you should keep to yourself."

Reid paced in front of my desk. "What about Zeke?"

"Zeke went into a deal with Ben, and it was a bust. Zeke lost his wife, his kids, his money, his car, and he got fired from the car dealership in Atlanta."

"Hold on. He's trying to sell a car to you."

"Yeah, that confuses me too. Maybe it's a new job."

"Or maybe he's trying to scam you. Maybe he learned a thing or two from Ben."

At the rate this investigation was going, he was probably trying to scam me. "It's very possible. Oh, like trying to sell me Ben's Corvette. What if I'd paid him and he disappeared with my money? Then Craig might have pressed charges against me for stealing the car."

Reid held up a hand. "Hold up. That didn't happen."

I took a deep breath. "You're right."

"What else did you learn?"

"In one of the tapes, Zeke said he wanted to work at a golf club or with some kind of company that makes golf equipment. And, drum roll please, Zeke was involved in the knock-off golf club scam."

"Zeke, Rory, Ben, and others conned people out of good money to sell them knockoffs. And you know that guy wears lots of trendy golf clothes." Reid turned and faced me.

"True, but I'm impressed you know what's trendy."

Reid shrugged. "I saw some of the same clothes in Rory's shop, and they're pricey. It makes me wonder if Zeke wears imitations or name brands."

"At this point, nothing would surprise me. He probably wears the real thing."

"So, what is the plan? You said you want to trap him."

"I do. Everything we have here is circumstantial. By tricking him into a confession, we'll have the proof Paul needs to arrest him. It'll also make it easier to get a conviction when the case goes to trial."

"I'm not crazy about you putting yourself in harm's way. If we carry it out, it won't be easy to get a recorded confession. Zeke will be on guard after his experience with Ben."

"Good point." I walked to the door, flipped the sign to indicate we were closed, and locked the door. "Let's take it step by step. First, how about I tell Zeke I found a box of interesting tapes?"

"Okay, but what exactly did Ben have on Zeke?"

"Ben threatened to hand over evidence to the authorities that Zeke was selling fakes. If he did, Zeke was in danger of losing his kids forever. I tell you, Reid, if someone threatened to prevent me from being with Ethan when he was a child, I would have done anything to stop that." My breathing grew shallow, and I stopped talking.

"Including murder?"

I thought about my answer. "If Ethan was in danger, like if he'd been kidnapped, or if David had left the country with him, I would've done anything. You know the expression, 'I'd take a bullet for you?' I feel the same way regarding my son."

Reid paced around the public area. "But you wouldn't have murdered the kidnapper?"

"Stalked him until I found Ethan? Yes. Found a way to help my son escape? Yes. Murder? No."

"Good to know. So, our plan is to tell Zeke that we've got the tapes."

"Yes, but I think we should go deeper. We'll tell him about the tapes and say we'll hand them over for a large amount of money."

Reid shook his head. "I don't like it, but we need to take precautions if we go through with this plan. We need to meet somewhere safe. Public. No dropping off the tapes in a dark parking lot at night."

"I agree. I don't want to get shot again." A shiver zipped up my spine. "So where do you think we should suggest for the swap?"

"We'll need Paul in the background to arrest Zeke when the exchange takes place." Reid frowned. "The police should be able to blend in or hide completely. We don't want to spook Zeke, but we also don't want him to escape."

"Don't forget the confession. That's the most important thing."

"That's the second most important thing. Mostly, we need to live through the confrontation." He moved to me and took me in his arms.

"You're right." I didn't want to ruin my future with Reid, but I couldn't let a killer walk away, either. I prayed we'd come up with a workable plan to catch the killer but not destroy our relationship.

Chapter Fifty-Seven

Paul came to Let's Get Organized and entered through the back door. We created a plan to nail Zeke McCarthy. It would be simple, really. Paul would work with a select group of local police officers. He chose people who hadn't been around the resort investigating Ben's murder. This would lessen the chance Zeke would recognize any of them.

Reid stuck with me.

I bought a burner phone and a voice activated recorder. It was small and looked like a portable battery charger. I wasn't certain if I'd use it, but the thing was too cool to pass up.

With the burner phone, I recorded a portion of one of Ben's blackmail tapes. Because Zeke had given me his business card, I had his contact number. With the burner phone, I texted Zeke a snippet of his conversation with Ben.

We'd decided to hang out at Seaside Hideaway's bar when we made the first contact. If we were lucky, we'd be able to watch him when he received the message.

After thirty minutes, Reid nudged me. "I think you should send the text."

"Yeah, we don't want to waste an entire day hoping he'll show up." I sent the message. "How long do you think we'll have to wait?"

"Not long if he's our guy."

I looked from Reid to my phone. It was vibrating.

Who is this?

I wasn't ready to reveal my identity. *That's not important. I have Ben's recordings.*

A few seconds ticked by.

My breath quickened while I waited for his response.

What do you want?

I couldn't contain my smile. "He's hooked."

Reid leaned close. "Do you have the next part of the conversation ready to go?"

"Yes." I sent another text. In addition to the clip of Zeke and Ben's conversation, I told Zeke he could have the tapes for one hundred thousand dollars. The exchange would be in person near the bike racks at the pier at sunrise.

I need more time.

My hands shook as we read the message.

Reid said, "We discussed this. Sunrise will be the safest time for the meeting. There's less chance for someone to get hurt."

"You're right. I'm going to the restroom in case he's watching us."

"I'll order refills."

I went into the closest public restroom and texted my reply. *If you don't make the payoff at sunrise, I'll turn the tapes over to the police.*

Fine.

I returned to Reid. We sat at a table with our seats angled so we could keep our eyes open for Zeke.

The man didn't let us down. He exited the doors from the lobby to the back patio. He looked toward the pool and bar, then turned and entered the pro shop.

Reid leaned close. "Now that's interesting. Instead of heading to the nearest bank for the ransom demand, he went to see Rory Ledger."

"It's troublesome and almost enough to make me wonder if Rory is involved. It's a good thing the police told him not to leave town."

"Rory lives in a nice trailer park, he invested in the golf carts, and he said Ben owed him money. Rory and Zeke were both involved in the golf club scam with Ben, but I don't see how Rory can help pay off our demand for money."

"Unless he tricked us." His niece would be brokenhearted. "Let's forget about Rory. If we hope to trap the killer, we need to stay focused on Zeke."

"I agree. We should wait a few more minutes and observe the pro shop."

The waiter appeared, and we ordered pimento cheese dip with homemade potato chips. A few minutes later, he returned with our food and refilled our drinks.

Reid dipped a chip into the cheese spread but stopped halfway to his mouth. "Oh. My. Goodness."

I turned and spotted Tom. "What's he doing?"

"No idea." He stuffed the chip into his mouth.

"Why do I feel like we should hide?" I scrunched down in my seat.

"You're being silly."

A dark-haired beauty exited the lobby doors and walked to Tom.

The pastor smiled and took her hand in his.

I gasped. "That's Camila, the head of housekeeping. Whoa, she fixed herself up to meet Tom. Man, Bess will be heartbroken."

The two of them walked to the bar and ordered drinks. I grabbed Reid's arm. "You don't suppose?"

"No."

"Let me finish. Camila found the secret room. Tom and Ben argued. Now Tom and Camila appear to be on a date."

"That's all it is. Wait here." Reid left me alone and strode to the bar.

I dipped chips in the pimento cheese and wolfed down one after another, trying to rein in my thoughts. All the evidence pointed to Zeke. Tom was innocent of Ben's murder. Breaking my best friend's heart? Guilty. Leading Bess on? Guilty.

Reid returned. "Tom's waving to you."

I waved back but couldn't smile despite my best effort. "What's going on?"

"Tom met Camila on one of his trips here looking for Ben. And the rest is history."

"He's pond scum."

"Settle down. We need to stay focused on our plan. We can discuss Tom later."

Sue appeared at our table. "I wanted to let you know, this will be my last week at the spa. I plan to move home, find a good counselor, and get a job. Thanks for believing me."

"Of course." I stood and gave her a hug. "Take care of yourself."

"You, too." She walked down the path to the beach.

We finished our snack but never saw Zeke leave Rory's shop.

Paul texted me. *You can return to your apartment.*

I looked at Reid. "Paul says the police are finished at my place."

"Great." Reid reached for my hand. "Why don't we check on Lady? I know Mom doesn't mind watching her, but I think you'll feel better with your dog."

"You're right. It's amazing how fast I've grown attached to the golden-doodle. Plus, I need to keep busy, or I'll make myself sick worrying about tomorrow morning."

"Let's roll." He reached for my hand.

To avoid giving Tom a chewing out, I kept my back angled toward the bar as we left the resort.

Chapter Fifty-Eight

Ethan met us at the apartment, and we updated him on the plan to catch Zeke. When we finished, Ethan said, "We should spend the night here, because it's so close to the pier."

Lady walked around the room and nosed the sliding glass patio door.

I opened it, and she watched people walking along the street. Restaurants and bars were open and doing a booming business. It was loud with excitement, music, laughter, and cars. "Reid, you should stay at your house and meet us here tomorrow morning."

"No can do. There's safety in numbers, and we're sticking together."

It did feel safer to have him stay with Ethan and me. "It'll be tight, but I doubt any of us will get much sleep. Are you sure you want to stay?"

"Absolutely." He pressed his lips together.

My burner phone vibrated with a text message. *Where will you leave the tapes?*

I showed my phone to the guys before texting a reply. *First, you will leave the money at the tourist map on the pier. Once I see it, I'll leave the tapes in the same spot.*

"Mom, do you think Zeke knows he's dealing with you?"

"It's possible. That's one reason I'm glad we're all together."

"Uncle Paul needs to know we're staying here tonight. I'll text him. Maybe he can have an extra cop patrol this area."

Reid nodded. "Layers of protection. I like it."

Lady stood on my little balcony and growled. Her growl quickly morphed into a bark.

"Lady, come here. Come on, girl. Let's get you a treat." I clapped my hands.

"Let me, Mom." Ethan walked out and urged her to come inside.

Once they were in, I closed the sliding glass door and dropped the security bar into place.

Lady whimpered, and I sat on the floor with her. I spoke soft, soothing words and rubbed her side. "You're such a good guard dog. What would I do without you?"

Her body seemed to relax, and I quit talking but stayed close to her.

Reid said, "Let's turn off the lights in case there's someone outside watching."

"Go ahead." I wrapped my arms around Lady.

Reid and Ethan looked out the window.

Reid said, "Do you see the guy in the hoodie by the coffee shop?"

"Sure do. I'm calling Uncle Paul." Ethan walked to my bedroom.

"I'm going to see if I can catch him. I'll pretend like I'm leaving, then—"

"No, Reid. We should stick together. You said it yourself."

He knelt beside me. "What if we can catch him tonight? I'm tired of sitting around, waiting on this nutcase to attack. Offense is better than defense."

"Maybe, but Zeke agreed to the plan."

"You only think he agreed. If he didn't come up with the money, he's desperate to get the tapes. He may think they are in the apartment with us. What if he tries to break in and gets them? Any number of things can happen before sunrise. Let's try my way. I love you." He gave me a quick kiss and disappeared out the door before I could say another word.

Lady barked, and I wanted to cry. This wasn't the way we'd planned to trap Zeke.

Chapter Fifty-Nine

Reid's truck beeped.

I could picture him clicking his fob to unlock his truck parked on the street in front of my apartment.

Ethan returned. "Uncle Paul is sending over Officer Diaz. Where's Reid?"

"He left to see if he could catch the guy." I stood from my spot on the floor beside Lady and led her to the bedroom. After getting her situated, I returned to the main room.

Ethan was at the window. "Reid is crossing the street with a group of people."

I stood beside my son and watched with a racing heart and a dry mouth. "We need to help him."

"Mom, I'm sure he believes he's doing the best thing to keep you safe."

"Where is Emerson Diaz? Shouldn't he be here by now?"

"Stay calm. I'm sure he'll be here soon."

Some of the crowd entered a restaurant with a live band. Reid continued toward the closed coffee shop and our suspect.

The guy wearing a hoodie spotted Reid and ran toward the beach.

A siren sounded.

The suspect pushed people out of his way, including a stroller. People screamed.

Reid tried to run through the crowd.

A police car stopped in front of the apartment building, and Emerson jumped out.

Ethan and I ran out the door and stopped by the official vehicle.

"Go that way." I pointed. "Reid's chasing the suspect. Dark pants and a dark hoodie. Average height."

"Thanks. Lock yourselves inside." Emerson ran in the direction I'd pointed.

Another police car parked behind Diaz's car. It was Officer Collins. Drake hopped out of his car. "What's happening?"

Ethan said, "Reid's running after Mom's stalker. We think it's Zeke McCarthy. Officer Diaz is trying to catch up with them."

I stood on the steps and watched. It stunk to be left behind.

Drake said, "I need to go after them."

Ethan looked from Drake to me. Our gazes connected. I'd seen the same pleading look a few times over the years. Even though I hadn't heard a question, I knew he wanted to chase the suspect.

"Go ahead."

"Lock yourself in the apartment, Mom. Then I'll help Drake." He lifted his chin.

"Be careful." I went into the apartment and locked the door. I double-checked the sliding glass door. It was secure. I hid the tapes in a kitchen cabinet.

What kind of mother was I to allow my son to go after a killer? I was a terrible person. Paul needed to know. *FYI. Emerson, Drake, Reid, and Ethan are all looking for a guy in a hoodie.*

I sat on the couch and prayed.

My phone vibrated. *On the way with more officers. Sit tight.*

The waiting would be intolerable, but I needed to guard the tapes. So, I stayed where I was.

Chapter Sixty

S it tight? Who was Paul kidding? I paced in the living area of my apartment. I itched to be out hunting for Zeke, but it made sense to protect the evidence.

People cheered in the bar across the street, and I felt safe with so many people around. I'd never lived in the country or on a mountain. I liked knowing people were nearby.

There was another loud cheer.

Must be the NBA playoffs. I followed basketball at every level of competition. It was a big deal in the state of Kentucky, and I'd grown to love it. After March Madness, the pro teams got my full attention.

Excitement for the game was normal, and I'd rather be cheering for my favorite teams than hiding. Standing in my apartment in fear of a killer was not normal.

What could I do that was productive?

I plugged in the burner phone to charge it in case Zeke tried to contact me. It seemed smart to charge my phone, too. After placing it on the charging station, I practiced recording on the new app I'd downloaded earlier.

The hair on my neck popped up. My heart raced like a thoroughbred racehorse. My good ear roared like a strong tide. I snatched my phone and opened the camera app to record whatever was about to happen. I slipped it into my pocket.

A board on the porch in front of my apartment squeaked. I seized the burner phone and called Paul. It rolled to voice mail. Oh, man, he probably didn't recognize my number. I called 9-1-1 instead.

The operator asked about my emergency. I whispered my address. "I'm Chief Paul Wright's sister. The killer is outside my apartment. Please tell Chief Wright to come here. I'm all alone." I repeated the information and hung up.

Despite my hearing loss, it was easy to hear the crowd across the street. Some cheered, and others booed.

I grabbed the audio recorder and rolled it in my hands. The manufacturer claimed the microphone would record clearly up to sixty feet away.

There was a thud on the apartment door.

I shivered.

Lady barked.

"Kate, I know you're in there. Open the door." Zeke pounded it again. "Don't make me break this down."

Where should I put the recorder in case he broke in? The kitchen counter might be obvious. I needed some clutter to disguise the thing. I found my purse and dumped it out on the couch. Next to the purse junk, I placed the recorder.

The door rattled, but the lock held.

I ran to the bedroom and squeezed open the door. Lady flew out before I could contain her. So much for barricading us in the bedroom.

There was more hammering on the door.

This place was old and had survived numerous hurricanes. Would it stand up to Zeke?

I dashed after my goldendoodle, who faced the door and barked. I snagged her collar with one hand. "Come on, Lady. Let's go."

We'd only made it a couple of steps when the door crashed open.

I whipped around and faced Zeke.

Perspiration dripped down his face. His eyes darkened, and his frown terrified me. "You don't make things easy, Kate. Where are the tapes?"

Lady lunged for Zeke.

I did my best to keep a grip on her.

Zeke waved his gun in the air. "Get your mutt under control. I'd hate for my trigger finger to slip."

"Stay calm, Zeke. I haven't been a dog owner for long, but it makes sense if you'd quit waving around your weapon, she'd stop barking."

He kicked the front door shut before putting the gun behind his back. "Your turn."

"I'll take her to the other room." I rubbed her head. "Please, Lady. No more barking, or he might shoot both of us."

My dog whimpered.

"Good girl. Come on." I pointed to the counter. "I'm going to get a treat. Nothing else."

"You're also going to get those tapes."

"Right." I held a treat in front of a reluctant pet, but she followed me to the bedroom. I tossed the dog biscuit onto the floor and nudged her forward. Once she cleared the doorway, I shut the door.

A smidgen of stress left my shoulders. My dog was safe. Now, to deal with Zeke.

His shadow fell over me, and it was almost scarier than when he'd busted the door.

Chapter Sixty-One

"The tapes." Zeke pointed the gun at me.

I didn't want to turn over the cassette tapes, but I didn't relish the thought of dying tonight. "They are in the kitchen."

I refused to walk past him in the small hall, so I waited for him to move.

He walked backward until he entered the living area. So, he wasn't a complete monster.

I followed him, forcing myself not to look toward the mess and the recorder. "What happened between you and Ben? If it didn't pick up our conversation, maybe the phone in my pocket would.

"His death was an accident. I came to town, planning to steal the tapes and stop him from blackmailing me. I wanted out of all business dealings with Ben, but he tried to get me to invest in the resort. With what? That's the exact question I asked him."

"Did he bleed you dry from his blackmail scheme?"

"I lost money on the golf club scam. It was crumbling, and we had to start refunding investors who caught on to the fake clubs. Between that and the blackmail, I lost all my money, my family, and my job. That wasn't enough for Ben. No, siree. He kept pushing me for money that I didn't have." He sighed. "Give me the tapes, Kate."

I moved into the kitchen and hoped he didn't realize I was recording him. "What exactly was on the tapes?"

"Hey, where's your phone?"

"In my pocket. I'm reaching for it now." I stuck my hand in the pocket of my jeans and retrieved my cell phone. "Here."

"Shut it off." The hand holding the gun shook.

I pushed the correct buttons to turn it off. Instead of powering it off, I ran my finger over the spot to call for help. "So, what is on the tapes?"

He met my gaze. "Ben got me talking about some of our scams and life in general. I trusted him, but he blackmailed me. If the police got the tapes, I'd never see my kids again. I couldn't risk it." Sweat poured down his face.

I opened the cabinet door.

"What are you doing?"

"The box is in here."

"Oh, right. Well, what are you waiting for?" He was losing his cool.

"Could you have turned around and blackmailed him?" I needed more answers, and if he killed me, hopefully, he wouldn't find the recorder.

"Not without the tapes, but that wasn't my plan. I was ready to go clean. You know what I mean?"

"Sure. Turn over a new leaf. I get it. What happened?" I pulled the cardboard box out of the hiding spot and placed it on the countertop.

"We were in Ben's office. He wanted to discuss a deal on the golf course. He always had a new way of conning people brewing in his mind. He was never satisfied. The day he died, Ben smarted off, claiming I'd never be free of him. He suggested I relax and accept reality. Can you believe it?"

"It would be hard to relax under that pressure." I began to feel sorry for Zeke; then I remembered he was the killer.

Zeke grabbed the box and lifted the lid. He uttered an ugly word. "That's a lot of tapes, but is this all?"

"Those are all I found, but they are not all of the conversations between you and Ben. There are other people he recorded."

"This box doesn't look sturdy." His voice lacked emotion. He almost sounded robotic, and that scared me. "The tapes might fall out. I need a garbage bag."

"Okay. I'll get one for you." From under the counter, I removed a white trash bag. Zeke was taking his sweet time, but so was Paul. What was happening?

Zeke couldn't let me live if he wanted to get away with his crimes. He'd even confessed to the murder of Ben. Zeke had the upper hand. He was bigger and stronger than me, plus he possessed a gun. "Why did you shoot at me the other night?"

"I couldn't take the chance that you'd listened to the tapes. There was nothing to stop you from blackmailing me like Ben had. Or you might have planned to give the tapes to the cops. It was too risky to let you live."

"I would never have blackmailed you, Zeke." I tried to hand the bag to him.

"You wrap it up for me. I can't let any of them spill out."

There was another cheer from the bar across the street.

Zeke looked toward the door. "Hurry."

With shaky hands, I opened the white bag, placed the box in it, and carefully wrapped the bag around it. "That should do."

He put it under his left arm while he pointed the gun at me.

"I'm sorry you've had such bad luck, Zeke. Killing me will only make it worse, though. If you tell the police it was an accident—"

"It wasn't exactly an accident, but I didn't plan it either. Ben wanted me to try a new golf club. We were in his office, and he had a new fairway wood. I was taking a few swings, but then he told me that my wife was dating someone else. Somebody better than me. He used that as leverage to try and convince me to join his latest con. Ben said it'd show her what she'd given up when I made a killing. He kept talking, turned his back on me, and I just took a swing. I was so mad. He didn't understand how much I love my wife and kids."

"Ben was truly cruel. I'm sorry about that." Again, I started to feel bad for Zeke. However, he was pointing a gun at me. "How'd you get his body onto the golf cart?"

"It was parked at the end of his secret passage. He was so blasted proud of that stupid hall. I dragged him to the door, and when the outside path was clear, I put his body on the golf cart."

"Why didn't you drive it somewhere else?"

"I didn't want to be seen with him, even if people thought he was alive. So, I grabbed the golf club and ran to an entrance that led to my hotel room.

On the way, I chunked the golf club into the sand dunes; then I hid until you found the body."

He walked to the damaged apartment door and turned his body to face me. "I really don't want to shoot you."

"Then don't. I'll talk to the police and help them understand you didn't mean to murder Ben."

With his gun shaking in his right hand, he took aim. "Sorry, Kate."

A shadow passed by the front window.

I ducked behind the counter.

The front door burst open.

Zeke fell forward.

The gun exploded, and everything went black.

Chapter Sixty-Two

I rolled into a ball on my kitchen floor. My good ear rang, and my heart raced as fast as a lightning bolt.

A hand touched my back.

I screamed.

"Katie, are you okay?" Reid crouched on the floor next to me.

I opened my eyes and met Reid's gaze.

"Are you okay?"

I shook my head, but wait. Was I okay? I was alive. Reid was looking at me with concern etched on his face. His eyebrows drew together. "Yes. Are you?"

"Yeah." He took my hands in his and pulled me into his lap, leaning against the kitchen cabinet. "I never should've left you. I'm so sorry, Katie."

"It's not your fault." I wrapped my arms around his neck and rested my head on his chest. "You came back for me. What happened?"

"Zeke gave me the slip. There was a runner in the pier parking lot wearing the same kind of dark clothes and hoodie. Zeke followed him around the corner. By the time I caught up, it was the other guy. He was cooling down from his run. I don't know who was more surprised." He sighed. "That's when I came back here. It was crazy to think a fifty-one-year-old man could catch a thirty-something guy. I should have stayed with you."

"Shh. It's all good now." I so much appreciated that he hadn't shifted the blame to Ethan, because Ethan had been the one to leave me alone with Lady. Not that I blamed him. If I had asked him to stay, Ethan never would've gone with Drake to catch Zeke.

"Mom!"

I rose and looked across the kitchen counter at Ethan. "Hey."

"Man, I never should've gone with Drake. I thought you'd be safe." He rounded the corner and gave me a hug. "I'm sorry, Mom."

"It's okay. We all did what we thought was best. Nobody is at fault. Oh, I forgot about Lady." I left him and hurried to get my dog. I scooted into the room and loved on her. "You are such a good dog. Thanks for taking care of me tonight."

She licked my face.

Oh, yeah. A laugh slipped out. I was more than okay. I had Reid, Ethan, Lady, and the rest of my family. "Let's attach your leash in case any of the police officers scare you."

There was a soft tap on my door.

I secured Lady and held tight, just in case. "Come in."

Reid entered my bedroom and petted Lady's head. "Paul wants us to leave so the crime scene people can go through your apartment."

"Okay, but doesn't he want to question us?"

"As a matter of fact, he does. The owner of Island Perk came outside to check on the commotion. He offered to let us use the shop as a base and even offered to fix coffee."

I tried to smile. "This could be the best interrogation ever."

"My thoughts exactly."

"Oh, I almost forgot. I may have recorded part of my conversation with Zeke." I went to the family room and picked up the audio recorder. "Paul needs to listen to this."

"I'm impressed. Let's find your brother."

Paul was speaking to an officer in the kitchen, and I waved at him. He soon joined me. "Can we talk at the coffee shop?"

"Sure, but if this worked right, I recorded my conversation with Zeke. I was going to record us with my phone, but he made me shut it off." I handed the little device to him. "And the garbage bag on the floor contains the cassette tapes Ben used to blackmail Zeke. Don't let anyone take it out with the trash."

"On it." My brother reached for the recorder and gave me a great big smile. "Nice work, sis. This could make the case much easier to prove. Thanks."

"You're welcome."

We exited my apartment through the busted doorframe. We walked down the wooden steps and up the sidewalk.

I stumbled at the sight of Zeke. One officer wearing gloves patted him down, and Officer Collins watched.

"Why is he still here?" I gripped Reid's arm.

"It's probably a process." He slipped his arm around my shoulders.

Lady barked and lunged for Zeke.

I tightened my grip on the leash.

Zeke turned his head. Our gazes locked. Instead of hatred shooting my way, his blank eyes lacked hope. Defeat dominated other emotions.

Sorrow seeped through me. Once again, I reminded myself that he would've shot me if the police hadn't arrived in time. I lifted my chin and walked past him. Still, it was sad to think about how greed had led to so much death and destruction.

Chapter Sixty-Three

Orange and yellow streaks filled the sky as the sun rose Tuesday morning. Reid texted me. *Waiting out front. Don't want to wake Bess. Take your time.*

The night before, Bess had invited me to spend the night with her. We discussed the case, our business, life, and Tom. She broke down when I told her about Tom and Camila. We continued to talk until we both fell asleep.

On the way. I'd convinced my brother to only take the burner phone and the audio recorder into evidence and leave my phone alone. There were no messages on it to be used at Zeke's trial, so Paul had agreed. I had slept fitfully, and the early morning garbage truck woke me before six. I had showered and was wearing shorts and a T-shirt on loan from Bess. There was nothing to stop me from meeting Reid.

I scribbled a note for Bess before taking Lady outside. I locked and double-checked the door.

"Good morning, beautiful."

I laughed, knowing how rough I looked. "Good morning."

He swooped in for a quick kiss before opening the passenger door. "Paul is at the pier, waiting to update us on the case."

"Great. I can't wait to learn more." I motioned for Lady to jump in first, then I got in Reid's truck and fastened my seatbelt. "Although, he told me a lot last night."

It didn't take long to drive to the pier. We passed my apartment, and the crime scene tape was still up.

Reid backed into a parking space. "There's your brother."

Paul wore athletic shorts and a T-shirt and was drinking a green health drink. He met us in front of the truck. "Morning, guys. Shall we walk?"

Reid nodded. "Sounds good."

Once we were on the beach, I released Lady and walked with my good ear toward Paul. "Did Zeke give you a hard time last night?"

"He was resistant at first, but it didn't take long to break him." Paul frowned at my dog but continued to discuss the night. "Of course, we had him dead to rights, intending to shoot you.

Reid said, "Twice."

"Right. He was the shooter at the lighthouse. Zeke admitted to everything. He seemed relieved to spill his guts. You know, keeping so many secrets for a long time can wear a person down."

"I'm curious. Did the audio recorder get our conversation?"

"Yep. The clarity was amazing. You did a good job, sis."

I paused for Lady to sniff around a sand castle.

"By the way, this time of year, dogs need to be leashed on the beach. In the winter, you can let her run free."

"Sorry, I never thought about it." I attached the leash to the goldendoodle's collar and gave her a treat. "What else did you learn last night? It seemed like Zeke was acting by himself in Ben's murder and covering it up, but did he have a partner?"

"Nobody else was connected to the murder." Paul finished his gritty-looking green drink. "I believe the FBI will investigate some of the scams, fraud, and possibly a Ponzi scheme. My primary goal was to solve the murder."

Lady finished sniffing, and I kept a firm grip on the leash as we walked. "How about Tom Cross?"

"I haven't found anything to implicate him."

"Good." Reid looked at me.

Paul's gaze bounced from Reid to me. "What am I missing?"

"Tom is interested in another woman. Not Bess."

"That's a shame."

Heat flushed through my body. "It sure is but let me ask you another question. Sam saw somebody on a sand dune. I reported it. Was it Zeke?"

Paul flipped through his notes and rubbed the back of his neck. "I'll ask, but I'm not sure it makes a difference to the case. We have the golf club used to murder Ben."

Reid said, "What about the book? *Atlantic Coast Guide*. How did that fit in?"

"From what Zeke told me, Ben hoped there was pirate treasure buried on the resort property. That was a little side hustle, though. The fake golf clubs were the main ongoing scam. Ben had Rory encouraging guests to buy the clubs. There was also the hotel room co-ownership con. The practice is legit in some countries, and Ben was evaluating the business model. According to Zeke, Ben would tweak the model and steal money from investors. I haven't figured it all out, and I'll probably let the FBI handle it too. They have more manpower than we do at the department. When it's all investigated and evaluated, there will be a lot of people to make whole."

"That's Craig Hauser's goal. He hopes to make up to the victims for Ben's actions." I kept a tight grip on the leash as we passed a family with small children. The kids were squealing in delight as they threw food in the air to seagulls.

Lady pranced by without a second glance or a growl.

"Good girl." I gave her another treat.

I remembered the eagle and the osprey. The osprey had worked hard for the fish, and the eagle had swooped down and stolen it. How many people had worked hard for their money only to have Ben swoop in and con them out of it? At least with the eagle, the intentions were obvious.

Paul stopped and looked at his phone. "I've got to go. For once, I don't have to warn you to be careful."

"Yay. See you later."

Reid and I continued walking as the sun climbed higher in the sky.

With no warning, Reid stopped and took my hands in his. "Let's get married."

I laughed. "We're engaged. Of course, we're going to get married."

Lady barked.

Reid shook his head. "I don't mean someday. Let's do it today. There's no waiting period between applying for our license and getting married around here."

My heart leapt with excitement. "Do you mean elope?"

"Yes. Last night was a close call. What if you'd died, and we'd never gotten married? I don't want to waste any more time. What do you say, Katie?"

My heart beat as fast as a hummingbird's wings. "No friends and family?"

"Nope. It'll take too long. Lady can come with us."

I had so many questions and arguments, but looking into Reid's blue eyes, all I wanted to do was agree. "Yes. Let's get married today."

He picked me up and spun me around.

I dropped the leash and laughed.

Lady let out a happy bark.

Before I knew what happened, we were driving to Savannah to meet a man who would handle everything for us. I sent a group text message to Bess and my family, telling them I needed a few days away, but I was fine.

Chapter Sixty-Four

We returned to Fox Island late Saturday afternoon, and I'd never felt so relaxed.

Reid stopped at a red light. "I've got a surprise for you."

"Another surprise?" I reached for his hand. "You're too good to me."

Lady popped her head up from where she had been snoozing in the backseat of Reid's pickup truck.

"You're going to like this."

"I've loved every single surprise the last few days."

The light turned green. Reid drove to my new house and parked in the driveway.

"Are we going to see the progress?"

"You could say that." He ran a finger down my cheek. "It occurred to me that the next best thing would be to carry you over the threshold. I promised the guys bonuses if the house would be ready by this afternoon."

"You mean—"

"Our new home is ready. We've even got your soaker tub."

"Oh, Reid." I leaned forward and kissed him, then leapt out of the truck. "I can't wait to see everything."

Reid and Lady joined me on the steps. "Don't forget your groom."

I cupped his face in my hands. "Never."

We kissed again, then he swung me into his arms and carried me over the threshold. "Katie Barrett, welcome home."

Lady ran through the house, and I hugged Reid. "We're going to have a great life here. I plan to focus on you and my business."

"What about murder investigations?"

"Let's hope there are no more murders in Fox Island."

"Touché. Are you ready for the grand tour?"

"You bet." I had a feeling life would be grand with Reid, and I was ready to start our new life.

The doorbell rang.

Lady raced past us and let out an excited bark.

"Funny how she knows the difference between dangerous and safe people." I met Reid's gaze. "Wonder who that is?"

He grinned. "The best way to find out is to open the door."

"Smarty pants." I opened the front door.

"Congratulations. I hope you're ready for a party." Bess hugged me. "All your alls families are coming along with most of the town. We're calling it a wedding reception and housewarming all wrapped into one big celebration."

I laughed. "Then I better freshen my lipstick. Come with me."

I led her to the main bedroom. "Bess, how are you doing?"

"You mean because of Tom and that other woman? I closed the store for a couple of days and rescheduled appointments. I sat on the beach and just thought and prayed. I'm going to be okay. We can talk more later. Today, we're celebrating you and Reid."

"I'm always going to be here for you." I hugged her.

"I know." She patted my back, then pulled away. "We need to return to your party."

We joined the others in the main room.

Reid came over and hugged Bess. "We're on your side, and I can share Katie whenever you need her."

"Thanks, Reid."

There was a knock on the door, and Ethan entered. "Welcome home, guys."

Soon, the house was full of people. Just like I'd predicted. Life was good. I'd helped solve another murder. I had reconnected with old friends and made a few new ones. My son lived here, and so did my brothers. I was getting to know my true self, not the people-pleasing wife and mother I'd been for years. I was married to the love of my life, and Reid accepted me for who I was. Yes, life was most definitely good.

About the Author

Jackie Layton is the author of cozy mysteries with Spunky Southern Sleuths. Her stories are set in Texas, Georgia, and South Carolina. She lives on the coast of South Carolina, where she enjoys walks on the beach and golf cart rides around the marsh. Reading, gardening, and traveling are some of her favorite hobbies. She always keeps a notebook handy to write down ideas for future stories. Be careful what you say around her, because it might end up in a book.

SOCIAL MEDIA HANDLES:
https://www.facebook.com/JackieLaytonAuthor
https://www.facebook.com/Joyfuljel
https://www.pinterest.com/jackielaytonauthor/
https://twitter.com/joyfuljel

AUTHOR WEBSITE:
https://jackielaytoncozyauthor.com/

Also by Jackie Layton

A Low Country Dog Walker Mystery Series:
  Bite the Dust
  Dog-Gone Dead
  Bag of Bones
  Caught and Collared
  A Killer Unleashed
  A Suspicious Breed

A Texas Flower Farmer Cozy Mystery Series:
  Weeding Out Lies
  Clover Covered Corpse

An Organized Crime Cozy Mystery Series:
  Clutter Free